FORBIDDEN PASSIONS

By KATHLEEN DRYMON

ZEBRA BOOKS
KENSINGTON PUBLISHING CORP.

ZEBRA BOOKS

are published by

KENSINGTON PUBLISHING CORP.
475 Park Avenue South
New York, N.Y. 10016

Printed in the United States of America

With love to my mother and father and also to Helena Muller for all the valuable help she has given me.

Chapter One

The morning sun bathed the room in a soft, golden warmth, one that usually would have brought joy and thankfulness to the heart of the young girl seated before the dressing table. But today a cold fright had laid claim to that most tender spot. "Have you yourself seen Father this morning, Biddy?" the young girl questioned her maid, as she gazed at her reflection in the mirror.

"No honey," Biddy answered, patting the last piece of hair into place. "All I know is he told that young downstairs maid to let you know that he wished for your presence as soon as possible in his study."

"I wonder what it is I could have done wrong now?" Katherine pondered aloud. "It seems as though the only time he ever wishes to see me anymore is when that wife of his has told him some false tale about me."

"Now don't you go a-fretting about what it is, honey, it can't be anything too bad," the old nurse said, patting her shoulder lovingly. "You haven't never done a bad thing in your whole life."

"You know how Joann is; she seems to fill father's head constantly with bad things about me," Katherine said, looking up at Biddy with a forlorn expression on her lovely features. "I just do not know what to do. She and her niece Rachel seem always to be plotting against me."

"Now don't you be a-worrying until you've seen your father and listened to what it is he wants to talk to you about," Biddy stated reassuringly.

"Oh, Biddy, I just do not know what I would do without you here beside me," Katherine exclaimed as she stood up and squeezed the old nurse tenderly around the waist.

Biddy had been with the Rafferty family

since before Katherine had been born, at the time when Mary Rafferty, Katherine's mother, was still living. After Mary Rafferty's death Biddy had been the one who had loved and raised Katherine. She loved the girl as a mother loves her own child and she had promised herself many a time she would not let any harm befall her young charge.

Biddy could not stand the new lady Rafferty or her niece, Rachel, and she also knew that Katherine was right in thinking that they were scheming against her. She herself had heard them on more than one occasion talking about her young mistress.

"Well, honey, you look just fine. You just calm yourself and do as your father wishes."

Slowly, with halting steps, Katherine made her way to her father's study. Her mind was in a blazing turmoil of thoughts about what she could have done to have caused this private interview with her father. It had been weeks since last he had requested her presence alone; and that last time had been no different from the others. Joann, her stepmother, had accused her to her father of boldly flirting with a married man, one Lord Darring, at a reception given for Lady Agnes Widmark. Of course it had been a lie. And, tears running down her cheeks, she had told her father so, begging him to believe her.

But telling her that he would not permit such behavior from his daughter, he had sternly reprimanded her, as though she had

9

never uttered a word.

Katherine had given up, hanging her head in a dejected manner as his voice berated her for her foul behavior. What was she to do? she asked herself. She could not argue with her father; she had always given in meekly where her father was concerned. And Joann took full advantage of this one weakness of Katherine's.

As though she were once again a small child, she found herself facing the massive door to her father's study. Bracing herself for whatever might come, she lightly knocked.

From within came the sound of her father's strong, dominating voice. "Come in."

Katherine entered, her hands clutching the folds of her gown as she viewed the dark scowl on her father's face. "You wished to see me, Father?" she questioned softly.

"Yes, Katie, take a seat; I shall just be a moment," he stated as he riffled through a stack of papers upon his desk.

Katherine, ready for the worst, looked to her father with surprise written across her delicate features. He had not called her Katie since she had been a small child. Perhaps this interview was not ruled by Joann's cruel hand and she had misjudged her father's motives. She took the chair he had indicated, her whole body seeming to relax somewhat with that one word.

She looked about her as she awaited his pleasure. This room had not changed at all; it was exactly as she remembered it when she was a small child. She thought back to when she had been a little girl; whenever she could sneak away from Biddy she would make her way to her father's study. She would come to this room and just marvel at the rows and rows of expensive books that lined every wall and the large imposing furniture that seemed to vibrate and come alive with her father's presence.

As Katherine looked over to her father he, too, seemed to be deep in thought. His papers lay to the side of his desk, forgotten for the moment; his brooding eyes seemed to be drilling holes through her.

John Vern Rafferty was a man of enormous wealth and high position in England and he prided himself highly on never having backed down from a duty or obligation in his life. At this time though, his thoughts ran rampant on how best to approach his only daughter on the subject of marriage.

He loved his daughter very much, though at times he knew he had been harsh to her. Still, he had always thought that he had held her best interests at heart. Now the subject of marriage had to be discussed and though he knew her feelings well, he was her father, and it was his duty to see she did not spend her life in spinsterhood.

Had he not given her plenty of chances to find her own husband? he argued with himself. Had she not promised over a year ago that she would find herself a mate? She had cried that she could not marry without love, and he, his father's heart going out to his only daughter, had agreed to give her at least another year.

The year had now been long up and still she had not found the man she would wish to take to wed. He had watched the way she had treated the many men who had come to call. She had led gentlemen around for the last few years as though they were a bunch of puppies chasing after her; and she, with her mother's lovely looks, had not chosen the one to whom she would throw a bone.

The dark scowl returned to his face as he went over his daughter's fragile features. She was so like her mother he could almost imagine her to be Mary sitting across from him now. Katherine had the same delicate features and firm-set chin as Mary Rafferty and that lustrous black hair, black as the night, with a satin texture which tempted a man's very soul with the desire to run his hands caressingly through its mass. And her deep violet-blue eyes were the same as his dear Mary's, the blue so deep one could lose himself in their depths. Never in John Rafferty's life had he set his eyes on a more beautiful woman than his first wife, and now her daughter was proving to be even lovelier than she.

With a jerk he pulled himself from his thoughts and addressed his daughter softly. "Katherine, my child, I do not know how to start. I must confess I am rather at a loss for words."

Katherine's deep blue eyes looked toward him, questioningly. "What is it, Father?"

He looked upon her with sympathy as he began. "I have called you here this morning to discuss the matter of your marriage."

Katherine looked at her father, not understanding his meaning. "My marriage? But, Father, you know I have not yet met the man I would wish to marry."

"Let me finish, Daughter," he stated flatly. "You are of an age now where you should be married and bearing children. I am getting old, Katherine, and I wish for grandchildren."

"Father, in time I am sure I shall find the right man for myself and marry," Katherine said softly, feeling a shiver of apprehension run through her body as she saw the set look on his face.

"That is of no matter, child." He waved her objections away with a turn of his hand. "I have given you plenty of time to find for yourself a suitable young man and you have failed. So, therefore, I have felt it my obligation to arrange the matter for you. Before you oppose my decision, let me remind you that plenty of young girls are married by arrangements made by their families. You shall not be the only girl to have ever been in a like condition."

"But, Father—" She stood up, pleading, tears starting to form in her eyes. "I shall find my own husband in time; just please have

13

more patience with me. I just cannot marry a man I do not love."

"No, Katherine, you are nineteen years of age now and I wish for you to take a husband soon. We have talked this matter over before; I'm sure you remember?" His eyes raked over her as though he misjudged completely her capacity to make this decision for herself. "The way you have treated the men who have come calling on you is shameful and I have my doubts of your ever finding the man you think worthy of your love."

Katherine started to protest, but her father once again waved her words into silence.

"Listen to me, child. I have already picked the man I would wish you to wed." His eyes critically roamed over his daughter, taking in her pale composure. "He is wealthy, Katherine, and his family has a very good name here in England. He lives in the colonies, but it shall not be long before we shall see each other. Perhaps we shall plan yearly visits."

Katherine felt an ice-cold dread clutch at her heart. "You cannot mean to send me all the way to America, Father?" she stammered, not believing her ears.

"Child, you shall find in time that we have made a good match for you; the Deveraux family are from a good stock, they are honorable and forthright. Your stepmother and I have talked this matter over at great length and we both agree that we have done very well by you and that you shall be happy

14

in time and adjust quite easily to your new life."

How could this be happening to her? Her thoughts were aswarm with the words he had just repeated. She faced her father with one last attempt to try to bend his decision. "This is Joann's idea, is it not, Father? Can you not see she hates me and will try anything to get me out of this house and out of her life? Please, Father, do not do this to me; do not send me to a land I do not know and to a husband I have never met."

"Nonsense, child," he said with a touch of anger tinging his words. "Your stepmother loves you and only wishes for your best and for you to find happiness. You shall learn, dear, there are a great many things one must do in one's lifetime that one has no wish to do; but I am sure you will find happiness in this new country to which you are going. There is really no use in arguing anymore on this subject, Katherine, for I have on this day sent my attorney to have the agreements between this gentleman's family and myself made ready."

Katherine stood as if stunned by a mortal blow; she could feel the tears starting to grow in her eyes and she willed them not to come. She turned, running from the room and up the stairs to the safety of her own room.

John Vern Rafferty stood silently by the door watching his daughter's retreat. His heart wrenched within him as he went over in his mind the look of pain in her eyes. "Damn, she'll just have to adjust to the idea for my word is already in writing and a Rafferty's word is his honor." He swore aloud.

Bradly Dwayne Deveraux had lived his thirty and one years of life as a bachelor and a man of wealth on his father's vast plantation in Richmond, Virginia.

His father, Joseph Deveraux, and his mother, Louise Deveraux, had built their plantation out of the wilderness in the hope of handing it to their sons. Their one dream had been to have a large family. But alas, Louise had died shortly after the birth of her first child.

To this child, Joseph Deveraux had given his most special care. He had taught him to be a man above most men, to deal fairly with people, and to stand firm on his beliefs. And before Joseph Deveraux died at the age of fifty-three, he had made his plantation, Moon Rise, one of the most prosperous in Richmond.

Bradly Deveraux was a stubborn man who was used to having things his way and not being forced into anything against his will. He had the tallness and rugged build of his father, which fit with this new and wild frontier to which he laid claim. His eyes and hair were those of his mother. Many men, when they were faced with his anger, had claimed that his eyes, light-colored and appearing almost silver gray, were able to see through to a man's very soul. His hair, a raven black, curled at the nape of his neck and made a striking contrast to his eyes.

The women of Richmond, from the most staid to the most outlandish, thought of Bradly Deveraux as a most handsome man and more than eligible. Many was the time Bradly had felt the bite of a woman trying to seduce him into her bed and into more. But all their plans to catch him had been for naught, for Bradly would take that which was given freely and would leave with only a good night, making no promises for tomorrow.

Now, as Bradly sat drinking from his third bottle of rum, he thought to himself, all of his caution with women had been for nothing. "Damn," he swore out loud. Who did his grandfather think he was, arranging a marriage for him?

That morning a messenger had arrived at Moon Rise with a packet from England, containing a letter from Bradly's grandfather, Peter Deveraux. Upon reading the letter Bradly had reached for a bottle of rum and started to drink.

"The old man is insane," he shouted to the walls. He had no right to sign any agreement concerning a marriage for him. Because the old man found himself in the position of being the eldest of the Deverauxs left, he thought himself capable of ruling his grandson's life. The old man knew how much Bradly loved him and thought to take advantage of this, Bradly stormed.

"This is preposterous," he mumbled, looking at the letter for the hundredth time. He could find his own wife when he so desired one. But even with these thoughts, he knew deep inside he would honor his grandfather's wishes. For outside of his own father, Peter Deveraux was the only other man Bradly had ever loved or respected.

Jezzie, Bradly's huge Negress housekeeper, stood outside of the study door pondering on what could be bothering her master. Ever since that messenger had brought him a letter he had shut himself up in his study, and she could hear him shouting and cussing so, she knew he must be drinking, which was not like her master at all. Curiosity was getting the better of her, but she could not think of a way in which to find out what was going on.

A loud crash sounded from within the room and here she saw her chance. As she went to the door and knocked she asked in a low voice, "Master Brad are you all right?"

"Come in, Jezzie," he shouted in a drunken voice.

"Yes, sir," she answered, thinking she would finally get to the bottom of this. As she looked at her master, who was now good and drunk she asked, "What's a-bothering you, sir? And why are you in here a-drinking yourself sick?"

Bradly stood looking at this large black

woman who had been in this house since before he had been born and who had taken care of him all of his life. "Jezzie, you shall be glad to hear that one of your wishes is finally going to come true."

Jezzie stood trying to understand what her master was talking about and shook her head from side to side. "I don't know what you be a-meaning Master Brad; old Jezzie she hasn't been a-wishing for nothing, Master Brad."

"Really?" Bradly asked with a drunken slur to his voice. "I received a letter from my grandfather this morning informing me of my coming marriage."

"What you be a-talking about, Master Brad?" she asked with questioning brown eyes.

Bradly looked upon her with anger contorting his features. "I am to be married; a bride shall arrive in Richmond within the next few months and that means there will be a new mistress at Moon Rise."

It took a full minute for the meaning of his words to form in Jezzie's head, but when finally his meaning took shape her face burst into a huge smile. "Lordy, Master Brad, if that's the truth why are you a-getting drunk and acting like you just lost your best friend? Think you would be happy, for this old house to have a new mistress. It sure will be nice to have a white lady back in this house once again. I just about gave up on you ever getting yourself a wife." She rambled on.

19

"Get out!" Bradly shouted, rising to his feet and almost falling in the process.

"Yes, sir, Master Brad, I'm a-going," she said backing out the door with a huge smile on her large black face. She shut the door and Bradly could hear her chuckling. "It sure will be something to have a new mistress and maybe she will be able to get the master out of his black moods that he gets himself into."

Bradly sat slumped over his desk cursing himself for ever telling Jezzie, and his grandfather for ever having started this whole business.

He could picture in his mind the type of woman he would be saddled with. She would probably be homely, without a trace of beauty; why else would her family need to pawn her off on a man halfway around the world?

Chapter Two

As the morning's brilliant sun shone down upon the land and each person went about his or her daily tasks amidst the hustle and bustle of the London streets, Katherine Rafferty sat alone in her elegantly furnished bedroom pondering over the fate that ruled people's lives and the cruel tricks it could hand out to one.

21

Katherine had tried with all of her might for the past month and a half to sway her father's decision to send her to a foreign country to marry a man she had never met. But all of her pleading and begging had been in vain. Her father had remained steadfast in his decision and had even told her of his wish for Rachel to accompany her as a traveling companion on her voyage.

Katherine let out her breath in a long sigh. "I don't even know my own father anymore," she told herself. "He acts as a stranger or a far distant relative, who does not care about my feelings or my wishes."

As these thoughts went through her head she thought back to the time when her mother had been alive. Her father had been deeply in love with her mother and Katherine knew he had loved her also. The three of them had been so happy until the night when her mother had been thrown from her carriage and killed while visiting a sick neighbor. Her mother's death had been a mortal wound to her father, and one which to this day had not healed. John Rafferty had thought his whole world had fallen apart at the death of his wife and he had taken to drinking and gambling. He would go out nights, leaving his ten-year-old daughter in the care of servants and her nurse, Biddy.

Katherine thought back on those days with a shudder which she could not suppress. She had been so lonely and scared thinking her father had deserted her, and the death of her mother had been unbearable.

She could remember waking up at night and crying for hours at a time for her father while Biddy would hold her and comfort her the best she could.

Then when she was sixteen her father had announced his intentions of remarrying. Katherine could look back and almost laugh at herself for thinking at the time of his annoucement what a good idea it was for him to remarry.

Katherine could remember her first meeting with Joann, who had just returned from her honeymoon. Katherine had disliked the other woman immediately. She had tried to be friendly, to get along with Joann, but her father's wife seemed to resent her and would not make any kind of effort to establish a rapport. Katherine had tried to stay out of her stepmother's way as much as possible and when Joann's niece, Rachel, had moved in with them, she had tried to avoid the both of them. They were so much alike she could not bring herself to be friendly with the girl.

Whenever an opportunity presented itself, Joann and Rachel would run and tell John Rafferty anything which Katherine did to their disliking. But this time she thought, Joann had schemed and won; she would soon be out of her way completely, thousands of miles away. But the one thing that Katherine could not figure out was why Rachel would wish to go all the way to America.

Rachel was in her room when a servant brought a message from her aunt, requesting her presence in the parlor as soon as possible. Rachel could not figure out what she could have on her mind, but perhaps it was about her stepdaughter, that little twit, Katherine. Her aunt was always coming up with some new plot against her. She had best hurry, she thought, for her aunt did not like to be kept waiting and Rachel had no wish to get on the wrong side of the woman. She knew her well and was aware that she had a very vengeful and cruel streak.

Rachel Profane was the daughter of Charles and Millicent Profane. After the death of her mother, Rachel had been left in the care of her father. She could get furious just thinking of her father. He had gone through all his money on gambling and loose women and at his death Rachel had had to seek out her aunt and take the charity that she offered her. If only I could have been born like Katherine, she thought, instead of a poor penniless beggar, having to beg for the morsels of bread I eat. Katherine, that bitch, she thought with rage, had everything—this house, lovely clothes, and all of her beautiful jewels—while a woman like herself, who more than deserved the good things in life, had nothing. Well, one day, she swore with vengeance, I'll have everything just like that little simple Katherine.

24

By the time Rachel reached the parlor to greet her aunt she was so upset by her troubled thoughts that she doubted whether she would be able to keep her emotions concealed. When she entered the room her Aunt Joann was deep in thought herself and didn't notice the turmoil going on within Rachel.

Rachel cleared her throat and started. "Aunt Joann, you wished to have a word with me? I was thinking of going for a walk through the gardens; it is such a lovely day and I hate to miss a walk on a day like this. Winter will be here soon and I do detest the cold weather."

"Rachel, if you would be good enough to take a seat for just a few minutes, I do have something of importance to talk over with you. Would you care for a cup of tea, dear?"

"No, thank you, Aunt Joann, I had a late breakfast this morning and I fear I overdid." Rachel could not figure out what was going on in her aunt's scheming head; she was eaten up with curiosity and could hardly wait for her to finish the small talk and get on with what she had on her mind.

"Well, Rachel," Joann began, "I called you here to have a little talk with you about your future welfare. As you know you came to this house virtually penniless and I have a proposition to offer to you."

"Yes, Aunt Joann?" Rachel asked, feeling a small rage she could hardly conceal spread through her body. The nerve of this woman, acting so superior and haughty, when she herself had been no better off before her marriage to Lord Rafferty.

"As I was saying, you have no funds of your own and John and I are in need of a companion for Katherine, someone to accompany her on her trip to the colonies. You shall have funds for the voyage and perhaps will be able to find yourself a husband while you are on this visit. There are, I hear, many young men in this new land and I hear there are plenty of rich ones."

"And if I do not wish to go to this foreign land as a companion for Katherine, Aunt Joann?" Rachel questioned, already knowing the answer.

"I am afraid dear you have no choice; you will find yourself out in the street if you do not comply. I will assure you though, that if you do not find yourself an agreeable young man I shall send you funds to get yourself started in some other venture of your choice."

Rachel knew that this last statement was a lie and that once she left she would be on her own, but what other choice did she have but to go along with her aunt. Perhaps she would find herself a rich husband in America, and she had to admit it would be an exciting adventure. Rachel knew Joann was waiting for her answer so she put on a forlorn expression and answered. "Very well, Aunt Joann, since I seem to have no choice in the matter and you are so set on having things to your own liking, I shall accept your offer and accompany Katherine on her trip. Does Katherine know of your plans?" she asked, with a sarcastic tone of voice.

"Yes, she does, dear, and I assure you she will be no trouble. Her father has talked to her on this matter, and she seems to give no resistance to his wishes. But let me tell you I am glad you are using your head and going along with my plans. You may leave now," Joann said rising from the settee. "I shall have to see about some other arrangements that are in need of my tending."

"Thank you, Aunt Joann. I think I shall go out for my walk now; I find myself wishing to think about my future for a while."

Joann was relieved when Rachel left the room; she had all but held her breath waiting for her answer about the trip. She could not help thinking what she would have done if Rachel had refused to go. John would have forbade her from leaving Rachel to take care of herself.

Yes, she thought, Rachel was just like herself, trying to make things go just as she wanted. She was sure her niece would fare better than her stepdaughter, Katherine. She had heard of Bradly Deveraux and she could not envy Katherine one bit. From what she had heard, Bradly Deveraux had a cruel temper and he had had one affair after another. She certainly would not wish to be in

Katherine's shoes when she was forced to marry this man.

Katherine arrived at dinner wearing a light-blue muslin gown with tiny sprigs of flowers on it. She wore her hair flowing free to her waist, and made a very fetching sight to behold as she entered the dining room.

Joann and Rachel were already in their places and were talking comfortably about the trip on which the two young ladies would be going.

As Katherine took her seat her father strolled into the room. "Good evening, ladies, I hope I have not kept you waiting. I was talking with James about the amount of liquor we would need for the ball tomorrow night."

Joann looked up with a smile. "You needn't have bothered yourself, John. I could have done it if you had mentioned the matter to me. I am afraid I have been so busy with the preparations for this ball that I have been running myself to a frazzle," she said, with as weary a smile as she could muster.

"I know you have been working hard my dear, but I do wish everything to be perfect for Katherine's last ball in England," he stated, looking down at his daughter. "Have you finished your packing, Katherine, my child? You know it will be but two more days and you shall be on your way."

"Yes, Father," she answered meekly, her words hardly reaching his ears.

"Are you not feeling well, dear?" Joann questioned with a sly grin. "It would not do for you to come down with a fever or something right before your voyage."

Katherine straightened her backbone and looked directly at her tormentor. "I feel perfectly fine, Joann, and I am in the best of health I assure you." She'd be damned if she would let this woman make her feel like some kind of a frightened kitten.

"I am glad to hear that," Joann replied, wishing she could reach over and slap that small white innocent face in front of her. "Rachel and I were just discussing your trip and Rachel has found she is in need of a few new items of clothing before she will be ready to leave. There are so few days left that I have promised her we would go tomorrow and pick out the things which she needs. And I do insist on your joining us on our outing, Katherine."

Katherine had no wish to accompany her stepmother anywhere. "I am afraid that I shall have to disappoint you, Joann. I must go to Madam Elizabeth's dress shop tomorrow and pick up a few dresses which she has been holding for me."

"Well, that is fine, dear. I had in mind to go by there myself, so we could all go along together."

Katherine started to protest, but her father settled the matter for her.

"Of course, you shall go along with Joann and Rachel. Katherine, do not forget you have only a short time more to remain with us so you would not wish to hurt your stepmother's feelings, would you, dear?"

Katherine could only accept the invitation as gracefully as possible, but she went through the rest of the meal feeling a dread for the day ahead.

Katherine excused herself early from the small dinner party and retired soon after to her bed. But she found little sleep until the early hours of the morning. Each time she would start to drift off she would be wakened by a dream in which a large beast tried to grab and devour her, while she fought with all her strength.

Katherine awoke the next morning when Biddy opened her door, carrying a small tray of rolls and tea.

"Miss Katherine, you had best get yourself up. Lady Joann and Miss Rachel are downstairs waiting for you. It's done past nine o'clock and you have a busy day ahead of you."

"I know, Biddy, but I am so tired," Katherine said, raising on an elbow and covering a yawn with her small hand. "I hardly slept a wink last night; I kept having the strangest dream."

"I'm sorry, honey, but you had better eat this breakfast and get yourself dressed," Biddy said, placing the tray upon a small table.

"Biddy, please tell Joann and Rachel I shall

be down as soon as I dress."

"I sure will, honey, but you eat before you leave this room. With all your shopping and then the ball tonight, you'll be sick if you don't eat and keep up your strength."

"Oh Biddy, you are just too fussy," Katherine said, laughing while she put on her robe and started to sip her tea. "I really am quite hungry; I could hardly eat a thing last night."

"Well, you just finish your breakfast and I'll be back up shortly."

Katherine descended the stairs wearing a light-yellow dress which set off her dark hair and fair complexion to its best. She wore her hair in a simple coiffure with yellow ribbons entwined throughout the curls, and tiny curls dangling at the nape of her neck and at each temple. She looked as fresh as a spring day but her spirits, which had risen, were now taking a fall as she approached the two women waiting for her at the bottom of the stairs.

"Katherine, you look most becoming," said Joann with a tinge of anger to her voice. "I presume you are aware you have kept us waiting this past hour?"

"I am sorry, Joann, but I overslept. I had the worst dreams during the night."

"Well, never mind now, let us be on our way. You are ready?" Joann asked looking at Katherine, hardly being able to contain the loathing she felt for the girl.

Katherine's spirits lifted after they had left the house. The excitement of the crowds of people running and hurrying about their business and the men and women shouting out their wares for sale always made Katherine's head reel with excitement. This morning the streets were full and as Katherine walked along with Joann and Rachel she felt a feeling of freedom and light-headedness.

Joann and Rachel both looked upon Katherine as if she were a child out for her first walk. They could not understand how anyone could enjoy the hustle and bustle of people shoving and shouting on the sidewalks of the London streets.

They were just about to enter the dress shop when Katherine heard the sound of her name being called. She turned as a young man came running up to her with his arms outstretched.

"Katherine! Is it really you? I could hardly believe my eyes when I saw you from down the street."

Katherine gave the man a brilliant smile. It was young Mark Prescot, one of the callers she had been receiving a few months before she had learned the news of her wedding.

"Why, Mark, how have you been?" she asked sweetly, giving him her hand. "I heard you had gone on a vacation to France."

"I had, Katherine, and have just returned this very day," he said devouring her with his eyes. "Tell me, how have you been, Katherine? Did you miss me while I was gone? I could hardly wait to get home so I could see you again. You look just grand," he said,

32

swallowing convulsively, as he dared to let his eyes wander to her bosom, which looked to be on the verge of bursting free of its tightly fitted bodice.

Joann cleared her throat, bringing Mark Prescot back to reality. "I beg your pardon, Lady Rafferty, Miss Profane, but I could hardly believe my good fortune in seeing you here on the street. I was going to call at your home this afternoon to speak with Katherine, but now that she is here I wonder if I might not be able to talk with her for just a few minutes?"

"Well it seems highly improper to me, but if Katherine wishes to speak with you for a few minutes alone, I suppose Rachel and I can go along into the dress shop and look around for a bit," Joann said in a haughty voice.

"Fine," Mark replied, not letting her attitude dampen his good spirits. "You are an angel of mercy, Lady Rafferty."

"Just a few minutes, mind you; it would not look proper for a young lady of Katherine's breeding to be seen about the streets alone with a gentleman," she added with a dark look. She turned and motioned for Rachel to follow her into the dress shop next to where they were standing.

As soon as the other two women were out of sight Mark took Katherine's hand and pressed it to his lips. "Katherine I have dreamt of nothing else these past few months but your sweet gentle face."

Katherine tried to disengage her hand from this passionate young man's grasp, but he held it as if it were his link with eternal life.

"Katherine, please hear me out. I know I am not the best young man in England, but I would like it very much if you would consider me as a future husband. I was going to beg you tonight when I came calling at your house and I would beg here and now on my hands and knees if there were room enough," he said with a huge grin.

"But Mark I cannot accept your proposal," Katherine murmured, not daring to look him in the eyes.

"What do you mean you cannot, Katherine?" he asked with a pleading look. "Is there someone else? Surely you knew how I felt about you?"

Katherine looked up at this tall good-looking man and her heart went out to him. "I do not love anyone—"

Before she could finish, he squeezed her hand tightly and said, "Please do not give me your answer now; think about it and I shall come to call this evening and we shall talk then. Oh, Katherine," he cried, "I shall make you the best husband."

Katherine pulled her arm free and looked into his green eyes which were full of hope. "Mark, you misunderstand me; I cannot marry you, for I am betrothed to another. If only I had known how you felt, if you had only mentioned something sooner," she said with tears starting to form in her eyes.

Mark stood as if he had just received a blow to his heart (and indeed he had; he loved this woman with all of his heart). "I do not understand. To whom are you betrothed? Where is this man?" he asked hardly above a whisper.

"You do not know the man, Mark. My father arranged my marriage for me and the man lives in the colonies—America."

"You are jesting! You cannot mean you shall be going all the way to that savage land, America?" he questioned, not believing his own ears.

"I assure you, sir, I am not jesting with you," Katherine replied, trying to get a grip on her feelings before she started crying here in front of all the people passing by them.

"Pray tell me, Katherine, you say you do not love this man? Is there any way to sway your father in this matter? Perhaps if I talk with him?"

Katherine shook her head in the negative, as tears started to make a path down her cheeks. "I am afraid my father will not relent in his decision. I am to leave the day after tomorrow."

"The day after tomorrow?" Mark asked incredulously. "Not so soon as that?"

"I am afraid so, and now I must be getting back to my stepmother or she will think ill of me," Katherine said, turning and running as tears flowed down her face.

Mark Prescot stood looking at her back as she fled to the dress shop. He would never again love as he did now, he swore to himself. All of his hopes and dreams he had put on her accepting his marriage proposal and now he was lost to love forever.

Katherine went through the rest of the morning following Joann and Rachel and not paying any attention to what was going on around her. The only thing she could think of was Mark Prescot's sad green eyes looking down upon her as if she had plunged a knife through his heart. She knew she would never have been able to marry him for she only felt a friendly affection for the young man. But meeting him, she had realized that if she could be more like all the other girls in England who married the first man who proposed, she would not be in the predicament she found herself in now.

By the time they had made their way back home Katherine was so miserable from listening to the other two women's talk and from her own self-pity that she only wished to retire to her room as quickly as possible.

As the three women entered the front door, voices could be heard coming from the study and at that same moment John Rafferty opened the door and on seeing his daughter, requested her to join him.

As Katherine entered the room her father took her by the arm and steered her toward a chair across the room whereupon sat an elderly gentleman with a smiling face and a mane of snow-white hair.

"Daughter, I would like to present to you Mr. Charles Vincent. He shall be traveling along with you and Rachel on your voyage to America. He is one of my dearest friends and has consented to see to your welfare until you are settled with your new husband. Charles, this is my daughter and my pride, Katherine," he added addressing the elderly man.

"It is my pleasure, Miss Rafferty," the older man said, rising and taking one of Katherine's hands. "I knew your mother, child, and I must say, you are her vision made over again. She was one of the most beautiful women I have ever had the pleasure of meeting. I shall look forward to the pleasure of your company on our long voyage, my dear."

Katherine liked the elderly man at once and knew she had found a lasting friend and ally. She gave him one of her most becoming smiles and expressed her hopes of a safe voyage. But as she spoke her words, she thought, Perhaps the voyage on the ship will not be too boring after all, with Mr. Vincent along.

John Rafferty looked upon them both and felt a feeling of relief; he was sure now he had made the right decision in engaging Charles Vincent to take charge of his daughter. He would protect her as if she were his own.

"Katherine dear, perhaps you would like to go to your room and rest for a while. I am sure you are exhausted after your morning of shopping. Mr. Vincent and I have matters to discuss and I do not wish you to be too tired tonight at your party."

"Very well, Father. I am rather tired. Mr. Vincent, it has been a pleasure meeting you," she said with a weary smile.

"The pleasure was all mine my child. Shall I say farewell until we meet aboard the *Good Hope,* the day after tomorrow?"

Katherine gave the kindly old man a smile as she took her leave. She felt a small amount of heaviness taken off her chest since meeting Mr. Vincent. Although still she did not look forward to this coming trip, she did not feel as despondent as she had a few hours ago.

As Katherine sat looking at her reflection in the mirror she let out a long sigh. Was this the same girl who only a few months ago would have been gaily awaiting the evening and the ball her father had arranged for her? But of course, this was not the same girl who looked back at her with those sad blue eyes. What did she have to be happy about? she questioned herself. She was betrothed to a man she had never met and was going to a foreign country. She would never be the same girl she had been; she would live out the rest of her life being used by others who had no thought about her or her feelings.

Biddy woke Katherine from her dismal thoughts. "Oh, Miss Katherine, you are the loveliest woman in all of England."

Katherine looked up into the mirror to meet her old nurse's eyes. "Thank you, Biddy, but I am sure you are exaggerating."

"No, ma'am, you're the prettiest by far. You look just like your mamma did at your age."

"If only my mother were here." Katherine sighed. "I would not find myself in this position, if she were still alive, and Father had never met Joann."

"I know, honey, but it don't do any good wishing for things that can't come true," Biddy said patting Katherine's hand. "For now you had best be getting ready to go downstairs. Most of the guests have already arrived and your father's sure to be in an uproar if you keep them waiting too long. Your father's gone through quite a bit to have a ball for you, before you have to be going away."

"I know, Biddy, and I do appreciate everything, but I really do not feel like a party."

"Now you come along, child, and stand up and take a good look at yourself before you go down there and turn all those young gentlemen's heads and put all those other women to shame."

"Oh Biddy, you are impossible," Katherine said, feeling somewhat better due to Biddy's gay manner.

As she stood and gazed into the mirror she knew she was looking her best. She was dressed in a red velvet gown, which enhanced her beauty to its fullest. Her bodice, which was daringly low-cut and tightly fitted, showed off her rich full bosom and small trim waist. She wore for jewelry only a small necklace with a tiny diamond stone in the center that matched the tiny diamond hair pins which Biddy had placed within each curl in her coiffure. Anyone who chanced to look upon this rare beauty she possessed would think of a rare stone that is fitted in its most perfect setting. She was by far the loveliest woman to be present at the ball that evening and when she descended the stairs everyone realized this.

As Katherine slowly made her way down the flight of stairs all movement below stopped, and all eyes rose to behold the vision of beauty descending the stairway. As she reached the bottom step, a score of young men rushed toward her to present themselves and to beg the honor of escorting her to the ballroom.

As she extended her hand to a handsome, soft-spoken gentleman, she thought, For sure all of the women will be glad to see me gone and married off. She saw a number of the ladies whispering behind their fans, as their eyes fell upon her.

The young man who had escorted Katherine to the ballroom was Dennis Wainwright. She had met him on one other occasion and thought him quite charming, even though a bit overdressed. He wore a deep-pink waistcoat, trousers that matched, and a striped vest in the same hue; a white high-collared lace shirt was worn beneath. Katherine thought its collar at any moment might choke him to death. He also carried a cane wherever he was seen and wore the most fashionable of shoes. Katherine thought him an overdressed popinjay, but tonight she would not find fault with any of the young men, she told herself.

As they made their way into the ballroom, Katherine's deep-violet eyes took in her surroundings. Her father indeed had gone all out to make this ball a success. The room itself was aglow with the many chandeliers which were blazing their light throughout the room. In a far corner, in a tiny alcove sat the musicians playing their beautiful music for the many people swirling across the dance floor. The smell of roses was strong in the air, for the French windows were opened wide and the cool night breeze was bringing the scent of the flowers from the gardens outside. Katherine took in all of the many men and women swirling to the music and thought, If never again I shall be able to attend another occasion such as this, I shall have this one night to treasure for the rest of my life.

Katherine danced her first dance of the evening on the arm of Dennis Wainwright, and as soon as this dance came to an end she was quickly claimed by another young man.

This went on and on until Katherine felt as though she would die from fatigue and then finally she was rescued by Dennis Wainwright again.

"Oh, I am sorry, Mr. Wainwright, but do you mind very much if we sit this dance out? I fear my feet are so weary I might just trip over your own, if I am forced into another turn on the dance floor right this moment."

Mr. Wainwright gave Katherine a large formal bow and stated, "Your every wish is my command, madam. Perhaps you would care to sit in the gardens for a spell and take some fresh air?"

"That would be very kind of you, sir," Katherine said as her eyes held him softly. "I do think, though, I could do with a glass of something cool to drink first."

"In that case, madam, I shall be proud to escort you to a bench in the gardens and then return to grant your wish."

"You are indeed, sir, most gallant," Katherine said softly.

Dennis Wainwright led Katherine to a bench in a secluded part of the gardens. "I shall be gone but a moment, Katherine," he said as he bowed to her, and even before she realized it he had vanished.

He was only gone a few moments and he returned with two glasses of sparkling champagne. "I hope you are feeling better now, Katherine," he said as he handed her a glass of the heady clear liquid.

"Oh much better indeed, sir. I am sorry for having to impose upon you like this."

"It was no imposition at all. What is a beautiful woman for if not to be waited upon? And please, Katherine, call me Dennis."

As Katherine took a deep drink of her champagne, she could feel the liquid relaxing her tired body. "I shall indeed call you Dennis if you wish, sir, for I have already begun to think of you as a friend and a savior," she said with a small laugh.

"But I would wish for more than mere friendship," he cajoled. "You are a very beautiful lady and I would wish for perhaps one small kiss for my gallantry."

Katherine looked up, shocked by this young man's words. "I am a betrothed woman and I shall not dishonor myself or my future husband by doing as you wish."

"You misunderstand me, my lovely Katherine," he whispered as he placed his arm around her shoulder. "I have only hopes of this night with you. I know you shall sail in two days, but what will it hurt for two old friends, as you put it, to be a little more than friends on this beautiful night? No one will ever know of our small interlude."

Katherine's smoldering violet eyes could not hide their loathing for this man as she gasped, "Get your filthy hands off me. I have no wish to be mauled by the likes of you!"

"But what would be the harm in one small kiss?" he coaxed, pulling her into his arms.

"You, sir, are overconfident of your powers over women," she sneered as she pushed against him. "And if you do not take your hands from my person I shall scream for help."

Katherine felt sickened by the moist feel

43

and liquor taste of his lips and pushed at him until he set her free again. When he withdrew his lips and relaxed somewhat against her, she shoved against him with one hand and brought her glass of champagne around and threw it full into his face with the other. "Now get yourself off my father's property before I kill you myself," she shouted, her lips drawing back into a feral sneer, and she clutched at the glass as if it were a deadly knife.

Dennis Wainwright looked upon this woman who stood as if she would desire nothing better than to slice his throat, with unbelieving eyes. "Very well, madam," he grunted, as he looked down at his clothes, which were sopping wet from the champagne. "I find myself in no condition to continue this evening anyway, but perhaps, dear lady, we shall meet again, in, shall I say, more pleasant circumstances." And with these words he turned and made his departure through the gardens.

With a feeling of relief she could not suppress, Katherine sat down on the bench. She had never thought he would have given up so easily, and she had no idea what she would have done if he had followed through with his pursuit. She should have known the type of man Dennis Wainwright was, she scolded herself. He was just like most of the other men in London—out for only their own gain, not caring about the outcome of their play or the measure of hurt inflicted on the

44

other person. Well, I am almost glad to be leaving all these fops in England, she swore, as she tried to straighten out her hair and clothes and to compose herself. For she would have to finish out the rest of the evening as if nothing had happened and all she could hope for now was a quick end to her last ball in England.

She spent the rest of the evening in a sort of daze. She went through the motions of dancing and putting on a gay face, although inside herself she felt as miserable as if she were a person about to face her executioner at any moment.

It was late in the evening before the last of the guests departed and gave Katherine their good wishes for her future life, but Katherine was finally able to make a quick retreat to her room and to her soft bed.

Katherine did not awake from her sound sleep until after the noon hour of the next day. Biddy woke her while she went from one end of her bedchamber to the other, packing and arranging last minute items for her trip the next morning.

Katherine sat up with a yawn and looked fondly toward the old woman. "Biddy, I shall miss you so much. Are you sure you will not change your mind and come with me to America?"

"We have been all through this once before, honey. I'm too old to up and move from my home and I sure wouldn't know what to do in some strange country. Why, I wouldn't know a thing or a person. But you, child, don't you worry; you're young and you will make out just fine, and, honey, I'm going to miss you more than I could ever tell you," the old nurse said with tears in her small green eyes.

"I know, Biddy, and I am sorry to keep at you about this; it is only that I wish things were different and I did not have to go all the way to America. I would even submit willingly to an arranged marriage if I could stay here and be near you and Father and everything I love."

"Now, don't you start feeling so down this early in the day, child. Old Biddy's got a feeling in her bones, and it's telling her that you're going to make out just fine in your new life. Now you had better hurry up and dress and eat, for we have a lot to get done today in order to have you on that boat tomorrow morning."

It was late in the afternoon before everything was ready and sent to the docks, to be loaded aboard the *Good Hope*.

Dinner that evening was a strained affair with everyone deep in thought. Katherine excused herself as soon as she finished the few bites of food which she could bear to eat and escaped to her bedchamber, to be alone with her own desolate thoughts.

An hour or so had passed by before her

father knocked at her door and entered with a tender smile playing on his features.

"Katie child, I came to wish you a good night and to talk with you for a few moments."

Katherine looked up with an expectant expression. "What is it, Father?"

"I love you, child, and shall miss you with all my heart—more, I am sure, than you shall ever realize. And also, Katie, I want you to know that I wish the best for you in all things." He spoke softly, finding it hard to express the words he wished to say to his only daughter.

"I know, Father, and I shall miss you and Biddy more than I think I shall be able to bear."

"I think you shall be happy, Daughter, and I hope you have many children to do you proud as you have done for me," he murmured softly, as his eyes held a plea for forgiveness. "I have also brought you a gift which I hope will be as close to your heart as it has always been to mine." He held out a gold chain and a locket of white gold with tiny diamonds forming a circle around a little emerald stone in the center.

Katherine reached out and took the necklace with loving hands. As she opened the locket she saw within, two tiny miniatures, one of her mother and the other of her father. "Oh, Father, I shall treasure it always and I shall wear it with fond and loving memories of

47

you and my mother."

"Your mother and I had the miniatures painted shortly after you were born and your mother loved to wear it. I know she would wish for you to have it, Daughter." As John Rafferty spoke, tears formed in his light-blue eyes.

Katherine ran to her father, hugged him tightly to her, and whispered, "I shall love it as Mother did, Father, and I thank you for giving it to me."

He kissed his daughter tenderly on the cheek and held her in his arms for a few minutes, regretting that he had not done this in such a long time and aware that he might not see his only daughter for a long time, if ever again.

"Katherine," John said softly, as he set her from him. "I must be leaving you to your bed now darling, for you shall have a busy day tomorrow and you must get your rest." He reached over and softly laid a kiss upon her forehead. "Good night, child, and may God send you pleasant dreams, on this the last night under your father's roof."

"Good night," she whispered softly as she wiped a tear from her eye, sat down upon the bed, and gazed lovingly at the locket in her hand.

Her father eased out the door and shut it softly behind him, thinking of the love he held for his daughter as he made his way to his study to pour himself a strong drink.

Katherine stared down at the miniatures of

her mother and father. She had almost forgotten the tenderness and love her father possessed. But she would never forget again, she told herself; nor would she forget the yearning look in her father's eyes as he had looked upon the miniature of his cherished wife—her mother.

Katherine awoke early the next morning and took her place in the dining room to have her breakfast. She was informed by a servant that her father had left earlier on business and had left a message that he would be back shortly to escort her and Rachel to the ship. As Katherine sat drinking her tea, Joann entered the room.

"Good morning, dear, I hope you slept well," she said with sarcasm dripping from her voice.

"Why yes, I did. Thank you for being so concerned," Katherine answered, not wanting this woman to see her low mood.

"I just wanted to stop in for a moment and offer you my best wishes on your voyage and your coming marriage."

Katherine lifted one dark brow mockingly. "Oh? You will not be going along then to see us off?"

"I am afraid not, dear. I have an appointment which I cannot break and I shan't be back in time to go along with John."

"Well, thank you for your wishes Joann, but I am sure I shall manage quite well for myself without anyone's wishes."

"I am glad to hear you say that, Katherine. I was afraid you were still upset by the whole affair."

"No, Joann, I have grown up some in the past few months and I do not see any sense in getting upset over matters I have no control over. And also I must confess I shall be glad to be away from here and away from people who have no wish for me to be around."

"Well!" Joann said in a huff. "Very well then, I shall take my leave now, until we may perhaps meet again," she said starting toward the door.

"Yes, Joann, until we meet again." Katherine felt relieved at being able to at last let the woman know that she was not taken in by her sweet words.

As Joann shut the door on her way out, she murmured to herself, "The little chit, she knew all this time that it was my idea for her to marry. Well, no matter, she and that little sponger Rachel shall be gone and out of my life forever and I only hope I never set eyes on either one of them again."

Not long after Katherine's meeting with her stepmother, her father returned home.

"Good morning, Daughter. I hope you are about finished with your breakfast. We should be leaving soon. Have you seen Rachel this morning? I do hope she will not keep us waiting too long. Mr. Vincent will be waiting for us on the dock."

Katherine gave her father a warm smile, remembering his words from last night.

"Would you care for a cup of coffee, Father? I am sure Rachel will be down soon."

John Vern Rafferty's heart melted as he looked at his daughter's lovely face. To never be able to see that adoring face again might prove more than he could bear. "No, child, I have already had my coffee this morning, but I have not yet told you how lovely you look today, Katherine."

"Thank you, Father, but I must confess I am rather nervous about going on a ship; it is something completely new," she said slowly as she fondled the locket around her throat.

"Have no fear on that account, dear. I am sure you will be quite comfortable on the *Good Hope* and the captain is as good a sea captain as can be found. But now, my darling," he said drawing her from her chair, "we must see what is keeping Rachel."

It was only a few minutes later when Katherine stood with her father and Rachel telling the servants good-by. "Oh, Biddy, I do wish you were coming along. I shall write to you as soon as I can." Katherine cried as she held the old nurse tightly against her.

"Now you hush yourself and dry those tears, honey. It won't be forever." Biddy wept against Katherine's soft hair.

"I hope I shall be able to return soon, Biddy, and I shall keep your memory in my heart always," Katherine said, releasing the nurse from her hold, and trying to dry her tears.

*   *   *

As Katherine, Rachel, and John Rafferty made their way through the London streets and toward the docks, Katherine craned her neck this way and that out the carriage window to take in all the sights of this last day in England.

It was a cool, crisp morning and the fog was just rolling out to sea, when Katherine felt the first tinge of salt from the ocean hit her nostrils. It was still early and the everyday life of the London streets had not yet begun; but here on the docks was a different story.

Wherever one would chance to look, the scurrying and activity of men at work could be seen. There were men unloading and loading boxes and crates from the ships to the docks.

As the carriage pulled to a stop Katherine looked on as a giant of a black man with huge muscles stood holding two huge crates, one in each arm.

Her father noticed the direction of her gaze, and rested a hand upon one of her own. "They are busy today, for there are three ships leaving port this afternoon. They must load their provisions aboard this morning, and I am quite sure that a man of that size is used to putting his back into his work."

"It is amazing, Father. I do not think I have ever seen a man as large as that," Katherine whispered, still looking at this gargantuan Negro from her window.

"You can see all kinds of different sights here on the docks," her father said. "But now I see Mr. Vincent, so we must be getting out of the carriage child."

Mr. Vincent stood holding the carriage door open as Katherine's father handed the ladies out to the ground. "Good morning, ladies. I hope you are both feeling up to your adventure today?"

"Good morning, Charles, I trust we have not kept you waiting?" John Rafferty said with a large smile for his friend.

"Indeed not, John. I myself have just arrived. And this, John, must be Miss Profane?" he inquired, looking toward Rachel with a fatherly smile.

"Yes, it is, Charles. Rachel, this is Mr. Charles Vincent. He shall be traveling along with the two of you to America."

Rachel held out one gloved hand and gave the elderly man a cold smile. "Mr. Vincent, it is a pleasure to meet you."

Charles Vincent was a good judge of people and he knew at once the kind of woman this Rachel Profane was. He could not understand why John Rafferty would choose her to accompany his lovely daughter on her trip to America. "The pleasure is mine, Miss Profane," he stated as coldly as she herself had spoken.

As the small group made their way to the boarding plank to board the *Good Hope*, Katherine surveyed the long sleek ship that would be her home for the next few weeks. She noticed at once the clean-cut and well-cared-for look about the ship, and she could only hope that it would be as seaworthy as her

53

father had claimed. As they made their way to the quarter-deck Katherine's preoccupation with the many different sights, was interrupted when she heard a loud clear male voice coming from the bow of the boat.

Mr. Vincent looked up and toward the voice. "Here comes our good captain now. Come along and I shall introduce you all to him. He looks a mite young, but I assure you, John, he is as good a sea captain as you will find anywhere."

As they came into view of a tall, golden-haired man with a trimmed beard and mustache, Katherine could hardly believe her eyes. She had expected to see an elderly man in rough dress, but instead saw before her a handsome young man, looking to be about the age of twenty-nine.

"Captain Eldridge, these are your two passengers and Lord John Vern Rafferty." Mr. Vincent made the introductions. "And ladies, this is your captain, Anthony Eldridge."

Anthony Eldridge was the only son of Lord Thomas Eldridge, who had given his son, upon his twenty-seventh birthday, the *Good Hope* as a present. Lord Eldridge deplored the fact that his son loved the sea, but he could deny him nothing, since he was his only child. Captain Eldridge ran a smooth ship and got on well with his crew. He also had a shady reputation with the ladies and prized himself on picking the most beautiful women for himself and being the envy of his friends and companions.

Captain Eldridge showed a smile of flashing white teeth to his companions and presented a formal courtly bow to the ladies. "Mr. Rafferty, Mr. Vincent has been telling me of you and your charming daughter and niece. And you," he turned in Katherine's direction, "must be Miss Rafferty?" What a beauty, he told himself, this was one voyage he would enjoy. With this lovely woman along it certainly would not be routine or boring as it had been on a number of occasions before.

Rachel cleared her throat, smoldering with jealousy as Anthony Eldridge stood holding Katherine's hand, and looking into her violet eyes longer than necessary.

"Oh, excuse me, you must be Miss Profane. It is a pleasure to meet you, madam," he replied automatically, taking her hand and lightly kissing the fingers before releasing it. This was the type of woman most men tried to avoid, he thought to himself. She was plain-looking and would try to bind a man to her if the opportunity presented itself. Well, he would put her out of his mind and just keep the image of the lovely Katherine there.

After meeting the captain of the *Good Hope*, John Rafferty made his farewells to his daughter and niece, reminding his daughter to write to him on the first chance she could find. Katherine and Rachel were then informed they would set sail within the next two hours, as soon as their provisions were all loaded and all the crew had boarded.

55

Chapter Three

Katherine and Rachel were shown to their cabin by the captain of the *Good Hope*. Katherine could see the eagerness in this man's eyes and manner and did not wish to add any more fuel to his fire. She thought it might prove best to stay out of his way as much as possible, but then his gallantry was very pleasing and he could help to make this boring voyage livelier.

As Captain Eldridge led the way to their cabin, Katherine gave him one of her most breath-taking smiles.

Anthony Eldridge's heart fluttered at this smile bestowed upon him. He had never seen beauty such as this in all of his travels, and he could not wait to hold her supple body and kiss those soft pink lips which seemed to be begging to be taken; and he had no doubts that he would in time take those lips with his own.

Rachel could tell the emotions which were playing inside the captain and she became more furious than ever. She swore to herself to make Katherine pay for this insult that the captain had shown her. She could not understand why men would prefer that simpering little mouse to her.

When they reached the cabin both the girls were surprised by what met their eyes. They had thought to be sharing a small room with hardly enough room for the both of them. But when Captain Eldridge showed them to a room containing a large canopied bed in the center, a dark blue carpet and an enormous built-in cedar chest in one wall, both girls just stood staring at the room before them. One whole length of a wall consisted of mirrors and on the other wall there was a porthole with a built-in settee beneath, upon which one could sit and watch the sea or the stars at night. It was a room which one did not expect to find on a ship such as this. It was large and spacious and hardly seemed to be on a ship at all.

Katherine was the first to speak after looking about her. "Captain Eldridge, is this the room for us?" she asked, hardly believing what she saw in front of her. "I was under the impression that a merchant ship such as this used all of its available space for its cargo."

"Yes indeed, Miss Rafferty, usually that is so but my father had this ship built and he had this room built especially for my wife when and if I should chance to choose myself a wife, that is. But for myself, I prefer to use a cabin, shall I say, less lavish."

"Really, Captain?" Rachel queried, trying not to let the couple forget that she, too, was present in the room. "I was under the belief that most seamen believe that a woman is a curse upon a ship."

"I assure you, Miss Profane, I have no such belief on that matter and as you can see for yourself, when I do take a wife she will spend a great deal of time here on the sea with me. Well, ladies, I must leave you now and see to my ship. If you will excuse me, perhaps you would like to rest for a time?"

"Thank you for your kindness, Captain," Katherine said softly. "I do believe I would like to rest for a while. I find I have grown quite tired."

"Well, ladies, until we see each other again at dinner," Anthony said, bowing in Katherine's direction.

*   *   *

As soon as Captain Eldridge had shut the door Rachel stood glaring at Katherine from across the room. "Really, Katherine, you were just shocking, the way you practically threw yourself at the captain. What were you thinking of?"

"Whatever are you talking about, Rachel? I have not given the captain any kind of encouragement, whatsoever!"

Rachel could see she had hit Katherine's core and thought she had best smooth things over for the time being. "I am sorry if I offended you, but I am sure you know a betrothed woman on the way to meet her future husband should have some morals."

Katherine was so stunned by these last words she could hardly find the words she wished to say. Finally she regained her composure and spoke very slowly and mean-ingfully. "How dare you! You and your aunt arranged for your passage on this ship against my wishes, and I am sure you knew this. But I shall have my wishes obeyed on this one subject. You may think what you wish, but do not open your mouth in front of me again about my morals. Do you understand? If ever you do make such a statement in my presence again you will rue the day! Do you hear?"

Rachel just stood in silence. She had never before seen this prim, soft-spoken woman looking so fierce. She had known when she had spoken her words that her anger had been ruling her better judgment, but she had not contained herself and now she knew she had best mollify this argument as quickly as possible. "I understand, Katherine. I was just thinking of your best interests."

"I will not hear any more on this subject, Rachel," Katherine said as she turned and walked from their cabin, feeling angrier than she could ever remember being. Could Rachel possibly believe that I would let her talk to me in the manner she had? she asked herself. Well, Rachel will learn and very quickly that I am not the same girl who lived under my father's roof and who never said a word back in anger to her or Joann.

Katherine found herself deep in thought standing at the rail of the deck when the merchant ship *Good Hope* left the docks of London and set her sails toward the sea and an unknown world. She had resigned herself earlier to make the most of her trip and now as she stood looking at her last glimpse of her home and country, England, she felt a bit better about her own fate. She would take what came to her and perhaps she would find a small amount of happiness in this new world to which she was traveling. Katherine stood thus thinking until the last bit of England faded into the distance and then made her way back to her room.

Katherine and Rachel were making their way to the dining area when Mr. Vincent approached them. "Good evening, ladies. I hope you were able to rest for a while and I also hope you find your quarters comfortable. I am sorry I could not see you to your cabin this morning, but I had matters which needed my attention."

"That was quite all right," answered Rachel. "The captain was good enough to show us to our room and it is perfectly satisfactory, I assure you."

Katherine remained quiet, sensing Rachel's tone, and she hoped Mr. Vincent would not take offense with her manner. She could not understand this girl. Why would she want to be rude to a man as kind as Mr. Vincent? "Is it not a beautiful night, Mr. Vincent? The stars seem to be close enough to touch."

"Yes, it surely is, Miss Rafferty. I believe you could search the world over and never would you be able to find a night more beautiful than right here on the seas."

"I do agree with you, Mr. Vincent. It is really breath-taking," Katherine said looking to the sky.

"If you two do not mind, I would like to dine; I find myself quite hungry," Rachel sneered, in an impatient voice.

"Why of course, Miss Profane. I would be honored to escort you both to dinner. I am sure it should be about time to serve."

Dinner that evening was a sort of formal affair, with Captain Eldridge acting host. His first mate, Mr. Foxworthy, was also present.

He was a young man, with a crop of bright-red hair, short and squat of build. He was a jolly, young man who had been all around the world and Katherine found his company quite entertaining. There were also two other members of the crew presiding; the additional company made the small gathering a gay affair.

Katherine ate her food with the gusto of one who was starving; and in fact that is how she felt. For the past few days she had only nibbled at small amounts of her meals and now she could hardly fill her empty stomach.

As the evening wore on, Katherine smiled and flirted with the captain and his guests. She did this mainly for the satisfaction of watching Rachel's anger from the corner of her eye.

By the finish of the evening Katherine found herself yawning, for she was exhausted, thanks to the good food and her long day. Mr. Vincent and Captain Eldridge escorted the ladies to the safety of their cabin and at the door wished them a good night. Then the men also withdrew to their own cabins.

Both of the women retired immediately to the canopy bed and within minutes they were softly brought to sleep by the easy motion of the ship.

The next morning Katherine awoke with the first rays of light. She could hear it lightly raining outside her cabin and she snuggled deeper under the quilt which covered her, feeling a slight chill from the cool air. She drifted back to sleep with the thought that she had always loved the feel of a winter breeze upon her face.

For the next few days it rained with a steady drizzle and both women stayed in their cabin and tried to stay out of each other's way.

Upon the fourth morning of the trip the weather had cleared and the sun shone down brightly upon the *Good Hope*.

As soon as Katherine found that it was not raining outside she made her way to the deck of the ship, relieved to be able to leave the confines of her cabin and more than glad to be away from Rachel's endless bickering about the weather. As Katherine walked she could feel the first cool air of the winter ahead.

Katherine stood looking out to sea and enjoying the peaceful mood which had settled over her, when she heard a soft rustle of movement behind her. She turned, not knowing who she would find, and there in back of her stood Captain Eldridge, gazing down at her with a yearning look in his eyes, which he could not hide.

"Captain, you startled me," Katherine said uneasily, seeing the way his eyes were appraising her body.

"Do forgive me for my rudeness, Miss Rafferty, but I saw you standing here all alone and I thought that perhaps you would care for some company."

"There is nothing to forgive, sir. I thank you for your kindness. It is such a lovely day,

I just could not resist taking a stroll, after being shut up for the past few days in my cabin."

"Feel free to stroll as much as you wish," Captain Eldridge said, moving to her side by the rail of the ship. "There is one small favor I would wish to ask of you, if it is permitted, that is?"

"And what is it you would wish, sir?" Katherine asked, looking up into his face.

"If you would allow it, I would like to call you Katherine."

"By all means, Captain, please feel free to do so."

"Thank you, Katherine. It is such a beautiful name, but not half as beautiful as the woman to whom it belongs."

Katherine could feel the color rise to her face. "Why, thank you for your kind words, sir, but now I really must be getting back to my cabin," she murmured not wanting this conversation to go too far.

As she started to walk by him and seek the safety of her cabin, Captain Eldridge placed a hand familiarly upon her arm.

"There is one more thing which I would wish to ask of you."

"What is that, Captain?" ·

"I was wondering if perhaps you might care to dine this evening with me in my quarters?"

With this question, Katherine raised one dark eyebrow and started to shake her head. "I am afraid—"

"It shall all be quite proper I assure you, Katherine," he said, not letting her finish. "I only wish for a small amount of your pleasant company and for us to get to know one another better. I promise I shall be a perfect gentleman," he added with a large smile.

Katherine could only smile in return and answer him with a yes. She could find no reason to deny him and she was sure he would do just as he said. Wasn't he a gentleman and captain of the *Good Hope?* she asked herself.

"Fine, fine." He smiled. "I shall have my first mate, Mr. Foxworthy drop in and escort you to my cabin. But for now, I must be about business. Until I see you this evening, Katherine, which I shall await impatiently," he said softly, gazing into her violet eyes and kissing one of her soft white hands.

All the rest of the day Katherine had a feeling of doom for the evening ahead. She wished time and again that she had said no to their tall good-looking captain.

But as the day wore on, she told herself she had no way out of this engagement, and perhaps her fears were for nothing. At least she would not have to endure Rachel's scheming eyes and demanding voice.

About an hour before the dinner hour, Katherine dressed herself. She chose a pale-yellow gown with a low-cut bodice, which was the style that most women wore at this time. She braided her hair with a light-yellow ribbon running its length; this she made into a bun at the back of her head and then made tiny curls at each temple. She set this off with a diamond necklace and earrings to match. As she gazed into the mirror she said aloud, "That will just have to do; it is the best I can do alone."

When the first mate, Mr. Foxworthy, arrived at Katherine's door he could only feel envy toward his captain. He had thought Katherine lovely the other night at dinner, but now he could hardly keep his eyes from her beautiful face. This was the kind of woman for whom any man would be glad to lay down his life, he told himself.

When Katherine arrived at the captain's cabin, Anthony Eldridge was there waiting for her at his door.

"Come in, Katherine. Would you care to have a seat?" he asked, indicating a small settee across the room. "You look gorgeous, Katherine, and I know you will enjoy the meal I have planned for us."

Katherine looked around at her surroundings as she took a seat upon the settee. She was not surprised to see that his cabin was just as charming as her own, but with more of a masculine feel to it.

"Would you care for a drink of sherry?" he asked reaching for a small decanter upon a table.

"That would be nice, Captain."

He poured them both a small goblet of the amber liquid from the decanter and handed

Katherine one. "Please, Katherine, call me Anthony. Captain Eldridge sounds so formal and I do wish for us to become good friends."

"Of course, Anthony, I would be happy to," Katherine replied, sipping slowly at her wine.

"Dinner shall be ready in a few minutes, but until then, let us drink a toast to the good fortune that brought you to my ship and brought us together." As he spoke, he downed his sherry in one long drink and reached for the decanter to refill his goblet.

By the time the first mate brought the trays of food, Anthony Eldridge had drunk four more glasses of the sherry and was feeling very high from the potent liquid.

The meal consisted of a succulent plump, roasted duck, several vegetables of a different variety, which had been cooked together in a delectable sauce, and for dessert there was a bowl of sundry fruits floating in a delicious red wine.

At first, Katherine put all of her attention on the food in front of her and when, finally, she looked at the man across from her she noticed he had not touched his food, but had sat drinking great amounts of wine and watching her as she ate.

"Is something wrong, Captain? The food is delicious."

"No, nothing is wrong, Katherine; it is just that your beauty takes all thought of food from my mind. You know, Katherine, you are the most beautiful woman I have ever seen."

"Thank you, Captain," she answered feeling a little frightened by the sound of his voice. She knew he had been drinking far too much and thought she had best take her leave before he became drunk.

"I am already beginning to feel grieved at just the thought of our departure when we reach Richmond." As he said this he reached over and took hold of one of her hands.

Katherine looked toward the captain, feeling a cold hand of fear run through her body. She pulled her hand free and started to rise. "Captain Eldridge, I think I should be going to my cabin now."

Before she knew it, Captain Eldridge was standing in front of her and placing his hands on either side of her waist. "Katherine, you must know what your presence does to my senses. I need you, Katherine. I want to hold you and caress your beautiful body. I must have you for my own, Katherine."

"Captain Eldridge, you go too far; please release me and let me go to my room."

Captain Eldridge did not hear her words; all his drunken mind could think of was possessing this lovely creature standing before him. He pulled her tighter to him and buried his lips on those soft pink petals of which he had thought constantly since he had first looked upon her.

Katherine struggled and pushed against him, feeling her lips aching from the rough kiss and the passionate abuse he showed in his own hunger.

When finally he withdrew his lips and started to make a trail of kisses from her soft slender neck to her full breast, Katherine could hardly contain the anger that ripped through her body. Would she forever be defending herself from cruel men who wished only to use her body for their own needs and not give a care to her feelings? She had been forced into a marriage and into this trip and neither did she wish for, but she would not be forced into giving her body to this drunken sot. He would have to kill her first! With these thoughts she pushed against his body with all the strength she possessed.

At her push, Captain Eldridge was taken by surprise and started to fall backward. As he did so he grasped out with a hand to steady himself and grabbed hold of Katherine's bodice, which tore to her waist with a rending of cloth.

Katherine clutched at her breast and made a run for the door, but Captain Eldridge was faster and caught her around the waist before she could get to her destination.

"No, my dear, you shall not get away from me that easily," he said, as he feasted his eyes on her breasts which were laid bare. All his mind could envision was to taste the lusciousness of those white soft mounds, which were straining from her heavy breathing and he could hardly wait to caress those beautiful pink nipples which were tautly peaked.

During his assault, Katherine reached out and touched upon a heavy glass object, which she surmised to be a vase. She did not hesitate a moment! She brought the vase as hard as she could down upon his head. Captain Eldridge fell to the floor with a loud dull thump.

Katherine stooped down to check and see that the captain was still breathing before she made her way to the door and to her own cabin. She reached her own cabin without being seen by anyone. She could well imagine Rachel's accusing eyes, if she were to see her state of dress.

Katherine had changed into a nightgown and was in bed by the time Rachel entered the room, and she went silently to sleep, thanking God for her good fortune in getting away from Captain Eldridge and not having to face Rachel in her torn dress.

The next day no incident occurred but Captain Eldridge wore a bandage around his head and had a grim look set on his face.

Katherine vowed to herself that she would make it a point to stay out of his way, and she would be sure to have Mr. Vincent or Rachel close at hand from now on, whenever he was near.

The days ahead seemed to drag on with idle chatter and the same boring routine. Katherine had already started her letter to her father and she could not believe how homesick she had already become.

Rachel proved to be worse company than

Katherine had thought possible. She was constantly irritable and edgy and would start screeching at whomever was at hand, indulging her wrath whenever she could not have things her way.

Katherine would spend as much time as possible walking on the deck with Mr. Vincent, or the two of them would just sit and talk for hours at a time.

They enjoyed each other's company and formed a tight friendship during those small talks which they shared. Katherine felt almost as close to this kindly old man as she did to her own father.

The *Good Hope* was only three days from reaching Richmond, Virginia, and everyone's spirits seemed to have grown better with the thoughts of being on land soon.

Each day seemed like the other to Katherine, but now with the ever-present thought of being so near to Richmond and Bradly Deveraux, she became more nervous than ever.

Captain Eldridge had begged for her forgiveness for his insults and his conduct toward her. There was really more to his apology than met the eye. He had met the man that Katherine was to marry and he knew that if Bradly Deveraux ever found out about his familiarity toward his future wife, there would be no way out but death for him.

Captain Eldridge knew Bradly Deveraux

could outshoot with a pistol any man that he had ever seen; and wasn't it widespread about the duels and the dead men Bradly had walked away from on the field of honor.

When Captain Eldridge had tried to seduce Katherine into his bed, he had such a high opinion of himself and his charms over women that he had thought that he and Katherine could share a brief affair and then both of them would go on to their separate ways. But since Katherine did not want any part of him he certainly was going to try to make amends, so Bradly would not call him out with either pistol or sword.

There were only two more days until the *Good Hope* would arrive at Richmond. Katherine was sitting in her room finishing her letter to her father and Rachel had gone walking about on the deck of the ship, when Katherine heard a loud crash which sounded like thunder, but which was so loud and close that it caused Katherine to drop her pen and sit as if frozen.

Rachel came running through the door and at its opening Katherine heard men shouting and cursing up on the deck.

"What is it, Rachel?" Katherine demanded, jumping to her feet.

"Pirates, it is pirates, Katherine, what are we going to do?"

"Are you sure, Rachel? Did you see them?"

"Yes, I did, and they are the vulgarest and

dirtiest bunch of men I have ever seen in my life. The captain said he would talk with them and try to give them the cargo if they would let us go. Dear God, Katherine, what are we to do? I have heard dreadful stories of what pirates do to the women they capture," Rachel cried, her voice ending with a raking screech.

"Stop your crying this minute, do you hear me? You do not know what these people want with this ship, and I am sure the captain will straighten everything out. Now you had better get a grip on yourself," Katherine said nervously, pacing back and forth on the blue carpet.

She herself had heard the many stories of the fates of the women who fell into murdering pirates' hands. There had been stories of women being raped by whole gangs of pirates and finally, when they were either dead or unconscious, being thrown overboard to the sharks. Katherine shuddered at this thought, but she knew she had better keep a grip on herself and not lose her head. Rachel would probably be in hysterics soon and it would do no good for both of them to fall apart.

"The captain said we should remain in our cabin and out of sight unless he sends for us," Rachel put in between sobs.

The pirate ship overtook the merchant ship *Good Hope* without a fight. Captain Eldridge knew he could not outrun the pirate ship and his ship was not armed to fight. He thought it best to try to persuade the pirate crew into taking his cargo and letting his own crew and passengers go in peace.

As the leader of the pirate crew ordered his ship tied alongside the *Good Hope* and he and his men boarded the merchant ship, Captain Eldridge felt his hopes for an alliance between himself and the pirate captain drain before his very eyes. These were the roughest looking bunch of cutthroats he had ever set eyes upon and the pirate captain looked as though he were Satan himself.

The captain of the pirates was a tall, lean, dark-tanned man with two pistols stuck in either side of his belt and a cutlass held threatingly in one hand. He had piercing black eyes, which snapped back and forth taking in his surroundings.

"What is the meaning of this, sir? Taking over my ship in this manner? My ship holds nothing of value except the small amount of cargo on board," Captain Eldridge said in a nervous manner, trying to appear brave in the eyes of this horrid-looking pirate.

"I don't have to give you reasons for my actions. I have captured your ship and everything aboard now belongs to me, and if you or any member of your crew try to interfere with me or my men I shall see you run through and tossed overboard," the pirate captain replied in a cold, contemptuous voice. As he turned and looked about him he asked in a menacing tone. "Have you any passengers aboard?"

Captain Eldridge cleared his throat and nodded his head slowly. "There are three passengers, sir, but they are of no concern and of no value. Please take what you wish of the cargo and let us go on our way."

The pirate captain looked as if he were a lord breathing down his nose at one of his peasants. "Who do you think you are, telling me what is of value? I asked if there are any passengers and I expect to see them up on deck immediately. I shall only tell you this one time and if you value your own life and that of your crew and passengers, I advise you to do as you're told and as quickly as possible."

"Mr. Foxworthy," Captain Eldridge shouted.

"Yes, sir?" the first mate said, stepping forward; he had been standing by listening to this conversation between his captain and the pirate leader.

"Please go and escort all of the passengers up on deck."

"Yes, sir, right away." The first mate saluted, turning and leaving the two men.

Katherine jumped from her chair when she heard the knock outside their cabin door. "Who is it?" she asked in a strained voice.

"It is me, Miss Rafferty, First Mate Foxworthy; the captain sent me to tell you he wishes all passengers up on deck at once."

"We shall be there in just a few minutes, Mr. Foxworthy," Katherine replied to the closed door. "Well, Rachel, come along; we must have this thing done with and I am sure everything will be just fine. Just try not to show them your fear and we might make out much better," Katherine said more for herself than for the other woman.

"But I am so scared, I do not think I will be able to endure this." Rachel sobbed, dabbing at her eyes and nose with a handkerchief.

"You can endure and you will, if you try to pull yourself together."

As they were making their way to the deck, Mr. Vincent approached them and took Katherine's hand. "Have faith, child; I shall protect you with my life if needed."

Katherine smiled up at this kindly old man, who had become like a second father to her these past few weeks. "Dear Mr. Vincent, I hope and I am sure that it will not come down to anything so drastic. Perhaps it will be all worked out when these pirates see we have nothing of any value."

"I certainly hope you are right, dear, but do stay by my side in any case."

"Have no fear; I shall not leave your side for one moment," Katherine said, as they arrived up on deck.

As soon as the pirate crew caught sight of the two women, chaos broke out. They each dropped what they were doing and rushed toward Mr. Vincent and the ladies, leering and smiling evilly.

Katherine stiffened her back and looked at the men coming toward them. If only I possessed a pistol I would shoot each and every one of these filthy dogs through the heart, she thought to herself. Never had she seen such dirty, terrifying men in her life.

The pirate crew came closer shouting obscenities to one another and sneering at the women in front of them. "I'll take the black-haired one first," sneered a burly-looking pirate who was stripped bare to the waist and had a gruesome-looking scar running the length of his face.

Katherine shuddered uncontrollably and Rachel started her weeping anew. Would this be her fate after all? Katherine questioned herself. To be sent from her home only to be used by a band of crude pirates until she was dead? How could this be happening to her?

As one of the pirates stepped forward and grabbed Katherine by the arm another did the same to Rachel, but the pirate captain strode over to the group and growled, "Release the women or I shall have you flogged within an inch of your life."

The pirate who held Katherine sneered. "Come on now, Captain, there ain't no harm in having a little sport with the women is there? You can have your fun first if you like, Cap."

When he had said his piece, the pirate captain said in a low, deadly voice, "I told you once, Jake, take your hand from the lady, unless you would prefer me to remove your arm for you?"

The pirate called Jake dropped his hand

instantly and a hush came over the pirate crew.

Katherine had no doubt that this pirate captain would have cut this other man's arm from his shoulder if he had not done as told. She could not imagine which would be worse; to be in the pirates' hands or to be taken by this brutal-looking captain.

"See to the cargo, men," the captain bellowed. "Look lively now, boys, we have not much time to dally."

After the pirate captain directed his orders to his crew and saw they were carrying them out he turned and looked at the women and Mr. Vincent. He looked first at Katherine, taking in her dark lustrous hair, dark-blue eyes, and voluptuous figure. Then, taking his eyes from Katherine's beauty, he let them roam over Rachel. He grimaced as he took in her disheveled brown hair, swollen red eyes from weeping, and her too-skinny frame.

Mr. Vincent was the first to speak. "Sir, I wish to appeal to your sense of decency. Please leave the women in peace; they have nothing of value which you or your men would wish."

The pirate captain looked at Mr. Vincent as though he had not noticed him before. "And who might you be to ask this of me?"

"I, sir, am Mr. Charles Vincent. I am responsible for these two women's safety until we reach our destination in Richmond, Virginia."

"And what are the names of the ladies?" the pirate demanded, rubbing his mustache with a finger.

"This young lady is on her way to meet her betrothed in Richmond," Mr. Vincent said, turning in Katherine's direction. "Her name is Miss Katherine Rafferty, the daughter of Lord John Vern Rafferty. And the other is Miss Rachel Profane, Miss Rafferty's father's niece."

The pirate captain stood as if contemplating each word that was said. "And who may I ask is this Miss Rafferty's future husband to be?"

"Of course, sir. The gentleman is Mr. Bradly Deveraux."

The pirate captain looked taken back by this name at first; then a huge evil grin appeared on his face. "So old Brad finally found him a woman that would have him, did he? Well, fancy that."

Katherine and Mr. Vincent both looked surprised to find that the menacing-looking pirate captain could know Bradly Deveraux.

"You look surprised that I know Mr. Bradly Deveraux," he said looking at the people facing him. "Oh, yes, Brad and I have known each other for some time; in fact we even have a small score to settle with each other, and one day I'm sure we shall see it to its end. But enough of this talk about Bradly; I think we have some business to discuss."

"Sir, I am afraid you are mistaken. I insist you leave these women alone and let us be on

79

our way. And I must warn you if any harm should come to these ladies, you, sir, shall regret it!" Mr. Vincent warned.

"Oh, but you are mistaken Mr. Vincent. We most certainly do have some business to talk over. You see we pirates make a very good living, on holding captured prisoners for ransom. First I think we should discuss the amount of ransom these lovely young ladies will bring."

Katherine looked on, not believing her ears, and the longer she listened to this man talking about her as if she were no more than a slave on an auction block, the angrier she became. "Sir, you cannot be serious. This whole affair is outrageous; my father will have you hunted down and hung."

The pirate captain looked upon this woman whose dark-blue eyes were even lovelier now that sparks of anger were shooting from them. "I assure you, my litte blue eyes, I am serious. I shall keep you and your friend as my guests until the required amount of money for the both of you has arrived."

Mr. Vincent looked at this pirate and stated flatly, "Sir, I will remind you once again that if any harm should befall these young ladies you shall regret your actions. Lord Rafferty has high powers in court and he shall, I am sure, petition the king for a fleet of ships to search you down and destroy the lot of you."

"Mr. Vincent, I give you my word these ladies shall be taken care of well, and will be in the best of health upon your return."

"And what is the word of a scurvy pirate worth?" Katherine asked angrily.

"The word of Marco Radford is as good as I can give you and that will have to be good enough, my lady. Now let us get down to the price of your worth, my dear ladies. I think ten thousand should be sufficient."

Katherine looked in horror. "That is outrageous. My father will need time to raise that amount of money."

"Perhaps, but Bradly Deveraux will find it quite easy to come up with."

"You cannot mean to ask Mr. Deveraux to pay this amount. Mr. Vincent will have to be allowed the time to go to England and seek the money."

"I am sorry, madam, but I'm afraid there won't be time for that," Marco answered. "Mr. Vincent will have to go to Bradly Deveraux for I shall wait no more than one week."

"But, sir, I emplore you, do not go to Mr. Deveraux for this money," Katherine begged, not knowing how she would be able to bear facing her future husband after this affair.

"Miss Rafferty, I'm sure old Brad would be more than glad to spend any amount of money for a woman such as yourself to warm his bed."

The pirate crew started to roar with laughter and vile remarks when Marco's words reached their ears, and Katherine felt her face turn crimson in color.

"I shall, sir, go straightaway to Mr. Deveraux in Richmond, but I warn you, I shall hold you to your word on the treatment of these ladies, Mr. Radford," Mr. Vincent said hurriedly, to take the attention away from Katherine.

"Done then," shouted Marco as he laughed along with his men. "I shall give you no more than a week to finish the bargain and if you do not return with the required amount of money you shall see how I keep my word when you find the bodies of these lovely ladies at the bottom of the sea."

Rachel who had remained quietly standing by started to weep profoundly when she heard these last words of the pirate captain.

"I assure you, Miss Profane, I shall make all the haste possible and see this matter to its end," Mr. Vincent said, placing a reassuring hand upon her arm. He then turned to Katherine and spoke gently. "Be brave, my child, I shall not linger a moment until I see you safe once again."

Katherine reached up and kissed him on the cheek. "I shall rest much easier, Mr. Vincent, knowing this matter is in your hands."

After these few words were exchanged, Marco shouted for two of his men to take the ladies to the pirate ship.

The men who were to escort the ladies were two of the worst looking amongst the gang of pirates. Both wore their shirts opened to their waists and they looked as if they would enjoy nothing better than to slice someone's throat. The one who took hold of Katherine's arm had a terrible odor about him and all of his front teeth were decayed. He wore a patch over one eye and held a rapier clutched in his hand. Rachel's escort was not much better and Rachel glanced fearfully about her trying to find help that was not to be found.

"Rachel, control yourself, everything will be all right. They will not hurt us; the pirate captain has given his word," Katherine said softly, not really believing her own words.

Katherine and Rachel were taken to a small cramped cabin in which there was hardly space enough for both of them to move about.

As they entered the cabin Katherine rushed to the porthole and watched as the *Good Hope* set its sails once again for Richmond, Virginia. Never before had she felt so downhearted as she did at this moment, watching the *Good Hope* depart. Would Mr. Vincent be able to get the large amount of ransom and to get it back to these pirates in time? Or would their fate lie in the hands of these monstrous men? As she turned and looked about her at the small untidy cabin, and Rachel, still sobbing, she felt herself wanting to just lie down and weep out all of her own misery and torment.

Katherine shook herself visibly. She must not give in to this feeling of being beaten; she must calm herself and be prepared for whatever was to come. The first thing to do, she told herself, was to calm Rachel, and then the two of them must make this filthy room more livable.

It was not quite as easy as Katherine had thought to calm Rachel's fears. The other girl was almost in hysterics.

"They shall kill us, I know they will!" Rachel wept uncontrollably.

"Rachel, you must get control of yourself," Katherine said sharply, losing her patience with the other girl. "Mr. Vincent will return with the ransom and the pirates will set us free."

"They won't, I know they won't. Those dirty, vulgar men will rape us and then they will throw our bodies over into the water," she screeched, her eyes wearing a glazed look, as if she were going mad.

Katherine had taken all she could bear from this sniveling woman and brought her hand back and struck her full on the cheek. "Now pull yourself together and quit acting like such a coward," she shouted, regretting instantly that she had struck the other girl. Never in her life had she struck another woman and she felt a deep regret for having lost her temper so violently. Katherine knew Rachel had good reason to be upset, but she knew also that it would do no good for either of them to fall to pieces.

Rachel sat as if frozen, holding her hand to her stinging face, which had turned a deep red.

"How dare you strike me!" she shouted, coming to her senses.

"I am sorry, Rachel, but there seemed no other way to make you stop your insane talk and quit your sobbing." Katherine apologized, knowing that she had been right in her actions, for now Rachel was back to her natural state.

"You shall regret you ever touched me, I promise you this, Katherine." Rachel spat, hate for the other woman filling her eyes.

Katherine let Rachel's words go by without comment and started to tidy up the small cabin. She was sure Rachel was just talking and when she had time to calm her anger and realize that Katherine had been right in slapping her, she would forget all about the whole affair.

The pirate captain, Marco Radford, gave strict orders to his men that they were not to go near the women, and he also told them that if they valued their lives they would obey him. He then posted one of his most trusted men to stand guard outside of the women's cabin door and gave him orders not to let them leave their room for any reason. He had thought over the matter carefully and had decided to release the women unharmed as he had promised, when Mr. Vincent brought the required ransom back to him. He had at first given thought to keeping Brad Deveraux's woman for his own pleasure, and with her charm and beauty it would indeed be a pleasure. But then he had thought of Mr. Vincent's warnings, about her father's wealth and power, and at the thought of having the king's men tracking him down he reconsidered the idea. Life was hard enough on the seas in this kind of business without having the kings' men looking for him. One day he told himself he would have Bradly Deveraux in his grasp and perhaps even have the little blue-eyed vixen, who will be Bradly's wife, but for now he would leave the women in peace and get the money which was to come from Bradly Deveraux. He could derive some small pleasure out of this, he told himself.

Katherine had expected the pirate captain to enter their small cabin at any time, but she was surprised when the second day of their captivity had passed and the only person who had entered the cabin was a young boy of about fifteen who had brought their meals and come back and taken their trays away. Katherine's nerves were as tightly drawn as a rope and she prayed nightly for Mr. Vincent's return.

Rachel kept to herself and would only talk to Katherine when necessary. Her hate grew stronger for Katherine with each hour that passed, and she swore to herself time and again that she would one day have her vengeance over this other woman.

On the third day of Katherine and Rachel's imprisonment Marco decided to pay a visit to his captives. "Good morning, ladies," he greeted them upon entering their room. "I trust you're comfortable and have everything you require?"

Katherine looked at him with contempt which she could not conceal, and turned her head away from his direction. But to her complete amazement, Rachel received him with a warm smile.

"Why yes, Mr. Radford, everything is fine, I must confess though I had expected things to be much worse under the circumstances, but I assure you that everything has been quite comfortable."

Marco gave this woman a knowing look. So he had figured this Miss Profane right. The only thing she cared about was herself and what she could get out of life. She would be a good ally for him in the future and she also would fit into his plans for Bradly Deveraux. "Well, I'm glad to see that you don't mind being my personal captive as your friend here does," Marco said pleasantly, looking in Katherine's direction and marveling at the rare beauty which she possessed. Yes, he thought to himself, Brad sure had the devil's own luck, with women and everything else, but one day that would change. "I came this morning to see if perhaps you ladies would care to go for a walk with me about the ship?"

Rachel's thin face lit up with the thought of being able to get out of the small cabin. "I would be delighted, sir. You are most kind for your invitation."

"And you, Miss Rafferty, would you care for a walk?"

"No, thank you, I shall remain here until I can leave your ship for good," she said feeling angry at Rachel, for accepting this pirate's invitation.

"Well, if you are sure, I shall take Miss Profane for a short stroll," he replied taking Rachel by the arm and heading her toward the door.

Katherine could hear Rachel's shrill laughter outside the door and could not imagine what could have come over her. She had been so frightened of these pirates a short time ago and now she was acting as if the captain of these dreadful men were some favorite friend. She just could not understand Rachel's moods.

Rachel and Marco had been gone only a short time, during which Katherine stood gazing out at the sea through the porthole, before she heard the knob on the door turn. She supposed it to be Rachel returning and when she felt a presence beside her she started to speak. "You certainly were not gone very long on your walk with that dreadful pirate, Rachel. Sometimes I just cannot understand you."

All of a sudden Katherine was seized by strong hands. "What is this?" she screamed.

"Blue eyes," came her answer.

Katherine realized that it was Marco's voice and as quickly she felt a sick feeling in the pit of her stomach.

"So you think of me as dreadful, do you?" he asked, his piercing black eyes looking into her violet-blue ones. "You have no reason to dread me, madam, for I have a very high regard for you."

"Where is Rachel?" Katherine questioned, swallowing convulsively.

"Do not worry about her. I have one of my men watching over her; nothing shall happen to her. But I did not come here to talk of her. Do you know you happen to be one of the most ravishing women I have ever seen, Katherine? I do not believe I have ever seen eyes as blue as yours," he stated, while drawing his hand through her dark curls.

"Take your hands off me!" she shouted and pushed at him vainly.

"Why do you try to resist me, my little blue eyes? Just hear me out. Why would you wish to marry a monster like Brad Deveraux? You need a man like myself, who would treat you as a queen and love you and no other but you," he coaxed, caressing her jaw with a light touch.

Katherine pushed once more at this man in front of her. "I would never give myself to you willingly, sir; you are one of the lowest things I have ever seen called a man."

Marco looked down at her, anger contorting his features. "You shall regret those words, madam, and you shall one day beg for my favors. I promise you this."

Katherine shrank away from his words and the anger on his face. She had forgotten her life depended on this man's every whim.

"I shall give you time to see for yourself and realize your own mistake in choosing Brad Deveraux, little blue eyes. For I can wait and you shall come to me with open arms; you can be sure of this."

Marco was so sure of himself and sure that Katherine would detest Bradly Deveraux for his bad temper that he decided he would let her go and see these faults. When she had had enough of Bradly she would flee and he would be waiting for her when the time came. A woman such as this was worth waiting for, he told himself, and in the end she would be his and only his.

"Never," Katherine fearfully stated. "Never shall I be yours."

Marco ignored her words and grabbed her in his arms in a tight embrace. When his lips sought Katherine's she struggled in vain against this tall, lean man who had a viselike grip and arms of steel. When finally his lips touched on hers she felt only revulsion.

He released her after a time and looked into the dark-blue pools in front of him. "You will belong to me one day," he stated with a bow and left the room without further ado.

Katherine stood in silence, looking at the closed door through which the pirate captain had just gone. As she thought of his departing words a shudder went through her body which she could not control. Did this barbaric animal really think that she would ever become his? He must be insane, he must have only wished to frighten her, she told herself. And he had successfully frightened her. That was one thing she knew for sure. She would have to tell Rachel to stay away from this monstrous man; there was no telling what he was capable of doing.

Katherine tried to ignore those dark piercing eyes and the evil smile which Marco wore when he returned with Rachel.

"Well, Rachel, I must leave you for now, but I shall come tomorrow and take you for another stroll."

"Thank you very much, sir," Rachel said softly, looking up to him with adoring eyes.

"The pleasure has been mine, my fair lady," Marco said, bowing and kissing one of Rachel's hands while his eyes caressed Katherine's beauteous body.

When the pirate captain left their cabin Katherine warned Rachel of Marco and told her of his behavior toward her, but Rachel was so taken in by this pirate and his charms that she refused to believe Katherine's words, and when Katherine tried to talk with the other girl about the pirate captain she would ignore her or shout out in a rage that Katherine was jealous of the attentions which he paid to her and was making up all this terrible talk about Marco.

So Rachel continued her morning walks with her gallant pirate captain while Katherine would wait alone in the cabin not knowing whether Marco would make a return visit to her or whether he did indeed care about Rachel. But Rachel needed to wake up and see what kind of a villainous man he was. With Rachel's dislike so apparent, she knew the girl would not listen to her. Thank God, Katherine said to herself, Mr. Vincent would be returning soon and the two of them would be away from this barbaric man for good.

On their sixth day of being held captive a boat was sighted approaching the pirate ship. The women were ordered to stay in their cabin and Katherine watched from the porthole as the *Good Hope* bore down upon them and then finally was secured alongside the pirate ship.

We are finally going to be rescued, Katherine thought with glee. After these terrible days of being held prisoner they were finally going to be free once more. Katherine ran to Rachel and grabbed her hands. "We are finally going to be free again," she shouted with happiness. "It is the *Good Hope* and Mr. Vincent. We are going to be rescued at last from these terrible people."

Rachel pulled her hands free and turned and walked to the porthole.

Katherine looked after the girl for a moment. Had she seen anger in Rachel's eyes?

No, she must be mistaken; it was just this terrible experience they had been going through and Rachel probably could hardly believe it was all going to be over at last. Katherine went on with her happiness and chatter as she put together the few articles which she had been able to bring with her to the pirate ship.

As Rachel stood staring out of the porthole she felt so angry she could hardly bear it. Finally, when she had found the one man she loved and who loved her in return, she had to leave him and go back to the same dreary life she had been living before she had met Marco. If only he would let her stay with him, they could stay together forever, she thought with a sigh. But hadn't he promised her that he loved her and that he would come for her soon and they would be together again? She would just have to put up with Katherine for a while longer. Then she would show them all, including that snotty-nosed Katherine, and perhaps she would even have her chance to get even with Katherine for the way she had treated her since they had left England.

It seemed to Katherine to take forever before Marco finally entered their cabin and stated, "Ladies, if you are ready, I will take you back to the *Good Hope*."

Just as they walked outside the door, Marco took Katherine by the arm and whispered for only her ears to hear, "Do not forget my words of the other day; you shall be mine one day, little blue eyes."

Katherine pulled herself free and walked ahead of the couple.

But Rachel, who had seen the exchange of words between Katherine and Marco, glared at Katherine with hate filling her eyes.

Marco saw Rachel's look and took her arm and gave her a large smile. "Have patience, my love, I will come for you soon."

Rachel's hatred melted away and her eyes filled with love for this man beside her. "I shall wait forever, if needed, only I pray you will hurry to me so I can be away from that hateful woman," Rachel said scornfully.

As Marco helped Rachel onto the deck of the *Good Hope*, he spoke softly to her. "Have no fear it will not be too long before we are again together, I promise you this."

When Katherine arrived on deck the first person she saw was Mr. Vincent.

As he saw Katherine approaching he held his arms out and opened them wide to fold her in; as he did so Katherine ran into them weeping. "There, there, child, you are safe now and no more harm shall befall you," he said softly, patting her head which was resting against his chest.

Katherine regained some of her composure and looked up and into her rescuer's face. "Dear Mr. Vincent, how can I ever repay you? Because of me you have been put through so much. I am so grateful to you for everything you have done."

"Think nothing of that, my child. I would not have it any other way. I have been charged with your care and I shall carry this out to the best of my ability. Besides, I have grown quite fond of you, child, and shall do everything in my power to see to your safety."

As Mr. Vincent turned he saw Rachel and Marco making their way toward him. "It is to your advantage, sir, that these dear ladies have come to no harm."

Marco smiled with an arrogant twist to his mouth. "Oh, but you have judged me wrongly, sir. I gave my word that these ladies would be safe and as you can see with those old eyes of yours they have been treated well and I have kept my word."

Mr. Vincent gave an angry grunt to this comment on his age, but held his tongue, afraid to rouse the pirate's anger, for he knew they were still in danger and this pirate could at any minute change his mind and kill them all. "Well, sir, you have your money now and if you would be good enough, we wish to be on our way to Richmond."

"Indeed," Marco replied. "Ladies, may I say your company has been the most gracious I have ever had aboard my ship." As Marco started to board his own ship, he turned and, looking directly at Katherine, said, "Until we meet again, ladies, I shall dream nightly of your beauty."

Katherine moved her eyes away from his feeling uncomfortable and frightened by his words, but Rachel, not knowing these words were meant only for Katherine, thought his words were directed toward her and her heart melted with love and happiness.

Aboard the *Good Hope*, Katherine tried to forget Marco's words. She kept herself busy working on a sampler she was sewing and she started another letter to her father, telling him of her experience and her rescue from the pirate ship. She spent a great deal of time talking with Mr. Vincent. She felt as if she owed him her life and now she felt closer to this elderly man than ever before. Captain Eldridge tried to stay out of Katherine's way and she thought this was just as well for she would not be as easy a victim as she had been previously. After her experiences with him and other men she vowed to herself she would not find herself in the same position another time.

Katherine enjoyed taking long strolls on deck before dinner; the weather was cool now and it lifted her spirits to feel the chilly air hit upon her face.

On their last evening aboard the *Good Hope* Katherine was on deck looking up at the stars and wondering what her future would hold for her, when Mr. Vincent approached her.

"So here you are, Katherine. I have been looking for you everywhere. I thought perhaps we could have a little talk. Here, child, keep your cape upon your shoulders tightly or you will take sick," he said, reaching up and pulling Katherine's cape together.

"Thank you, Mr. Vincent," she replied, with a smile for his fatherly affection. "You wished to speak with me?"

"I did not wish to mention the subject before, but I feel I must tell you a few things about your future husband."

Katherine looked up in alarm. "What is it?"

"Nothing to worry about, child," he said patting her shoulder. "It is just that you know I have a great fondness for you; it is almost as though you were my own dear child. And that is why I thought I would venture to speak with you."

"Go on, Mr. Vincent. I would like to hear about this man I am to marry," she said in a small voice.

"Well, you know, Katherine, I had to go to Mr. Deveraux for the money with which to ransom you and Rachel."

"And he gave it to you grudgingly; is that what you are telling me Mr. Vincent?"

"No, no dear, if you will let me finish."

"I am sorry, Mr. Vincent. Please continue."

"As I was saying, Mr. Deveraux did not become angry over the money, dear, as much as he did over who held you captive—Marco Radford. It seems there is indeed bad blood between the two men. And I must tell you I have never met a man with a temper such as Mr. Deveraux possesses."

"Oh," Katherine replied, her worst fears

coming to light. Her husband would be a bully and a tyrant.

"Shall I continue?" Mr. Vincent asked, noticing Katherine's face turning pale.

"Yes, please do." She would rather know now what to expect than find out later after she was married what kind of man her husband would be.

"Well, it was almost all I could do to keep Mr. Deveraux from coming along with us to rescue you and Miss Profane, but I was afraid for your and Miss Profane's safety to depend on the outcome of these two men meeting and this is why I insisted upon his staying in Richmond. But I must tell you, child, your future husband has a very bad temper and you will fare much better if you try to avoid it."

"Thank you, Mr. Vincent," Katherine said with a sinking feeling inside her chest. "I shall heed your warning, but for now if that is all I would like to retire to my cabin."

"I did not mean to make you upset, child. I only thought you should know this one thing."

"I assure you, Mr. Vincent, you have not upset me. You have been so kind to me, I do not know what I shall do when we have to part."

"You will make out just fine, dear. Mr. Deveraux may have a bad temper, but he is also a man of honor and strength and once he realizes the rare and precious gem you are, he will treasure you above all else."

Katherine looked up at him with tears shining in her eyes and hugged him tightly to her. "Thank you so much, Mr. Vincent, but now would you please walk me to my cabin? I fear I have grown very weary all of a sudden."

He realized she needed time to herself and he put his arm out for her to take. "Yes, my dear, I think you shall find a great deal of happiness, in time."

Time—Katherine did not want to think of time; all she could think of was tomorrow. She would be in an alien country, in unfamiliar surroundings, and she would meet the man she most dreaded to meet.

Katherine was awake before dawn the next morning and lay abed listening to the activity aboard the ship. They were only a few miles from Richmond and the crew was in a bustle of activity to get the ship ready for their landing. Katherine felt as if she had not slept at all that night and her nerves were a jumble of emotions. She dreaded having to meet her future husband and to be forced into doing things she had no wish to do.

Rachel was in a much better mood with the thought of being on land once more and the hopes that Marco would be coming for her soon. Marco—just the thought of that romantic, good-looking man being all hers set her skin to tingling, but she knew she had to be patient for a while longer and she could only hope that Katherine's future husband would not be as impossible to bear as Katherine was.

Katherine donned a satin gown of violet-blue; it matched the color of her eyes to perfection. The bodice was snug fitting, which made her waist appear even smaller than it was and her bosom fuller. She wound her hair atop her head and set a silver-gray fur hat on top. As she surveyed herself in the mirror she thought, That is good enough for some backwoods colonial. Katherine looked toward Rachel who had just finished her own toilette and asked, "If you are ready, Rachel, we can go up on deck?"

"Yes, I think I have finished. If you are ready we can be off. I really cannot wait to be on land again. I feel as though I have always been on this boat," Rachel replied, acting a little better mannered than usual.

"I agree," Katherine answered. "I must say it will be good to walk as far as one wishes in one direction again." Katherine put on her dark-blue cape and held her fur muff which matched her hat, and then the two girls left their cabin.

Chapter Four

Katherine stood on the deck of the *Good Hope*, beside Mr. Vincent. She could see a flurry of people moving about on the dock and she strained to see if she could make out Bradly Deveraux. But there were so many men and women walking about that she could not tell which one was to be her future husband.

"You look very enchanting, dear," Mr.

Vincent said as he noticed her agitation. "Mr. Deveraux will be very proud of you, I am sure."

"I am a little nervous, Mr. Vincent. Do you think I will like living in this new land?"

"Katherine, I am sure you will like it here; there is something about this new, rough land which seems to inspire love in everyone who comes to it and almost no one wishes to leave."

"I certainly do hope you are right," Katherine replied nervously.

"Well, here we are about ready to tie up to the dock. Are you ready to meet your new home?" Mr. Vincent gave her his arm for support.

"Wherever did Rachel get off to?" Katherine questioned him, looking about her.

"Do not worry, dear," Mr. Vincent said in a reassuring voice. "I see Captain Eldridge taking her to the dock now."

"Well, in that case I suppose we should be going also," Katherine said, deliberately speaking in a strong voice to cover her qualms. "Whatever are all these people about here on the dock?" she asked, looking at the many different people roaming about.

"They are awaiting news from home," was his reply. "The *Good Hope* carries a packet of mail from England and people are always anxious to hear from friends and family. I am afraid when we came into Richmond a few days ago we were not here long enough, except to get the money for your ransom. Actually we did not even put the *Good Hope* in port; I was brought to town in a small boat."

"I did not know the *Good Hope* carried mail," Katherine replied. "But that reminds me, I must see about sending my letters to my father. I promised to send them as quickly as possible."

"Katherine, I would be honored to take care of this small service for you."

"That would be very kind of you, Mr. Vincent. Are you sure it would not be an inconvenience?"

"Nonsense, my dear, it would be an honor to do this small favor for you."

"Then I shall with pleasure leave them in your care," Katherine replied with relief at having this task out of her hands.

Bradly Deveraux was in a foul mood the morning he drove into Richmond to meet his future bride, Katherine Rafferty. He had never been more furious with fate than he was at this time. He could well imagine the kind of woman his grandfather had chosen to be his wife. She would probably be homely, middle-aged, and the type of woman his grandfather thought would keep him in line. And as if this whole marriage was not enough, she and her companion had had to be kidnapped by that scum of a yard dog, Marco Radford.

Bradly could feel his blood run hot at the thought of Marco. He could well imagine

103

Marco's laughter at the good luck he had come across at having Bradly Deveraux's future wife in his clutches. Bradly could just picture the usage of the two women in his hands; and then this Miss Rafferty was to come to him as his wife. The thought of having a woman in his bed after she had shared one with Marco repulsed him more than he could bear. Then also, there was the money for the ransom. Bradly knew he could well afford the amount, but it burned him to the core to have Marco having one dollar of his money.

Bradly and Marco had been enemies for almost five years now and Bradly had sworn he would kill Marco the first time he laid eyes on him again. Bradly could remember it as if it were only yesterday. He had been going almost nightly to a bordello house in Richmond, seeing a young, beautiful girl called Julie. She was young and had an innocence about her which attracted Bradly. True, he had not been in love with her, but he had been very fond of the girl and had enjoyed her company.

They had shared a very good relationship until the one night when Bradly had visited Julie earlier than usual and had left early to attend to some business he had to settle with a neighbor. This had been the worst of nights for Bradly to have had to leave early. For shortly after he had departed, Marco Radford had made a visit to this same house and had somehow found his way to Julie's room. Bradly had searched his mind again and again,

104

trying to figure out why she would have allowed him in. Every woman in Richmond knew of the cruel treatment Marco was used to dealing out to the women he took up with. But it did no good now for Bradly to wonder why she would have entertained the blackguard, for on the next morning another girl had found the dead body of Julie, brutally murdered.

Bradly had searched for almost one month for Marco, but had been unable to find a trace of him. He had heard rumors that Marco had joined up with a band of cutthroat pirates, but he had not been sure of these rumors until a week ago when he had been visited by Mr. Vincent and been informed of his betrothed's abduction. Marco Radford had not been seen in the past five years in Richmond, but Bradly told himself that the first chance he got he would shoot him down like the filth he was.

By now Bradly had made his way into the streets of Richmond and saw that he was nearing the water, he could see the *Good Hope* had already arrived and people were already descending the landing plank.

Bradly made his way through the mass of people scurrying about and the first person he saw getting off the ship was Captain Eldridge with a tall, almost skinny woman on his arm.

Bradly could tell from where he stood the type of woman she was, and he thought to himself that it was just his luck to be tied to a screeching, nagging woman who would constantly badger him; he knew without talking to this woman that she would be just this type. He would have to let this woman know right from the beginning that she would have no more than his name and his roof over her head. Yes, he thought, he would not even so much as touch that scrawny body of hers. He would continue finding his pleasures with the women of Richmond who had always taken kindly to his attentions.

He decided, at last, that he had best make his way over to the captain and Miss Rafferty. Now that his mind was made up about his future wife his whole body seemed to relax with relief.

Bradly walked over to Captain Eldridge and was making his greetings when Katherine and Mr. Vincent descended the gangplank and made their way toward Rachel and Captain Eldridge.

Mr. Vincent cleared his throat to draw the attention of the small group. "Ah, Mr. Deveraux, I see you have already met our good captain."

"Yes, I had the pleasure of meeting Captain Eldridge a year or so ago on another voyage," Bradly answered in a polite voice.

"Well, sir, then may I introduce you to my charges?"

Bradly smiled, sure of himself and that he had his emotions under control. "Please do so, Mr. Vincent."

Katherine had walked up behind Mr. Vincent to get a better look at this man whom Mr.

Vincent had pointed out to her, as Mr. Bradly Deveraux. This man was very different from what she had expected to be marrying. He was so tall and large that he looked like a great beast of the wilderness, who had been tamed and civilized. Yet he seemed to be so cool and collected that Katherine knew at once he would always be thus under any circumstances. Bradly was dressed in a fawn-colored jacket and matching tight-fitting breeches. He wore a snow-white shirt with lace ruffles down the front and at the cuffs. Katherine had seen many young men in England in lace and ruffles, they always had reminded her of sissies, dressed in all their splendor, trying to act as men. But this man whom Katherine saw now in front of her looked so powerful and masculine that she could hardly take her eyes from him.

Katherine was pulled from her thoughts by Mr. Vincent stepping aside and speaking her name. "This, sir, if I may present her to you, is Miss Katherine Rafferty."

Bradly stood stunned. He could not believe his own eyes, and he could hardly believe this small, lovely woman could be the one he was to marry and not the other woman who looked as though she were ready to snap at the slightest wrong word. Bradly had been caught off guard for a slight moment, but quickly found his voice. "I trust, madam, your voyage was not too trying an experience for you," he said, making a bow and taking her hand and kissing it lightly.

"Thank you, sir, but I assure you Miss Profane and I are fine." Even his voice sounded powerful and told her that he was used to giving orders and by the looks of him he was also used to having them carried out.

Bradly raised a dark brow at her answer; then a thought came to his head: Could she mean that she enjoyed Marco's attentions? He knew Marco's ways and he knew he would never let a woman with her beauty get away from him without sampling her charms.

Mr. Vincent called Bradly out of his thoughts. "May I also present Miss Rachel Profane, Miss Rafferty's companion and also her father's niece."

"I am very glad to make your acquaintance, Mr. Deveraux," Rachel said sweetly.

Perhaps he was mistaken about this woman, Bradly thought to himself; however, he would all too soon find that he had been right in his first assumption of this Miss Profane. "It is my pleasure, Miss Profane. I have brought my carriage along and if you ladies and also you, Mr. Vincent, would care to get out of this chilly wind, we can be on our way. I have made arrangements for you all to stay at an inn for tonight and then tomorrow the wedding shall be performed at a nearby church, at one o'clock."

Katherine felt stunned. Everything seemed to be going so fast. It seemed only yesterday she had been in her own safe room in her father's house and now she only had one day left before she would become the wife of a man she not only did not know, but who gave her a dreadful fright inside whenever he cast a look in her direction.

Richmond was a small, thriving town and as Katherine walked toward the carriage to which Bradly was leading them, she glanced about her taking in the sights and the different people walking about. She noticed a number of men wearing fur caps and leather jackets, pants, and leggings, but there were also men and women strolling about in suits and fancy gowns. And there were Negroes carrying packages as they trailed behind their mistresses or masters or ran about to do their masters' bidding. Yes indeed, she thought, this America held all sorts of people in its midst and she could only hope that she would be happy and content to live here amongst the strange and unfamiliar surroundings which would have to become her new home.

Katherine looked at the lushness of the carriage into which Bradly helped her and Rachel. The seats were of a deep, plush dark velvet and Bradly placed robes upon their laps of a rich material of the same velvet hue as the seats. One thing Katherine knew for sure now was that she would at least live in luxury and not have to do without the things to which she had been accustomed.

Bradly and Mr. Vincent took the seat across from Rachel and Katherine, and Raymond,

Bradly's Negro driver, took his seat and proceeded to drive toward the inn.

"I hope you enjoy your stay at the inn," Bradly said, breaking the quiet which had settled over the group.

"I am sure it will be fine. I am really tired from our voyage, but I must say, Mr. Deveraux, I really did not expect to be wed so soon," Katherine said in a honey-sweet voice. Perhaps, she thought, she had best try to be as kind as possible in order not to rile this large animal-like man's wrath.

Bradly looked hard at Katherine as though trying to read her mind. Could it be that she did not wish this marriage any more than he did? But that couldn't be, he reasoned with himself. She only had to protest to her family before the arrangements had been made and signed and she would not be here now marrying a man she knew nothing about. A woman with her beauty and charm must have had all kinds of men back in England willing to marry her, for her looks alone. No, he thought, she was just like all the other women; ready to grab the wealth of a man even if she had go halfway around the world to gain it. "Madam, I have already made arrangements for the wedding for tomorrow in the church, and I have not much time to spare here in Richmond. I must get back to my plantation and see to its running."

"I do understand, sir. It is only that I had hopes of more time in which to prepare myself and my wardrobe."

"I am sorry," Bradly said rather stiffly. "You must understand, madam, I have business to take care of on my plantation and I wish for you to get settled as quickly as possible."

Katherine stifled an angry retort to his cold and uncaring manner, afraid to cause him to even this anger on her. Mr. Vincent's words of last night had frightened her more than she cared to let herself admit and now as she looked at this beast of a man she had no wish to have him show his temper to her.

Mr. Vincent smiled to himself; things seemed to be going fine between Katherine and Mr. Deveraux. Bradly seemed to be in a better mood than on his first meeting with the younger man and Katherine was heeding his advice. He was sure she would be able to soften Mr. Deveraux's manner, and for Katherine's sake he could only wish this to be the turn of things.

The carriage pulled in front of a small two-story building with a sign on the outside which read RICHMOND'S FINEST.

"I picked these lodgings for you because a good friend of mine is the owner and it is neat and tidy and usually very quiet here," Bradly spoke, looking directly at Katherine.

Katherine was shown to a spacious room where she immediately felt at home. It was clean and tidy and was furnished with bright, cheery colors. When she looked at the large bed, she could hardly wait to undress and lay her weary body down. She found she had grown very tired from her morning and the turmoil her body and mind had been in these many weeks had taken its toll. When she finally stripped down to her chemise and lay upon the soft downy bed, she still could find no rest. Her thoughts kept going over the morning and her meeting with Bradly Deveraux. What would her life be like being married to a man such as he? She could not deny even to herself that he was very handsome, but would he use her cruelly and not give a care to her feelings? His manner so far had been cool and aloof. Would he remain so? Perhaps he even had another woman he was in love with and did not wish to wed her; she had never even considered this before. She knew it was his grandfather who had signed the marital agreements with her father. Perhaps Bradly did not have any say in the matter and did not wish this marriage either.

"Oh, the shame and embarrassment I have been placed in," she cried aloud to the empty room. This man who was to be her husband would probably resent her and show her his dislike at every turn.

With these miserable thoughts in mind, Katherine turned on her stomach and wept uncontrollably into her silk pillow. With the passing of time, her weeping finally subsided, and a peaceful sleep overtook her trembling form.

*   *   *

Bradly Deveraux had left his future bride at the inn; his final words had been about having a carriage arrive to pick her up and take her and her companions to the church the following day.

When leaving the inn he had ordered Raymond to take him to the Drake tavern. Here at the tavern he started to drink, to try to clear his mind of the plaguing matters which were tormenting his brain. But the deeper he drank into his cup the more the image of a lovely, dark-haired woman with violet eyes and snow-white satin skin kept coming to mind. How could he, he thought to himself, have this woman in his home and as his wife and not take her to his bed and caress those high full breasts and sample that which would be rightfully his? But as quickly as this thought entered his mind he quickly shunted it. If only his grandfather had chosen some homely, mousy spinster to be his wife. How could he ever take this woman to his bed after that cur Marco had already sampled her soft, beautiful body? If only she had acted as though she had been put upon; but the lovely little bitch had acted as though she had not minded at all being taken by that scum of a pirate.

As the night wore on, Bradly drank more and more as he tried to clear his mind of Katherine Rafferty. But with the strong liquor the vision of the lovely Katherine became more vivid in his thinking.

Clayton Johnson, a close friend and neighbor of Bradley's, arrived at this inopportune time at the Drake tavern, and upon seeing Bradly sitting by himself in a far corner of the room, walked over and pulled out a chair at Bradly's table. "How you doing, Brad old boy? It looks as though you have been here quite some time," Clayton said good-naturedly, taking in the empty bottles on the table and Bradly's glassy-eyed appearance.

Bradly only gave a loud grunt to the other man's words and took a large drink from his mug.

"I guess you're getting one last night of drinking in before you get yourself married up, eh? Let me buy you a drink to your coming marriage, Brad," Clayton offered in a friendly tone.

"Damn it, man, can you not leave a man in peace?" Bradly shouted angrily, slamming his fist atop the table.

"Sure, Brad. I just thought I'd be neighborly, that's all," Clayton stammered, getting up from his chair and backing away from the table. Clayton Johnson had known Brad since they had been boys; he knew the other man had a fierce temper when he was pushed too far. Clayton had seen Brad at one time get into a fight with a river man who was almost half again Bradly's size; but Bradly had almost killed the man with his bare hands and as the image of the river man's bloody face came back to Clayton's mind he hurried toward the bar, not wanting any part of Bradly Deveraux, when he was in a mood such as this.

Bradly stood up and knocked over his chair, reeling drunkenly. He hadn't thought he had drunk that much and he could not remember what Clay had said to make him so angry. "Damn that blue-eyed witch anyway," he murmured aloud. He finally made his way out of the tavern and Raymond, who had been sitting in the carriage these past hours, ran to give assistance to his intoxicated master.

Raymond had never seen his master this drunk before and as he helped him into the carriage he muttered aloud, "It sure must be something mighty wicked that's a-bothering Master Brad; yes, sir, mighty wicked indeed."

Katherine awoke the next morning to the humming of a small Negro woman preparing a tub of bath water. When the older woman looked toward the bed and saw Katherine looking in her direction, a large, friendly smile appeared upon her face. "Morning, ma'am, I brought you up some nice, hot water for you to soak yourself in."

"Would you know what time it is?" Katherine asked, worriedly, looking at the sun-filled room.

The Negro woman burst into tiny giggles. "Old Macey, ma'am, she ain't never learned to tell no time."

Katherine looked at the Negro woman with a smile. "Macey, could you please go down and ask someone what time it is, for me?"

"Why, yes, ma'am, I sure will, right away. I'll go find out the time." And with these words she fled the room on her errand.

When Macey returned with the news of the time being ten o'clock and that Mr. Vincent had sent a message of good morning, Katherine scurried out from under the covers and from the bed. "I only have a couple of hours!" she exclaimed. "I'll never be ready in time." Katherine sighed, while she tried to get out of her silk nightgown.

"Here, ma'am, I'll help you. I'm real good at helping ladies with their clothes and such."

"Oh I do thank you, Macey. I would greatly appreciate your help," Katherine said, feeling some relief at having another pair of hands to help her.

"My master, he say, you're going to be married today and old Macey she going to make you the prettiest bride there ever was."

Katherine leaned back in the tub of warm water and let it work its soothing effects upon her taut body. After soaping her with a delicate rose-scented soap and toweling her dry, Macey set her down in front of a tray of creamed fruit and hot tea.

Katherine could only nibble at the food in front of her, for her nerves were jittery and her hands kept shaking. After her scant breakfast everything was such a rush that Katherine's head was in a flurry.

Macey rushed from one end of the room to

116

the other until Katherine could have sworn she was twenty little women instead of just one. First she perfumed Katherine's body from head to toe with the same rose-scented perfume which Katherine loved and always used. Next she did Katherine's hair. This she piled atop her head and took strands of tiny pearls and interwove them through each curl. Macey then took a light-blue powder and lightly placed a small amount upon each of her eyelids. When this was completed, she put a touch of rouge on each cheek and rubbed a glossy lip rouge upon her lips. She then helped Katherine into her wedding gown—the gown she had brought with her from England and which had belonged to her mother.

Katherine had thought at first to buy a new and more fashionable gown, but her father had insisted upon her wearing this one which had adorned her beloved mother. And as Katherine looked into the mirror she was glad she had taken her father's advice. The gown was layers and layers of snow-white lace with a tight-fitting bodice, trimmed with tiny pearls. As Katherine looked at the gown in the mirror, she thought the bodice was almost too tight. It was a good thing she did not weigh a few more pounds or her breasts most assuredly would pop right out of their confinement. At this thought, she gave a small smile at her reflection. She could just envision Rachel's and her future husband's shock and gaping mouths if she popped out of her dress while walking down the aisle.

Macey, who had seen Katherine's smile, could not contain herself another minute. "Oh, miss, you are so beautiful, you're sure to be the prettiest bride that old church has ever had in it."

"Thank you, Macey," Katherine said softly, not feeling very pretty. In fact she searched her mind to find how indeed she did feel, but she only felt numb as though she were watching someone else going through the motions of preparing for her wedding day. Katherine gave the woman in the mirror a hard, penetrating look. Could this calm- and cool-appearing woman really be herself? She felt as though she were detached and watching from far away another part of herself going through the motions.

As Katherine stood gazing at her reflection, a knock sounded at the door.

Macey scurried off to answer it and shortly announced Mr. Vincent and Rachel.

"My dear, I hope you are ready; a carriage is waiting outside for us," Mr. Vincent said entering the room. But when his eyes rested upon Katherine, he stopped and caught his breath. He found himself staring at the young woman in front of him and rushed over to take one of her hands. "Forgive me for staring child, but you are a vision of loveliness to these poor old eyes of mine. Never have I seen such beauty as yours before and if I were a young man again I would be first in line to fight for your hand."

"Thank you, sir, for your kind words, but I really feel anything but beautiful; I am quite nervous," Katherine murmured demurely, the color rising to her cheeks at his generous compliments.

"Oh really, Katherine, you act as though you were still a child. I do not understand you at all. Here you are going to marry one of the richest men in Richmond and I am sure one of the most handsome and you claim you are scared. What on earth are you frightened of?"

The color drained from Katherine's face as she glared at the woman in front of her. How could Rachel be so unfeeling and so harsh? she asked herself.

But Mr. Vincent to her relief came to her rescue. "Miss Profane, I am sure anyone with any feelings can understand Katherine's reluctance and nervousness to wed a man she has just met and to have to start a new life in a foreign country. And if you cannot show a little compassion, I for one would take it kindly if you would keep your thoughts to yourself."

Katherine looked upon the elderly man with gratitude brimming in her eyes.

Rachel could hardly keep her anger under control at this old goat's words and tone of voice. Who did he think he was, trying to protect this little vain, simpering woman, who was scared of everything?

"I do hope you understand me, Miss

Profane," Mr. Vincent added in an angry voice.

"I understand perfectly, sir. I did not mean to say anything wrong; I only thought to offer Katherine some advice," Rachel said softly, trying not to let her anger show. She would have to control her tongue, she told herself— at least until Marco came to take her away from these cruel people and make her his.

"Well, if that is settled may we leave? The carriage is still waiting and I would hate for you, my dear," he said looking at Katherine with a tender expression in his eyes, "to be late to attend your own wedding."

The church, where the marriage was to be performed, was a small white structure, on the outskirts of town.

As the carriage pulled into the drive Katherine was relieved to see only a very few carriages outside. She had hoped the wedding would be a small affair and at least one of her hopes had come true. Katherine entered the front door of the church on the arm of Mr. Vincent.

As the music started to play everyone within the church turned to get a glimpse of the woman who would become the wife of one of the richest men in Virginia—Bradly Deveraux.

Katherine could feel the eyes upon her and willed herself to glance neither to right nor left, but to look directly in front of her. And there in front of the altar stood Bradly

Deveraux, in all his splendor. He was even taller than Katherine had remembered and also more sinister-looking.

Katherine felt her knees starting to shake and was relieved to feel Mr. Vincent's sturdy arm holding her own tightly, to give her the support she most desperately needed.

As they reached the end of the aisle, Mr. Vincent moved away from Katherine and left her at Bradly's side.

Katherine looked deeply into Bradly's face and he bestowed upon her a large smile, which more frightened her than helped to calm her fears.

As Bradly had watched Katherine come down the aisle on Mr. Vincent's arm, he thought he had never before seen beauty as he saw it in this woman. She looked to him to be a goddess, serene and composed, floating on a cloud of white lace. He had never imagined himself marrying a woman with even half the beauty that this woman possessed.

The preacher started to speak and Katherine stole another glance at this man who within a few minutes would be her husband. He looked on with a cool gaze, while she herself had to hide her hands in the folds of her dress to hide their trembling.

She went through the ceremony as though she were still the woman in the mirror that she had earlier watched dress. She felt as though she were not taking any part in what was happening about her, but as the ceremony came to an end and Bradly Deveraux took her in his arms and bestowed a warm and lingering kiss upon her lips, she came alive with feeling and could feel her pulse quicken and her body melt against that of her husband.

As quickly as Bradly had taken her in his arms, he released her. He had meant only to show her that he would be the master and that she did not affect him one way or another, but with that kiss he had awakened a need within himself to take that beautiful face between his hands and to ravish it with kisses and to hold that supple body closely and to share the secrets beneath the folds of her gown.

Bradly quickly quenched these thoughts. He could never allow himself to fall into her bewitching powers. He then turned, gave his guests a large smile, and offered his arm to his new bride.

He led a shaky and frightened Katherine back down the aisle. She could not understand her reactions to his kiss. She had been kissed by a number of men before but never had she felt so utterly consumed by a kiss in her life. She could only pray that her husband had not noticed her reaction. She did not wish for any man to know he could hold such power over her.

Bradly halted Katherine outside the church steps and waited for the few guests to make their introductions and give their good wishes to the new bride and groom.

Katherine felt so shaken inside she feared

she would become faint. She hardly heard a word as Bradly's close friends took her hand and welcomed her to their town. She doubted if she would remember a single name. Her senses were so filled by the nearness and masculine smell of this man standing beside her and holding her arm that she felt herself wanting to run as far as possible and hide herself away.

Clayton Johnson was one of the guests who had arrived to witness the marriage of his best friend. He slowly made his way toward the newly married couple. He wanted to be sure of Bradly's mood before he met his bride and wished her well.

"Clay," Bradly shouted and grabbed his arm. "Aren't you going to meet my wife?"

Clayton's face broke out into a hearty smile—one mostly of relief. Bradly must have forgotten the scene the night before in the tavern and Clay certainly was not going to be the one to bring it up and remind him of his bad temper.

"Here, let me introduce you to my wife, Katherine. This is my nearest neighbor and closest friend, Clayton Johnson. You will probably see a lot of him and his wife, Jean, at Moon Rise."

Katherine looked at the young man standing in front of her. He was of medium build and had light-brown hair and brown eyes. He was dressed in a dark brown suit, seemed well at ease, and possessed a gay manner. She knew at first glance that she liked this grinning young man and she hoped his wife would be as friendly and appealing as he. She would need all the friends she could muster at this time. With Bradly as a husband and Rachel living under the same roof with her, she would be needing someone with whom to talk who would be kind and not hateful. "It is very nice meeting you, Mr. Johnson," Katherine responded, as Clay took her hand in his. "I do hope you and your wife will feel free to visit anytime you care to."

"Clay did you bring Jean with you? I would like her to meet Katherine."

"I'm afraid not, Brad. She has come down with a cold and I wouldn't let her make the trip. Even though she fussed and shouted, I insisted she stay at home. I don't want any harm to come to her while she's carrying my son," Clay answered.

Katherine could tell at once he cared a great deal for his wife and also that he was quite proud that he would become a father.

"I'm sure Jean will be over as soon as she feels up to it. Katherine, I hope you and she will become good friends. She's always saying that all our neighbors are too far away to visit. With you being the closest I'm sure you will be able to visit back and forth."

"Tell your wife, Mr. Johnson, I shall be waiting for her to call as soon as she is relieved of her cold," Katherine answered, giving him one of her most breath-taking smiles.

"I certainly will," Clay said, looking at the beauty Brad had gotten himself for a wife. If he didn't adore his own wife as much as he did he would almost feel envious of Bradly. With his loving Jean waiting at home for him he could only feel gladness for his friend and hope that his marriage would be as happy as his own.

Rachel, who had been standing by talking to an elderly woman about the terrible voyage they had just made, excused herself and approached Katherine and Bradly.

Bradly saw her making her way toward them and quickly introduced Clayton to her.

"It is nice to make your acquaintance, sir," Rachel replied rather stiffly. "But I must say I do not think I can bear any more of this infernal dust and wind. It is just dreadful. I do not see how you can all stand around and talk out here," she said gruffly, dusting at her dress with a gloved hand.

"I am sorry," Bradly said with irritation, "but I guess you are right and it is about time for us to be on our way."

"Are you going straight to Moon Rise, Brad, or are you going to stay in town another night?" Clay questioned.

"We are going straight to Moon Rise, Clay. I wish we had more time to stay here, but I'm anxious for the ladies to get settled and I don't like being gone too long from the plantation."

"Well, I guess I'll be seeing you all soon, Brad. As soon as Jean gets better we'll be on over. It sure has been a pleasure meeting you ladies, and I'll tell you both now that Jean will be tickled to death when I tell her that old Brad's gone and brought home two women for her to chat with," Clay said, with a bow and a smile. "May I escort you to the carriage, Miss Profane?"

"Surely, sir, that would be most kind of you, Mr. Johnson," Rachel replied in a better manner.

"Shall we be going, my pet?" Bradly bent and asked Katherine.

Katherine did not have time to answer for Bradly was already leading her toward the carriage.

When they were seated inside, Rachel on one seat and Katherine and Bradly sitting across from her, Mr. Vincent came to stand by Katherine's window. "My dear child, I wish you all the happiness which my heart possesses."

"Will you be able to come to Mr. Deveraux's plantation to visit me?" Katherine asked in a beseeching tone of voice.

"No, my dear, I am afraid my boat will sail in a couple of days, and as soon as I arrive in England I shall go posthaste to your father's home with your letters and to inform him of your beautiful marriage."

"I-I did not expect you to be leaving for England so soon," Katherine said, her eyes starting to mist over. "I shall miss you more than I can express with any words. You have been so kind to me."

"There, there, child; perhaps it shan't be for too long. Maybe one day we shall meet again."

"I know," Katherine cried with tears streaming down her flawless cheeks, "but it will seem like an eternity before we see each other again."

"Time, my dear, goes by quickly and you will see that you will be so busy with your new life, you will hardly have the time to think of an old man such as me."

"I shall never forget you," Katherine cried and flung her arms around his neck.

"Hush, child," Mr. Vincent said softly, releasing her arms and kissing her forehead tenderly. "I must be going now, child. I am sure Mr. Deveraux wishes to be on his way," he stated, backing away, feeling tears starting to sting his own eyes. "God bless you, child, and may he grant you every happiness," he said softly, turning and walking away from the carriage.

Katherine sat weeping softly and looking after him until his frame disappeared from her view. Would she always feel so desolate and would everyone she love always be torn from her? she questioned herself.

Bradly ordered Raymond to start the carriage going and then he sat quietly watching Katherine as she wept silently into her handkerchief. He had never felt great compassion for any woman before, but as he watched

Katherine in her state of sorrow he wanted to bring her into his arms and comfort her tear-stained face. However, he could neither find the words to comfort her, nor had he the courage to try.

Katherine looked up after a time and met Bradly's eyes, which held her own in a strong compelling gaze. She was confused for a moment, for she had thought she had seen a tenderness and understanding there of which she had not thought him capable. She felt her face turn hot at his intense stare and turned back toward the window.

Bradly sat inhaling the delicate rose fragrance that seemed to encompass his senses, and his mind went over once again Katherine's deep-blue eyes and her black tresses. He felt a fire start to ignite inside himself and his pulses quickened; he shook himself and cautioned himself not to dwell on this woman who was now his wife. He would have to think of other matters and get a grip on himself. He could not let himself forget the fact that Marco Radford had already lain with her and he would not play second to that bastard.

Bradly had informed the ladies earlier that it would be a long ride to Moon Rise and they would most assuredly arrive after dark. The only words which were spoken during the ride were those of Rachel; complaining about the weather or the bumpy ride. Then finally, after finding no sympathy from the couple within the carriage, she laid her head back against the

128

seat and tried to put her headache out of her mind and only think of Marco and his return.

After a few hours of the bouncing ride, Katherine fell asleep, her head falling upon Bradly's shoulder. Bradly's face turned into an angry scowl, but he remained still so as not to disturb his sleeping wife. He should have ridden outside with Raymond, he scolded himself, and left the inside of the carriage to the women. But he had to admit he did enjoy the feel of this small, fragile woman's head upon his shoulder.

It was well after dark before Raymond turned the carriage down the dirt road which led to Moon Rise plantation. The road was shaded by huge oak trees on either side; Spanish moss hung from their limbs, which stretched out over the road.

There was a full, bright moon shining down upon the land and the countryside looked as though a magical hand had painted a masterpiece upon a huge canvas.

As the carriage came into view of a huge red brick house, with light coming from within and smoke curling out from the chimneys, Rachel craned her neck to get a better view of the house she would be living in—she hoped, for only a short while. She had pictured in her mind a small house built of logs or even wood, so when she glimpsed the magnificent house set back among huge, ancient oaks she was even more jealous of Katherine than ever.

The carriage pulled to a stop before the

front veranda and Raymond scampered down from his seat to open the carriage door for his master.

"Katherine," Bradly said softly, "we are here."

Katherine awoke with a start. "What, what is it?" she questioned, as she looked about, trying to take in her surroundings.

"We're at Moon Rise, Katherine."

Katherine realized all too quickly where she was and on whose shoulder she had laid her head. "I-I am sorry," she stammered. "I must have fallen asleep, I did not mean to—"

"That is quite all right. My shoulder did not have anything better to do than to support a lady in distress," Bradly said with a small grin upon his face. "But now, if we're ready, may we make our way into the house and warm ourselves?" Bradly added, as he opened the door and climbed out of the carriage.

Katherine looked around her when she stepped down and was surprised at the vastness of the house and the property which surrounded it. She had not really thought too much about what Moon Rise would look like, but she would never have thought of anything as grand and beautiful as it actually was.

As the small group made their way across the veranda and through the front door, a huge, dark Negro woman came bounding out from the dining-room door. "That you, Master Brad? You sure enough took your good old time in bringing the new missus here. Let me get a look at her, Master Brad; move out of my way, so I can see what you got for us." Jezzie chuckled with a large, toothy smile, while she pushed Bradly away from in front of Katherine.

Bradly stepped to the side and took hold of Katherine's elbow. "Jezzie, this is my new wife and your new mistress, Katherine," he said, giving the old Negress a warm smile.

"Why, Master Brad, she ain't but a tiny little thing, but Lordy ain't she pretty?" Jezzie laughed, looking Katherine up and down. "Old Jezzie, she'll have her fit in no time at all, Master Brad; you just leave everything to me. Yes, sir, I'll get some meat on those bones in no time at all."

"Jezzie, you act as though every woman should be as healthy as you," Bradly said good-naturedly.

"Yes, sir, I sure enough do, Master Brad, but I can see by the look in your eyes that you be liking this little thing just the way she is." Jezzie laughed.

After completing her survey of Katherine, Jezzie rested her eyes on Rachel. "Master Brad, who's this other lady you brought back with you?" she questioned, looking pointedly at Rachel.

"This is Miss Rachel Profane, Jezzie. She shall be staying as a guest of Miss Katherine's."

"Well, I sure didn't know nothing about any other lady, Master Brad," she stated with

131

her hands upon her hips. "You know I like to know what's going on and who's going to be staying here."

"Jezzie," Bradly said with a tinge of anger in his voice, "if you will see to our meal and have someone show your mistress and Miss Rachel to their rooms, I would greatly appreciate it."

"Yes, sir, Master Brad. I bet the missus be right tired and hungry after that long ride, but old Jezzie she been keeping your meal hot and I'll be having that little Lucy girl take them and show them to their rooms. Yes, sir, Master Brad, you sure got yourself a pretty little thing, didn't you?" She grinned at Katherine.

"Right now, Jezzie, get that fat bottom of yours out into the kitchen." Bradly smiled, not being able to stay angry at Jezzie for any amount of time.

When she went back through the dining-room door Bradly burst out in a roar of laughter. "That, ladies, is Jezzie. She rules this house and tries to rule everyone's life here on Moon Rise, but you shall come to love her, I am sure, as we all do."

"I, for one, cannot believe you would allow a slave to talk in such a manner to you, Mr. Deveraux," Rachel stated coldly. "She should be taught her place and to stay in it, I believe."

"Miss Profane," Bradly said, trying to control his mounting anger at this woman, "Jezzie means no harm by the way she talks. She has been running this house the past thirty-five years and also, Miss Profane, I shall tell you this one thing: I will not tolerate anyone questioning me on the treatment of my people. If you will honor this one wish of mine I am sure we shall all get along fine."

"I am sorry, Mr. Deveraux, but I am used to servants staying in their own places. Of course I shall do as you ask, this being your house."

"Good. I am glad to see we will not be having any trouble on this matter," Bradly replied, turning and looking about for Katherine.

When Bradly and Rachel had started their discussion, Katherine had walked into the sitting room, wishing to avoid any arguments. Upon first entering the room, she had caught her breath at the lavishness before her. It was decorated entirely in white and gold, and a huge white sofa with gold trim stood in the center of the room facing a wall-length fireplace. The carpet was a deep white Persian; it looked as though one could lie down and sink into its softness. At the large French windows were hung sheer white drapes, with gold-leaf designs interwoven, along the borders.

Katherine had never thought to be living in such luxury. This house was even more impressive than that of her father, which she had always thought to be beautiful. As Katherine walked about and admired the small porcelain figurines placed upon a small table in one corner of the room, Bradly walked up softly behind her and spoke in a low, husky voice.

"Well, Katherine, what do you think? Do you think you will enjoy living at Moon Rise?"

Katherine jumped, surprised to find him so close behind her. She had been so engrossed with looking about the room that she had not heard his approach, and now due to his close survey of her she found herself blushing and at a loss for words. "Your home is indeed quite beautiful, sir," she finally got out.

"I'm glad you approve, madam," Bradly said, not knowing why, but he really was glad that she thought of his home as being beautiful. "But enough of looking over your new home for tonight, I imagine you would like to be shown to your room. Miss Profane has already been taken to hers and I thought you would care to freshen up a bit before dinner, unless you are overtired and would rather have a tray sent up to you?"

"I am a little tired. If it is not too much trouble, I think I would like a hot bath and a tray brought up to my room," Katherine answered, hoping that perhaps with him thinking her too weary he would leave her to herself tonight. She knew she would have to submit to him when the time came, but she dreaded what would take place when he did insist on his husbandly rights.

"Good then, but if you do not mind I would like to join you there for dinner. Miss Profane has already excused herself with a headache and I would like to talk to you about some matters I feel we must discuss." Bradly spoke slowly his light silver-gray eyes watching her face with an intensity that made Katherine tremble.

There was no way in which Katherine could refuse him. He had posed his words as a question, but Katherine knew full well that he would make it a command if she offered any resistance, so she could only accept his presence gracefully.

Lucy, a young, light-colored Negro girl, showed Katherine up the stairs and to her room. "This is the master chamber," the girl said entering a door and walking over to a large brass tub sitting in front of a fireplace in which a crackling fire burned. "I'll prepare your bath right away, ma'am," the small girl said, placing a few more small logs upon the hearth.

"Thank you, Lucy," Katherine said to the girl as she looked around the room in awe. She had never before seen such a large bedroom. It was at least twice the size of the room she had always slept in at her father's house, and as she looked about her she could hardly believe her own eyes. In the center of the room stood the largest brass bed she had ever seen. Katherine walked over and placed a hand upon the large goose-feathered mattress. Lord, she thought, one would sink in all this softness upon lying down on it. As she walked about and admired the beautiful sitting room which adjoined the master bedroom, Lucy called out to inform her that her bath was ready.

Katherine lingered in the warm water, feeling her tired body relax. As she soaped herself, she went over in her mind everything that had happened since this morning when she had been awakened by the small elderly woman at the inn. She was now Mrs. Bradly Deveraux, and she could barely remember one word which had been spoken during the marriage ceremony. She searched her mind trying to recall the words the preacher had spoken, but her head was a blank except for the end of the ceremony when Bradly had taken her in his arms and bestowed that searing kiss upon her lips. Her face turned a deep red as she sat there rinsing the soap from her arms. She would have to force that kiss from her mind, she ordered herself. She would become a stumbling idiot if she kept dwelling on the power that kiss had held. She forced herself to think of the house that was now to be her home. She already felt a great warmth and fondness for the place and for the servants who ran it. Perhaps with time, she would find some happiness here at Moon Rise. With these thoughts, her mind eased somewhat. She rose out of the now-cool water and wrapped the towel Lucy offered her around her body.

After she was dry, Lucy helped her to slip into a sheer light-yellow gown with slits which rose to each thigh and with tiny, yellow ribbons which laced up the front. Over this, she put on a matching yellow robe. Then Lucy brushed out her hair until it shone, and tied a yellow velvet ribbon about the rich, black curls.

Just as her toilette was completed, a knock sounded at the door and without an answer it opened. Bradly stepped into the room, his eyes taking in Katherine's appearance from her dark, lustrous curls to the small slippers that adorned her feet. "Dinner will be up shortly," he said in his deep, husky voice, which almost made Katherine lose her will.

Katherine sat facing the mirror of the dressing table and watched as Bradly made his way to a large comfortable chair across from the fireplace.

"Lucy, you may leave now. Your mistress will call if she has any further need of you." He spoke kindly to the Negro girl.

"Yes, sir, Master Brad," the girl replied, hurrying out of the room.

As soon as the door was once more closed, Bradly rose and walked about the room, reminding Katherine of a great panther stalking about in a cage. "I hope you like this room, Katherine. My mother had it furnished to my father's taste and my father had the bed built to suit himself. I have found no reason to change anything, but if something does not meet your fancy, feel free to do so."

Katherine lowered her head, looking at her

clasped hands and replied, hardly above a whisper, "Thank you, I am sure everything will be fine."

Bradly, who was watching her sidewise, raised one fine dark brow. "Come now, Katherine, there is no reason to be frightened. I am your husband now. Come sit over here by the fire and we can talk until our dinner arrives."

Katherine rose on wobbly legs and took the seat next to that in which Bradly had earlier been sitting.

"I hope you're hungry, Katherine. Jezzie is determined to see you eat all you possibly can and she has fixed one of her best meals this evening," Bradly said, taking the opposite chair and trying to put her more at ease.

"I am rather hungry. I fear I have not eaten much today," she murmured softly, now feeling the full craving of her appetite.

"I also hope you and Jezzie will get along well. She was waited a long time for me to take a wife and I'm afraid she had almost despaired of my ever taking one. She has always run this house and she also raised me from a small child. I guess that explains best her manner and voice, so please do not take anything amiss in her words. I myself still find her scolding me as though I were still only five years old."

"I assure you, sir, I thought her most kind and I am sure we shall become good friends," Katherine replied, finding it easier to talk with this man sitting across from her. Katherine sensed the tenderness in his voice when he spoke about his Negro housekeeper, so she ventured to speak. "Sir, you say Jezzie raised you from a small child. What happened to your mother?"

His cold, gray piercing eyes looked upon her with a look of contempt and anger and Katherine regretted immediately her questions and intrusion.

"I am sorry. I did not mean to pry; I only thought—"

"You needn't apologize; it is no great secret and you would learn from Jezzie soon enough. I was just not prepared for your questions. My mother died giving birth to her only son—me. And that is why Jezzie has raised me from an infant and I in return have a great affection toward her."

"Oh, I am sorry about your mother and I can understand your feelings toward Jezzie."

"I'm sorry, too." Bradly spoke softly, as if to himself. "My mother was said to have been a wonderful and warm woman and I regret not having been able to know her."

Katherine could understand his feelings even better than he could know. She remembered her own mother's death and Biddy being there to care for her. She also remembered the many times she had wished to be able to talk with and confide in her own mother, but it was too late for that and she could now only remember her mother's image and soft-spoken voice. Katherine felt a small bit closer now to this man to whom she was married yet barely knew.

But all too quickly their friendly talk came to an end as the dinner trays were brought into the room by two identical twin Negro girls, about sixteen years old, each wearing calico dresses with white, starched aprons.

The meal was delicious and Katherine was surprised at the tastiness of the wild herbs and spices used in the foods.

After the wonderful dinner, Bradly poured them both a glass of light wine, which Katherine accepted and drank both quickly and eagerly, hoping to brace herself for the night ahead and to steady her shaking limbs. As she placed her glass upon the table laden with their empty plates and the bowls of food which still contained more of the good repast, Bradly refilled her glass and handed it back to her.

"You had best take your time and drink this one slowly or you may find yourself a little calmer than you wish," Bradly said with a little smile, as if he could read her mind.

"I assure you, sir, I shall be just fine," she replied in a haughty voice; but taking his advice, she only took a tiny sip from her glass.

"Come sit down, Katherine. I find it more pleasant to converse when I am comfortable and have a chair to relax in."

Katherine walked over and sat down in the chair she had occupied earlier.

Bradly pulled his chair up closer to hers and placed his large frame in it. "There are some things I wish to ask you, Katherine, and I wish for you to answer me with the truth."

Katherine looked hard at him, trying to read his meaning from the set look upon his face. "Yes?" she questioned already feeling a little light-headed from her drink.

"First of all, I wish to know why in hell a woman with your beauty and charm would wish to marry a man she does not know and be willing to travel halfway around the world to accomplish it?" he asked, his anger mounting at the thought of himself having been trapped into marriage. Even though his wife was by far the most beautiful woman he had ever seen, he still had been trapped into marriage, and this sorely bruised his pride.

Katherine sat frozen, gripping the arms of her chair as his words seeped into her brain. She had been forced into this marriage against her will and now in addition to everything else she had endured, this man was sitting here acting as though she had set out deliberately to trap him into marrying her. "How dare you!" she shouted, jumping to her feet in a high rage. "Do you think for one minute that I would *wish* to travel to this terrible, backwoods country and to marry such a brutal, beastly man as yourself?"

Bradly looked up at this small woman whose eyes were flashing with tiny sparks of anger. Never would he have imagined this small wisp of a woman possessed such a temper. "Then why would you have agreed to such a proposal?" he questioned, watching her stomp about the room.

"I—I agree? I never wanted this or any other marriage arranged for me. I was forced into this marriage by my father and stepmother," she cried angrily, her face flaming red.

"I suppose you were forced into marrying me," Bradly said, rising from his chair, "as you were forced by Marco Radford?" He said his words slow and menacingly.

"What?" Katherine asked not understanding the full meaning of his words.

"You know perfectly well, madam, what I mean and I shall have an answer from you now."

Katherine stood stunned as the realization of his words came to her. "Sir, you are a loudmouthed, arrogant fool and I have no intention of answering any of your vile, filthy questions," she cried, anger overruling her better judgment.

"By damn, you will answer my questions, madam. Even if I have to beat the answer out of you, to gain that which I wish to know, I shall. I am master of this house, and you for better or worse are now my wife."

"I, sir, had no choice in the husband I was forced to marry and I have no intention of answering your vile questions, so if you must show your superior strength by beating me, do as you wish, for I have not the strength to fight you back," she said, trying to stand up to him and not show her fear.

Her words were like an ice-cold pitcher of water being thrown in Bradly's face. Never before had he threatened a woman, let alone raised a hand to one. But this proud beautiful woman before him had aroused new feelings within him and he could barely control his words or his senses. How could this woman who was now his wife bring his anger to such a high peak? Before he realized how or why, he found himself tightly embracing Katherine and bringing his lips down upon those which were tempting him so.

Katherine fought and shoved against his unwelcome attack.

Finally, Bradly's lips found their target and he covered hers with his own.

Katherine pushed against him in a panic, but then as suddenly as Bradly had grabbed her, she felt herself melting against him and kissing him in return, savoring the taste, feel, and smell of this strong virile man.

Bradly released her abruptly and moved back a few steps.

Katherine stood dazed and breathless, grabbing hold of the back of the chair beside her.

"Madam, I have told you I am master of this house and I shall also, madam, be master of you when and if I wish it."

Katherine stood as though stunned. She could not believe her own body would betray her as it had. How could her body betray her and respond to this horrible man's passion and kisses? What had come over her?

Bradly looked upon her a moment longer, his gray-silver eyes as cold and hard as steel. Then without another word, he turned and strode from the room.

When he had vanished from the room and the door was tightly shut, Katherine flung herself upon the great bed and wept until her tears would come no more. "Oh, body, how could you do this thing to me?" she cried aloud. How could she have responded to his kisses and gentle caresses after the terrible things he had said? But even as her mind took on these thoughts, she could still feel the touch of his lips upon her own. She had to admit to herself, she had enjoyed his lips on hers; and she also had to admit that no other man had ever made her feel as Bradly had with that one searing kiss. She had not thought it possible for her body to feel so encompassed by such strange emotions or the feelings she had of wanting something more. She had never met a man as virile and masculine as he. She knew she would have to keep a tight restraint upon her body and not give it another chance to betray her again.

Katherine finally found sleep and dreamed the night through, of black hair and piercing gray eyes.

Chapter Five

The next morning Katherine awoke to a cool, sunny morning. Lucy was bustling about, putting the room in order and humming gaily to herself.

"Good morning, Lucy," Katherine said softly.

"Oh, ma'am, I didn't mean to wake you," the girl replied guiltily.

"That's all right, Lucy; it is time I was getting up and about anyway," Katherine said sweetly, trying to put the girl at ease.

"Yes, ma'am. Would you be wanting your breakfast up here in your room, Miss Katherine?"

"No, thank you, Lucy. I think I shall join the others downstairs, if I am not too late."

"Yes, ma'am. I'll just straighten up a little and then help you to dress."

Katherine dressed in a high-necked, dark-blue velvet gown, with white lace at the throat and wrists. She then had Lucy brush her hair and put a dark-blue ribbon in it, to keep it in place.

She made her way down the stairs and into the dining room almost with eagerness at the thought of seeing and being close to her new husband. What could be coming over her? she questioned herself. She had never before felt this way at only the thought of seeing a man.

The dining room was empty; to her surprise, though, she could hear voices and noises through a door leading out of that room. So, without a second thought, she opened the door and entered a room that was obviously the kitchen.

Jezzie was standing in front of a large wood stove, stirring a number of pots and fussing at the two twin Negro girls cutting vegetables at a long wooden table.

On seeing Katherine, Jezzie spoke in a surprised voice. "Why, Miss Katherine, what you a-doing in this old hot kitchen?"

Katherine gave the friendly old woman a smile and sat upon a high stool next to the door. "I came down to breakfast, Jezzie, but no one seems to be about."

"Yes, ma'am. Everyone done ate. Master Brad, he left early this morning," the big Negress said, hanging her head upon her ample chest. She had overheard the fighting and arguing coming from Katherine's room last night, as she was pretending to be dusting in the hallway, outside of her master's bed-chamber, and she hated the thought of her master saying such terrible things to her new, sweet, little, innocent mistress.

"Where did he go off to, Jezzie?" The words popped out of Katherine's mouth before she could stop them.

Jezzie's heart went out to her new mistress; she knew her master sometimes let his temper get the best of him. She walked over and patted Katherine's hand. "Now don't you fret none, honey. He be a stubborn man some-times, just like his pappy was. The master be just like him, but both the master and his pappy got a heart of gold for those they care about."

Katherine sat staring at her tightly clasped hands, lying upon her lap.

Jezzie hated to see this sweet young thing feeling so badly, but she knew she had to give her mistress the message as her master had ordered. Sometimes Jezzie wished she could take her master and switch his backside as she had done when he was a small boy. This, she knew, was only wishful thinking and now she had to tell her mistress. "Well, honey," she said, lowering her eyes and shuffling her feet, "the master, he say to tell you he was going into Richmond on business and he would be back in a couple of days."

"Oh," Katherine said, feeling a great letdown, but not knowing why in the world she should feel this way. Katherine regained her composure and gave Jezzie a small smile. "Thank you for telling me, Jezzie." She was not about to show anyone in this house how Bradly Deveraux affected her. "Has Miss Rachel been down to breakfast yet?" she asked, trying to change the subject.

Jezzie gave Katherine a large toothy smile, relieved that her mistress was not too distressed. "No, ma'am. She sent word that she was still suffering with her head and that she wished for a tray to be brought to her room."

"Well, Jezzie, what can I do to help?" Katherine asked, looking about her.

"Ma'am? You ain't got to do nothing. We got girls that do all the work in this old house."

"Well, I certainly do not mean to sit by and watch while others do all the work. If this is to be my home I must help to see that it is kept in order."

"I don't know, Miss Katherine. It ain't fitting for a white lady to be a-doing work when she gots plenty of black girls that can do it."

"Oh pooh, Jezzie! If you would be kind enough to fix me something to eat—I fear I really am starving—then afterward you can show me through this grand house and perhaps we will be able to find something for me to do."

"Yes, ma'am." Jezzie chuckled, shaking her head. "I'll fix you something right up." She could see there wouldn't be any arguing with this little, stubborn woman and she rather liked the idea of having a mistress that wouldn't be scared to get her hands dirty.

Katherine ate her breakfast at the long wooden table where the two girls were cutting vegetables, and every now and then taking sly glances at their new mistress. Never before had they sat in front of a white lady, let alone at the same table with the new mistress of Moon Rise.

Katherine almost ordered Jezzie to sit down and drink a cup of coffee, as she ate her breakfast and in between bits of the delicious food questioned Jezzie about the plantation and her master. The latter, Katherine was really more interested in, but only asked a few questions about Bradly, so Jezzie would not know how much she did care and wished to know about her new husband.

Jezzie, having given Katherine a knowing smile about the way of the heart, went into a long history of the Deveraux family, one which she never tired of telling to anyone who wished to hear. She started from when she had first come to Moon Rise and all that had stood where they were now sitting was trees and weeds.

Katherine sat spellbound, listening to the large woman as she told of Louise Deveraux's death at the birth of her only son and how she, Jezzie, had practically raised Bradly single-handedly. Then, at the end of her story, she did add reluctantly that Bradly's father did take a hand in the matter now and then.

Katherine had to smile at the old Negress, as she sat and listened to her trying to take all the praise for Bradly being what he was today. She could not imagine the old woman being any more proud of Bradly if he had been truly her own son.

With breakfast completed, Jezzie led Katherine through every room in the house, talking all the while, pointing to almost every piece of furniture and explaining where it had come from and who had purchased it.

Katherine found she never had met a woman quite like Jezzie. She seemed to know everything there was to know about the house, the family, and all the servants here at Moon Rise.

It was late in the afternoon when Jezzie led a tired Katherine to the front sitting room, the tour completed.

Katherine was exhausted; having had barely any exercise on the ship from England, she found her legs were aching and her whole body seemed weary to the bone. "Oh, Jezzie, I'm afraid I shall have to wait until tomorrow to see the outside of this wonderful house. I am so tired now I only wish for a hot bath and my bed."

Jezzie gave her a sympathetic smile. "You'll feel fine tomorrow, honey; you just go on up to your room and I'll send you a good hot meal."

"Thank you, Jezzie, but I think first I should see how Rachel is feeling. Perhaps she would care to join me for dinner," Katherine said, rising from her chair and starting toward the stairs.

"I'll send that Lucy girl up to help you with your bath directly, Miss Katherine."

"That will be fine, Jezzie, and I do thank you for showing me through the house and everything you have done for me."

"Oh, nonsense, child, you just get yourself up to your room and rest a bit before dinner." Jezzie smiled, feeling a close bond being formed between her and her new mistress.

Katherine went to Rachel's room and knocked lightly on the door. She was concerned because she had not seen her all day. Perhaps she was really ill and not just suffering from a mild headache.

Rachel's voice came almost as a shout. "Come in."

Katherine entered looking about the dark

room. "Rachel, are you feeling well?"

Rachel, realizing who had entered her room, held back an angry retort. "I am fine; I wish only to be left alone so I can rid myself of this throbbing headache."

"Is there anything I can do? Perhaps open the drapes and windows to let some fresh air in?" Katherine questioned, starting toward the window.

"No," Rachel hissed, startling Katherine. "I only wish to be left alone. Perhaps you could tell someone to send a tray to my room; I do not wish to starve to death here in this heathen country."

"As you wish," Katherine stated. Trying to overlook the girl's foul mood, she started back to the door.

"Katherine," Rachel sneered, before she had turned the handle.

"Yes, Rachel?" Katherine questioned, not knowing what was to come next.

"I hear your new husband has already left Moon Rise. It could not be that he has already found displeasure with his new bride, could it?"

Katherine bristled under this attack, but held her tongue. "Mr. Deveraux had business he could not put off," she said walking out of the room, Rachel's laughter following her down the hall.

Katherine found she was near to tears as she opened the door to her chambers. Why did Rachel constantly try to pick and to hurt her?

She knew it was useless even thinking about it. How many times had she asked herself this same question since she had known the girl? There was just no understanding her.

She felt even more tired now after her meeting with Rachel and was happy to see Lucy had already started to prepare her bath.

"Miss Katherine, let me help you out of that dress," Lucy said, walking over to her when she saw her enter the room.

Katherine smiled fondly at the girl and gave herself over to her hands. At least there were kind people here who thought of others and not only of themselves.

Katherine almost dozed off as she rested her head on the rim of the tub and soaked her aching body in the warm water. But pulled herself awake and out of the tub, when she found Lucy placing a tray of food upon a small table in front of the fireplace.

She ate what she could of the warm repast and then, with a mind full of worries, she snuggled deep between the silk sheets on the large brass bed.

Sleep that night was hard to come by, even though Katherine felt more tired than ever before in her life. Her thoughts kept going over Rachel's words and then, when she could put them from her mind and would almost drift off to sleep, she would be pulled back awake by the thoughts of what had occurred the night before. Finally, in the late hours of the night, she found rest, but her dreams were plagued by Bradly's hands caressing her, his eyes looking into hers and his lips devouring her own.

On her second morning of residing at Moon Rise, Katherine awoke late in the morning. She dressed herself and hurried down to the kitchen, hoping to eat breakfast with Rachel so that perhaps the two of them could become better friends.

Jezzie was in her usual place, before the stove, cooking, and the two girls were scrubbing the work floor to a high polish.

"Good morning, Jezzie," Katherine greeted her. "Has Rachel been down yet for breakfast?"

Jezzie nodded her large head and gave Katherine a large smile. "She done been down and left to go out riding about on Master Brad's property."

"I guess her headache is better then. I was hoping we could have eaten together, but I must have overslept."

"That's all right, honey; you need all the rest you can get, and I doubt if that girl will be too long unless she goes and gets herself lost." The old Negress chuckled.

Katherine already had the impression that Jezzie did not care too much for Rachel and she could not much blame her. However, as long as Rachel was Katherine's guest, she at least felt that she should try to become closer to her.

"You just sit yourself down and I'll fix you

154

something right up. You're so small it's a-
going to take all my cooking to put some meat
on your bones."

Katherine only smiled, already knowing it
did no good to argue with this woman. "I
wonder, Jezzie, do you think I could get
someone to saddle me a horse, so I could ride
for a bit after breakfast?" Katherine asked,
already anticipating a good long ride.

"Why sure you can, honey. Master Brad's
got a whole pasture of good, fine horses,"
Jezzie answered, already placing a plate of food
in front of her mistress.

Katherine wolfed her meal down, in a hurry
to be gone.

"You had better slow down, honey, so you
can taste that food before you," Jezzie rebuked. "Those horses will still be there when
you're done."

Katherine looked up shamefaced, feeling as
if she were still a small child and Biddy was
scolding her for being bad.

Jezzie led Katherine out to the barn a short
time later and told Raymond to help her to
saddle the horse she wanted. Then the old
woman hurried back to the house, mumbling
that her food was sure to be ruined if she
didn't hurry back.

As Katherine looked about her in the stalls,
her eyes fell upon a small cream-colored mare.
"Raymond, would you please saddle that one
for me?" she said, pointing to the fine-looking
creature.

"Yes, ma'am, that one a real good horse;

155

she be as gentle as a lamb," the Negro man said, walking over to the stall and proceeding to saddle the mare.

"What is her name, Raymond?" Katherine questioned as she walked around the horse and admired her flawless flanks.

"She be Golden Girl, ma'am. Master Brad has had her since she been a filly and he tamed her down and taught her how to carry a saddle."

Katherine mounted Golden Girl, her blood rushing in her veins at the anticipation of being able to ride once again. She had always loved to ride and indeed, had had her own horse in England. She had rode at every chance she had had until, on her fifteenth birthday, Joann had informed her very calmly that she was not to go about the countryside on the back of a horse again. She had stated that whenever Katherine wished for an outing she was to ride in a carriage like all proper young ladies. Katherine could still remember the outrage she had felt for months after Joann had laid down her new law. Katherine had sought out her father in order for him to intervene, but he had sided with his wife and from that day forth Katherine had ridden in the carriage and had not sat astride a horse.

She kicked her horse's sides and left the barn. She also left behind her the thoughts of England and Bradly and Rachel. She was free once more, sitting on the back of Golden Girl, her hair flying in a long, black mane behind her and her face turned toward the wind.

Golden Girl also was glad to be free and stretched her long, fine legs out before her.

Time seemed to stop for Katherine as she rode about Moon Rise. She looked about at all the sights this strange, wonderful, and almost savage land held. She had never thought she would enjoy being in another country, but now as she rode atop Golden Girl, she felt at peace with this great country and knew she would miss it dearly if she were ever to have to leave.

It was almost dinner time before she once more found herself in front of the large, imposing house that belonged to her husband.

When Katherine, her hair in disarray and her cheeks pink from her long excursion, went in, Jezzie met her at the front door and from her set expression Katherine knew she was angry.

"Miss Katherine, where you been all this time? I was worried to death; I thought you had been thrown from that horse or something and was just about to send someone looking for you. Why you wanting to worry us all to death? And Master Brad he be powerful mad if'n he come back here to find you hurt."

"I am sorry, Jezzie. I did not mean to upset you. It is just that I completely lost track of all time. I promise I will not do it again, and as far as Bradly Deveraux being mad, I for one know that he would probably be glad if I were to come to harm and he could be rid of me."

Tears started coursing down her face. She could not understand it; only a few minutes ago she had been so happy and carefree and then the minute she thought of Bradly she became so emotional.

"There, there child, old Jezzie didn't mean to be so hard." The old woman put her arms about her mistress. "You go on upstairs and wash your face and I'll have Lucy bring you up something to eat," Jezzie cooed, her face a mirror of concern.

For the next two days Katherine kept to the same routine, helping Jezzie with the housework and riding Golden Girl until late in the afternoon. Each night she would fall asleep exhausted, willing her mind not to betray her into dreams of Bradly. She had barely caught a glimpse of Rachel in the preceding days; either the other girl was out and about riding or she was in her room with one of her headaches.

On the fourth day after Bradly's departure, Katherine went down to the kitchen to help Jezzie and the two Negro girls. Today was baking day and Katherine wanted to watch and help with anything she could. She wore a white muslin dress with tiny sprigs of yellow flowers on it. She had tied a yellow scarf atop her head and her hair hung freely down the length of her back.

Jezzie had already started with her baking and the lower portion of the house smelled of baking bread. Katherine could feel her stomach growling from the delicious aroma. "Here, Jezzie, let me do that; perhaps you could find something to eat for your starving mistress," Katherine said, walking over to the wood table and taking the rolling pin out of Jezzie's hands.

"Yes, ma'am, I'll get you something right quick," the black woman said with a large smile, abandoning her rolling pin to her mistress.

"Has Rachel been down to breakfast yet?" Katherine questioned, drawing her hand across her forehead and leaving a line of white flour in its stead.

"Yes, ma'am," was her answer, as Jezzie brought a pot of hot tea and a plate of hot cinnamon rolls over to the table. "You just sit yourself down now and eat some of these rolls, Miss Katherine."

"Thank you, Jezzie, I certainly will. They smell delicious."

Katherine bit into one of the cinnamon rolls while Jezzie took the rolling pin back up and rolled out the dough for one of her delicious apple pies.

The two women had become fast friends and Katherine felt almost as close to Jezzie as she had been to Biddy, her old nurse. Jezzie was always making Katherine laugh by telling her stories of Bradly when he was a boy.

She was in the middle of one of these stories about how Bradly, only six years old, had been missing all day—worrying everyone on the plantation half to death—before he had come home with a large grin, his whole body covered from head to toe with mud and a large line of fish in his hands. Katherine burst out laughing as the large woman proceeded to tell her of the tongue-lashing she had given him and the way he had just stood grinning until he finally said, "Well, Jezzie, if you're finished now I think I shall go up and take a bath."

"Yes, sir, that boy, that boy was something else when he was a young'un." Jezzie chuckled.

Both women were laughing out loud when Katherine heard a deep, throaty laugh and whirled around in her chair. "Bradly," the name escaped from her lips before she could stop herself.

Bradly Deveraux, with a small smile playing upon his lips, entered the room and made a large formal bow in Katherine's direction. "And what do we have here? Another one of my slave girls from the cabins out back?" he asked, looking with smiling eyes at Katherine's attire, his eyes lingering at her breasts.

Katherine blushed deeply, sensing a new warmth radiating from those cold, gray eyes.

Bradly, seeing Katherine's color rise, was quick to put her at ease. "Madam, you are more beautiful this morning than I could envision in my mind on the dusty ride home."

"I-I am sorry," she stammered softly. "I have been helping Jezzie, and I am afraid my other gowns are much too fancy to do housework in," she said, looking at her gown

160

with flour dusted upon it and feeling as if she were a child who had been caught with a stolen piece of candy.

Bradly looked toward Jezzie, who had remained quiet during the conversation. "May I ask you, why your mistress must help with the housework? Have you not enough girls who can help you, Jezzie?"

"Yes, sir, Master Brad, old Jezzie she got plenty of girls to help in this old house, but the missus, she wanted to help and she a-going to have things her own way. Yes, sir, Master Brad, she be almost as stubborn as you." Jezzie giggled.

"Is that so, Jezzie?" Bradly questioned, his features softening once again.

"Yes, sir, Master Brad, that's the way of it." The old woman grinned, shaking her head.

"Well, Katherine," Bradly started, taking a napkin and gently wiping the flour off her forehead. "This is your home and as such you may dress in any manner you wish."

"Thank you, I do not know what I would have done if you had forbidden me to help in here with Jezzie. It would surely bore me to death to have to just sit all day with nothing to do."

"Forbidden you, madam? Never; as I have just told you this is your home and you may do as you please. But for now, my little worker, I would like you to see about my bath and fresh clothing. I swear I must have half of Virginia's dust upon my backside. Also, Jezzie,

I'm in need of something to fill my belly," he said good-naturedly and then strode out of the room, whistling a lively tune as he made his way up the stairs.

Katherine looked up at Jezzie, hardly believing that this was the same Bradly who had stormed out of her room only a few nights ago. "I do not think I shall ever understand that man, Jezzie."

"Well, honey, understand him or not, you had best hurry and get his room warm and a bath ready. He sure can get mighty uppity when he has to wait for something."

Katherine jumped to her feet and rushed toward the door, not wishing to spoil Bradly's good mood. "Jezzie, please have the boys bring hot water up to his room."

"Yes, ma'am, I sure will."

Katherine rushed up the stairs to Bradly's room. He had moved into one of the guest rooms since Katherine's arrival and now, as she entered the room, she found Bradly squatting down, building up a roaring, warm fire and still whistling the same tune.

As he rose and saw Katherine enter the room he gave her a warm, generous smile. "I hope you have been getting along all right during my absence?"

"Oh, yes," she answered, finding it easier to talk with him while he was in a pleasant mood. "Jezzie has really been marvelous and I have been keeping myself quite busy."

"I'm sorry I had to rush off as I did, but I

had business to settle and it really couldn't be helped," Bradly said, as he filled his eyes with the vision of her.

"I understand," Katherine said softly and lowered her eyes from his penetrating gaze. "I do hope everything went well in Richmond."

"Fairly well, but that's enough of this talk. Come over and sit down and tell me what you have been doing while I've been gone."

"Well, I have helped Jezzie mostly here in the house, but I have visited a few of the slave women."

Bradly raised a dark brow at this.

"They are so kind, they treat me as though I really belong here and I am growing quite fond of all of them," Katherine said nervously, trying to explain herself.

"You do belong here, Katherine, and I shall not let you go away and leave Moon Rise." He said this with such a powerful voice that it frightened Katherine, while at the same time it sent a small shiver of pleasure through her.

"Go on now, Katherine, what else have you found to do?" he added in a more gentle voice.

"Not much really; I have helped to tend Jezzie's garden and also I have been taking long rides in the afternoons."

"You enjoy riding?" Bradly asked in surprise.

"Oh, yes, I love it. I had my own horse in England and my father told me once I could ride as well as any boy."

"You shall have to show me your riding

abilities tomorrow afternoon, if it pleases you and you wish to have company on your outings."

Katherine gave him a small smile. "That would be nice." To her surprise she found she really did mean every word she had just said and already she could not wait to be all alone with this large, beastly man.

The two boys entered the room, carrying steaming buckets of water in their hands.

Bradly rose and started to pull his shirt over his head.

Seeing him undressing, Katherine started toward the door.

"Will you join me for lunch, Katherine?" Bradly asked, as she started to leave the room.

"Yes, if you wish."

"I do wish you to join me, but for now you had better go see about its cooking, unless you would rather wash my back for me?" He grinned, as he undid his belt and made to pull off his trousers.

Katherine's face turned a flame red, as her eyes traveled down to Bradly's pants. "I-I will see to your meal," she choked and fled the room; Bradly's roaring laughter followed her down the stairs.

After Bradly had bathed and changed his clothes, he and Katherine ate a small lunch on the patio in the flower garden.

Katherine found it hard to believe that this was the same man who had threatened to beat her, only a few short nights ago. He was so polite and considerate to her now, it seemed impossible to believe that night had actually occurred at all.

After the meal was completed Bradly rose and took Katherine's hand and as if they had been young lovers they strolled through the gardens, talking to each other of childhood memories and the life each had lived before.

As Katherine talked of her own childhood in England and told Bradly about her mother and her nurse, Biddy, she sat down upon a stone bench; tears started to well up in her eyes. She had never felt so homesick or wished so hard for her mother to be alive and beside her as now.

"What is it?" Bradly questioned her anxiously, kneeling down and taking one of her small hands in his own.

"I am sorry," Katherine whispered, embarrassed by her show of tears. "I did not mean to act like this; I was only thinking of my mother and how happy and simple life had been when she was alive."

"You still had your father with you, Katherine," Bradly said tenderly.

"You do not understand; when my mother died my whole world seemed to fall apart. All of my father's love died along with my mother and when he took himself another wife, everything changed." She wept, trying to pull herself out of this feeling of self-pity, which had overcome her. "I am sorry I did not mean to bore you with my past life," she said finally, subduing her tears.

"I was not bored, madam. I wish to know everything I can about you."

Katherine lowered her head and tried to quiet her trembling.

"I think for now you had better go and lie down and rest awhile. I do not wish you to take sick from overdoing." Bradly spoke as though to a naughty child.

"I think I would like to rest for a time," Katherine answered, relieved to find a way to be alone and pull herself together.

As Katherine made her way down the hall, toward her room, Rachel stepped out of her own room.

"Oh, Katherine. I hear your husband has finally returned home. You must try to be more becoming, so as not to chase him off again." She grinned.

"Yes, Bradly is back home, Rachel." Katherine ignored the girl's hateful comment. "Will you be joining us for dinner this evening?"

Rachel made a small pout of anger at Katherine's ignoring her comment. She had wished for some fun with this simpering, little mouse, but it did not seem to be the day for it, so she proceeded to answer Katherine's question. "I do feel a small headache coming on, but perhaps it will be gone by dinner time."

"I was hoping to talk with you about your headaches, Rachel."

"What?" Rachel asked angrily.

"It is just that I thought perhaps you should see a doctor and let him examine you. It is not healthy for you to be in constant pain with your head."

"I have no wish to see a doctor and I do wish you would mind your own business." With these words Rachel turned her back on Katherine and made her way back to her room, slamming the door behind her.

Katherine did not feel like trying to figure the girl out now, as she went on to her room, stripped down to her chemise, and fell across the bed and into immediate sleep.

It was dark and far into the night, the only means of light coming from the small fire, still burning eagerly in the hearth, when Katherine awoke in the master bedchamber.

She had only meant to rest for a short time, but now as she sat up, she realized with a start that the house had a deadly quiet about it.

She pulled her legs to the side of the bed, slipped into her slippers, and then made her way to the closet to find her dressing robe. Why didn't Lucy awaken me? she questioned herself. Surely it must be past the dinner hour. She felt her stomach's hunger and, planning to go downstairs and see if Jezzie was still about in the kitchen, she left the room.

Just as Katherine was about to take the last step on the stairs, Lucy approached her, coming from the kitchen area. "Lucy, for goodness sake, why did you not wake me for dinner?"

"The master told me not to disturb you, Miss Katherine," the negro girl apologized, hanging her head down. "I'm sorry, ma'am, but Master Brad, he say you be needing your rest."

"That is all right, Lucy, I did not mean to upset you; it is only that I am so hungry."

"Yes, ma'am, but Master Brad said to come let him know when you woke and he would bring you your tray hisself."

"Oh?" Katherine asked, looking thoughtfully at the girl. What could be Bradly's reason for being so kind and concerned for her?

"Yes, ma'am," Lucy returned. "Master Brad said for you to stay in your room and rest and he'd bring your supper right up."

"Well, I guess I have no choice about it, but, Lucy, please tell Jezzie to be sure and give me plenty. I fear I am starving."

"Yes, ma'am, I sure will," Lucy said in a gayer tone.

Katherine went back to her room, sat down at the dressing table, and started brushing her long, dark tresses. She could not figure out what had brought about Bradly's good mood or kindness toward her, but she had to admit she did prefer kindness to his overbearing and brutal behavior of the other night. As she sat thus, deep in thought, Bradly entered the room carrying a large tray, laden with delicious-smelling food.

He stopped short when he saw the sight in front of him. Never before had he seen a woman such as this, her hair tumbling about her shoulders and a look upon her face, which was that of a goddess of some faraway haven.

"You look beautiful, sitting there like that, Katherine," he said in a voice which even surprised himself with its warmth and feeling.

Katherine turned about with a start; she had not heard the door open and had not expected him to enter without knocking first.

Bradly took in the surprised look on her face and misread it for fear. He tried at once to calm her. "I did not mean to frighten you; I brought you a tray. I hope you were able to have a nice rest this afternoon."

"I would really have preferred to have dined downstairs," she said trying to appear cool and calm.

"Katherine, let us not argue and fight this evening. I only wished for you to get some rest; you looked rather tired this morning and I do not wish for you to take ill."

Katherine looked upon him, not being able to suppress a small smile at his standing there holding the tray of food and acting as though she were his only concern. He did not appear anything like the Bradly Deveraux she had met only a few days ago. "I am sorry, sir, if I sounded rash and I must admit I have not been sleeping too well lately, so I do thank you for your concern and for my rest."

169

Bradly set the tray on a small table and placed this in front of Katherine. "Is anything bothering you, Katherine? Are you displeased here in my home?" he asked with concern, his silver eyes seeming to bore into her very soul.

"Oh no! I love it here, I already feel a part of belonging. It is only that it is all new to me. I shall be fine in time I am sure," she answered truthfully.

"Good; I am relieved to hear you find no fault with your new home. Now, madam, you must eat your dinner. Jezzie told me to inform you to eat every morsel off your plate."

Katherine gave a little giggle at this. "She treats me as if I were a child, but I must confess I have already begun to love her."

As she sat before her tray and laughed, Bradly watched Katherine with a yearning look. With her wine-red robe and her black curls cascading down her back, he could not suppress the thought of how it would feel to have that silken skin beneath his hands and to caress those shining, black curls. Without thinking he reached out and started to finger a small stray curl by Katherine's forehead.

Katherine looked up from her plate and saw the passion and warmth that was beginning to grow in the depths of his eyes. They sat thusly for a time, each lost in the tenderness and feeling seen in the other's eyes.

Finally Bradly broke away from her gaze and from his thoughts and asked softly,

"Would you prefer to eat alone or would you care to talk while you dine?"

Katherine could not bear the thought of his leaving and ventured, "If you are not busy, sir, I would enjoy your company."

"Indeed, madam, I have nothing better to do than to entertain you, I assure you," he answered, relieved she had not sent him from the room.

"Did you and Rachel dine together this evening?" Katherine questioned, trying to break the silence that overtook them.

"Yes, we did; and I must say, I was tempted to have Lucy awaken you and summon you down to join us. I do not know why, but I don't seem to get on too well with your cousin."

"My cousin? She is nothing to me except my stepmother's niece and honestly I do not understand the girl either," she said, angry that anyone would think that Rachel was her relation.

"Then why on earth did she come along with you to America?"

"I really do not know *her* reasons, but as for myself I had no choice in the matter. My father and stepmother wished her to accompany me and she has."

"You seem to have had very little choice in any of the decisions concerning your welfare," Bradly stated reflectively.

Katherine looked up from her plate, ready to rebuke him for his words and to defend herself, thinking he was making fun of her as he had the first night they had been alone. But when she looked into his face she met only tenderness. "No, I really did not have anything to say on any of the matters which led me to America," she answered softly, returning to her meal.

Bradly sat quietly looking at her and wondering to himself how this small wisp of a woman could have gotten into his blood as she had. His few days in Richmond had been a disaster; wherever he went and whatever he did, her image would come floating into his mind. And then when he had run into her friend, Mr. Vincent, in an inn and the old gentleman had told him of her reluctance to make the voyage and of her aversion to marrying thusly, he had stormed at himself for the way he had accused her of wanting a rich husband and trapping him into marriage. All of this he had falsely accused her of; but then there had been Marco. He knew Marco Radford well and he did not think he accused her falsely in this one area—but then again he could not be sure; she had neither denied it nor admitted it.

"Katherine!" he said, so loudly that Katherine jumped in her seat. "I am sorry I shouted, I only wished to apologize for my behavior of the other evening. I have not been able to get it out of my head—the terrible things that I said to you—but you must understand my reasons. First, let me tell you I am a very rich man and I have never liked being forced into anything against my own wishes. I did not wish for this marriage; it was forced upon me by my grandfather."

Katherine started to speak, feeling her anger starting to rise. "And do you think, that I, sir, wished to be wed to a man I did not know?"

"Let me finish, my dear," Bradly said softly, holding up one hand. "Yes, I must admit, I believed you wanted this marriage, but while I was in Richmond I ran into Mr. Vincent; his boat did not leave when expected and stayed in port an extra three days. Mr. Vincent told me of your circumstances in England and he also told me of your reluctance to come to America and to wed."

"He told you? But why would you not believe me?" she asked, her face turning pale.

"I do not really know why I did not believe you, Katherine, and I do apologize for it. I have a bad temper and when I get something formed in my head I just turn angry instead of thinking clearly. I really do hope you will forgive me for treating you in such a harsh manner," he beseeched, his eyes almost pleading.

Katherine sat back in her chair. Did she have any right to be angry? She herself had been forced into doing things against her will and she knew she would have probably acted in the same manner as he, if she were a man. She gave Bradly a small smile. "I do forgive you, sir, and I understand perfectly how you must have felt. I only wish I were a man and could give vent to my own anger and feelings."

Bradly laughed in a relieved voice; he could not fathom why this woman's forgiveness had meant so much to him. It was as if he had been holding his breath awaiting her answer. "Thank you, Katherine; it means a lot to me that you forgive me for my cruelty and that you can understand my reasons for acting as I did. But for now I had better bid you a good night and let you get your rest."

"Must you leave so soon? I am not really tired and the only other person I ever get to talk with is Jezzie. Rachel is always out riding or in her room with a headache." Katherine implored him to stay.

"Do you know what her plans are?" Bradly questioned.

"I am afraid I really do not know what her plans are; she does not confide in me. I know this must be a terrible burden to you, all of a sudden being thrown into a marriage and then having a house guest also."

"No, Katherine, Rachel's no trouble at all. As you know, this house is so large there could be five extra guests here and no one would be aware of it, unless they made their presence known."

"I am glad you feel this way. I would not wish to be the cause of any extra trouble to you," Katherine replied sweetly.

Bradly stood and pushed his chair back. "I am really glad to have you here, Katherine, if you can believe me after the fool I made of myself the other night."

Katherine smiled and rose from her chair. "I thank you, sir, for your kind concern about my rest and for your bringing my meal up for me; the food was delicious."

"You are welcome, my dear, but it was my pleasure to be of service," he said, with a large grin and a bow that made Katherine's own features break into a smile.

Bradly stood looking at this vision of beauty standing before him. "Katherine, your beauty overwhelms these poor eyes of mine," he murmured in a low, husky voice.

Katherine blushed deeply and started to feel faint because of the closeness of this strong virile man. Before she knew what had taken place she found herself in the circle of Bradly's arms.

"My love," he whispered, as he held her tightly and softly stroked the length of her back.

Katherine's senses reeled at the touch of his body and the sensuous feeling of his strong hands. Before she knew what was happening Bradly had bent down and scooped her up into his arms. When he started toward the large brass bed, Katherine regained some of her senses. "Bradly, please put me down," she begged, in a frightened voice.

"Hush, my love. I shall love you and make

you forget all about that scum of a pirate, Marco."

Katherine stiffened in his arms with these words. "Put me down this minute! You shall not touch me; you are worse than any man I have ever had the misfortune to meet!" she shouted and pushed at him with all the strength she could muster.

"Oh?" Bradly raised one dark, fine eyebrow. "But you are wrong, my love; you are my wife if you still remember, and I shall have my husbandly rights of the marriage bed and I shall have them tonight."

When she saw his intent, Katherine started lashing out at him with all of her strength and she called him every foul name she had ever heard.

But ignoring her futile attempts at freedom, Bradly strode to the bed and threw her in the middle.

Katherine saw her chance for escape and tried to scamper to the other side, but her attempts were useless, for Bradly had anticipated her move and threw himself on top of her. "I am master here, sweet, and you shall find I have my own way and get what I want in my own house."

"No, do not do this thing to me, please," she cried, with tears streaming down her soft downy cheeks.

Bradly looked down into her eyes, which were tightly shut and desire streamed through his loins anew; he had never in his life wanted any other woman as much as he wanted this one. "Katherine, do not fight me in this. I shall have my way and it would prove much easier if you would calm yourself and try to enjoy it."

Katherine could feel nothing but rage and hurt to her body and pride from being forced into consummating her marriage in this brutal manner. "Never! Do you hear, I shall never willingly submit to you, you are the most vulgar and detestable man I have—"

Before she could finish her sentence Bradly's lips found hers.

At the touch of his lips against her own Katherine tried vainly to break his hold upon her. She knew all too well the power those lips had upon her and she was determined not to be an easy prey for him. But alas, all too soon the sensation of his lips and his probing tongue made Katherine's mind swim and her body start to respond of its own will.

Bradly could sense her resistance wearing down and he kissed her lips even deeper.

Katherine's body was afire with sensations she had never known before. She strained toward him as his hands caressed her body and his lips made a trail of soft kisses down her soft neck to her taut breast. Katherine never knew when or how Bradly had relieved her of her chemise or robe; all she knew was the feeling of this bronze, godlike man atop her.

Bradly's eyes held a soft glow as he looked down at the lovely body beneath him. "You have the most beautiful body I have ever laid eyes on," he whispered softly, as he nibbled lovingly at her ear lobe. "You were made for love, my sweet, and I shall show you all the delights of your body, I promise you."

At his words, Katherine felt a shiver of passion run through her and her body waited in anticipation for what was next to come.

Bradly shed his clothes as he kissed and caressed her body. "My love, I want you with every fiber of my being," he said softly, as he raised his body over hers and spread her thighs tenderly.

When she felt the pressure of his manhood trying to make entry between her thighs Katherine's eyes widened at the realization of what was about to happen and she tried one last time to pull herself free, but to no avail.

Bradly looked down into her frightened eyes the moment he plunged his hardness into the object he had so lustfully craved.

With his first plunge into her unwilling body Katherine gave a sharp cry of pain and Bradly realized that his wife was indeed a virgin; but at the same time he told himself it was far too late for him to stop now.

Katherine felt as if she were being torn apart at his first thrust and tears streamed down her face.

Bradly looked into her tear-stained face as he slowly moved back and forth. "I am sorry, love; it will be better, try to relax," he whispered softly.

After the first pain of losing her virginity,

Katherine felt her own body starting to respond to his. She started to strain toward him and move with the same rhythmic pressure as Bradly's body. She searched her mind for the answer to her thoughts; how could her own body betray her, respond, and want this beast of a man's touch and kisses? After this brief mind-searching she lost all reason and her thoughts flew from her mind. All she was sure about was the pleasure she was receiving from him. She felt a fire in the depths of her body, and she knew only that this fire had a need to be quenched.

But all too quickly Bradly gave a large sigh of pleasure and relaxed upon her soft yielding body.

It was some time before Bradly spoke. "Katherine, my love, I have never known a woman more beautiful or more passionate than you. I am sorry for the things I accused you of, but I promise you I shall make it up to you in a thousand different ways."

"I do not want you to make anything up to me," she said, sobbing and pushing against his heavy chest. "You take my body by force and treat me as a common slut and then you expect me to forgive you? Never; I would have given willingly that which you have taken by force, if you had only been kind and gentle. But no, you have forced me and accused me of all kinds of vile things that were false. Well, sir, now that you have taken that which you desired, I wish only for you to leave my room."

"Nay, my love. I shall not leave our room and you had better start getting used to the idea of my presence in this bed from now on," he replied softly, looking deep into her violet eyes which were shooting sparks of fire from their depths. "I must confess I did not find the idea of marriage too pleasing to begin with, but now I have tasted the joys of your beauty, I find the idea more than enticing. And for you, lying there and acting as if you were sourly set upon, must I remind you of your responses to my kisses and caresses? I know you are a woman of passion even if you do not, and I also know it will only be a short time before you become a real woman and know the full joy that my body has to offer you."

Katherine could not bear to hear his words and turned her head so as not to see him, and to shut out his condemning voice. She felt the guilt of her body's betrayal and shut her eyes tightly, wishing to forget.

"Do not turn your head from that which I speak, love," he said tenderly, turning her head around and caressing her fragile jaw line. "Let your body glory in its union with mine, Katherine, for I shall not leave you and I shall always be here to share this large bed with you."

Katherine lay sobbing and not daring to look into those piercing, silver eyes above her.

Bradly's large, strong hands, which were as gentle as a butterfly's touch, softly stroked her nipples, which rose tautly in anticipation. "This time, love, I shall take my time and you shall know the pleasure my body can give."

Katherine started to protest, but her words were smothered by Bradly's lips taking her mouth. She could feel her resistance already waning and her body melting from the fires beginning to grow within her.

"I shall love you as I have never loved another before," he said, releasing his lips from hers. "You are like a goddess who only needs the first fires of love to make you complete."

Katherine could only sigh and shiver from the sensations of fire coursing through her veins, and when he finally did mount her she gloried in the feeling of this bronzelike god atop her. She found herself responding fully to his every thrust and, circling her arms tightly around his neck, she was soon swept into the whirlpool of brilliant embers bursting within her body. She strained her body toward him and was totally consumed by the feeling of belonging to this man completely. From her lips burst his name: "Bradly." She rose up to meet his thrust, a look of wonder on her face.

Bradly looked into her eyes and kissed her soft lips, knowing he had brought her to fulfillment. He at last spent himself and lay holding her tightly, while rubbing his hand through her soft dark hair.

"I had no idea it would be like this," she said breathlessly.

"I know, love," he said looking into her soft, liquid eyes, "but now I have had the sweetness of your body I am afraid you shall

181

have to fend me off night and day."

"Nay, my lord. It is you who shall have to do the fending, for I fear I could grow quite fond of your play upon this magnificent bed," she answered wickedly, and gently ran her fingers through the short, dark hair upon his chest.

"Oh? Does the wench play a different tune now that she has had the pleasure of my body? I am glad to hear of it, for I shall never grow tired of the delicious fruits of your wonderful body, and I must say it would prove awfully tiring to have to resort to rape each night," he said laughing.

They lay there quietly for a time, each content with the feeling of the other close by.

It seemed to Katherine an eternity had passed before Bradly spoke. "Did you have anyone whom you were fond of in England, Katherine?"

"No," she answered truthfully. "My father claimed I was much too picky in my choice of men."

"I'm glad to hear that, my love, for you shall find I am a very possessive man and keep that which is mine."

Katherine looked at him with widened eyes. "And am I one of your possessions, sir?"

"You are indeed, madam; you are my most treasured possession and I shall never let you forget it, for I shall never let you slip away from me," he said in a more serious tone.

Katherine snuggled closer to him, happy to

feel the security of his arms. "And what, sir, of you; are you mine also?"

"I do not do things in half-measure, Katherine. I am your husband and I must confess you have captured my heart and my soul. I am yours now and through eternity and no other shall know that which I promise only to you."

Katherine kissed him softly on the cheek. "I did not know a beast such as you could be so tamed by a mere girl such as I, my lord."

"Nor did I, my sweet, but your witchcraft has turned me into a blundering fool. I could not even go about my business in Richmond without your vision coming into my mind. Your face has been haunting my brain day and night, since the moment I first laid eyes upon you."

"I am sorry if I have been tormenting you, sir," Katherine said playfully, nipping at his neck. "But I do think I shall keep bothering you, my lord."

"I hope so, my love, for I shall treasure you always," he said, taking her lips with his own.

The night continued to be filled with love-making and whispered words. Katherine was thrilled by Bradly's knowing hands titillating the secret places of her body. And Bradly could hardly contain himself when Katherine reached out to explore her first male body. Neither found sleep until the early hours of the morning, when the dawn light was streaming through the windows.

Chapter Six

Bradly awoke when the noon sun was shining throughout the room. He had a feeling of contentment as he turned slowly to observe his young, beautiful wife.

Katherine lay deep in slumber, with one slender hand lying upon Bradly's massive chest.

Bradly had never felt such desire for any

other woman as he did for this one. He felt as if he could not get enough of her tender, sweet body. He had never thought of himself as the type of man to love or protect any woman, but from the time of their meeting he had wanted to take her in his arms and never let any harm befall her. All of a sudden the realization came to him as if it were a strong blow: this was the woman he wanted to spend the rest of his life with, to raise his children with, and to love and protect always.

Katherine felt a movement next to her and awoke abruptly, eyes widened, trying to take in her surroundings.

"Good morning, sweet," Bradly said, placing a loving kiss upon her brow. "I'm sorry if I woke you, but I'm not used to sleeping, even this late."

At first Katherine felt shy and uncomfortable lying in the same bed, naked, with this man who was now her husband. But Bradly's tender, soothing voice and loving expression soon relaxed her, so that she lay back against the silk pillows. "I am afraid we overslept, Bradly, and I am a bit hungry."

"I quite agree, love. I find myself starving also, but not for food," he murmured nibbling playfully at her neck.

"Bradly! It is broad daylight." Katherine squirmed deeper under the covers.

"You shall have to get over your shyness and quickly, love, for you will find I am not the type of man who wishes to hide his passion or his wife's beautiful body in the dark of the night," he whispered softly, pulling the covers from her and exposing her body for his eyes to behold.

Before Katherine could make any kind of a protest she found herself once again swept into the feelings of the night before. Never again would she be the same, she told herself, and never in her life would she ever find any man who could move her body and soul as this man did. For the first time in months she felt a warm, peaceful feeling overcome her as she gave herself fully to her husband.

Afterward, lying in each other's arms and feeling deliciously wonderful in the aftermath of their love-making, Katherine wound her arms around Bradly's neck. "You, sir, are a rogue; first you wish to beat me and now you try to starve me to death."

Bradly gave a roaring laugh. "You have me all wrong, my darling. I would never attempt to beat your lovely body. I am a selfish man and I would not wish to harm my play-ground—and as far as starving you to death, I will personally see that when you are not lying in my arms you shall have food in front of you, for you shall need your food to keep your strength up." He gave her a warm smile and pulled her tightly against him.

"Are you never sated, my lord?" Katherine asked chidingly.

"Not where you are concerned, Mrs. Deveraux; I honestly do not seem to be able to get enough of you."

At that moment a knock sounded outside their door.

"Come in," Bradly shouted, irritated at being disturbed.

Lucy entered the room carrying a tray of food; as she saw the sight upon the bed she immediately lowered her eyes. "I'm sorry, but Jezzie said that perhaps you all would like something to eat," the girl said nervously.

"Thank you, Lucy, and tell Jezzie thank you also. I am quite famished."

"Will you be needing anything else, ma'am?"

"Yes, Lucy; as soon as we're done eating I would like very much to have a bath."

"Yes, ma'am," the girl replied, glad to be gone from the room.

After breakfast, when Katherine had finished her bath, Bradly asked her, while she was toweling herself off, if she would care to ride about the plantation with him.

"I would love that, Bradly." Katherine's face lit up with joy.

She was now so impatient to go riding with her new husband that she ran to her closet and found a dark-blue riding habit.

Bradly lowered himself into the tub of hot water and relaxed against its rim, watching his young wife and thanking the good fortune that had brought her to him.

When Katherine had finished dressing, she

turned and faced Bradly, still sitting in the brass tub. "Oh, Bradly, please hurry. I just cannot wait to get out and ride Golden Girl."

"Just sit down and be patient for a moment, love," he said, rising from the tub. "You act like a little mouse with your scampering and rushing about."

Katherine lowered her head and replied softly, "I am sorry, Bradly. I did not mean to rush you."

Bradly reached over and took her face between his hands. "You have nothing to be sorry for, my little bird. I also am anxious to be off and about."

When the couple left the house and started on their ride, Bradly was surprised at the way Katherine could ride a horse. He did not, in fact, know of many men with the horsemanship which she showed. Even more surprised was he, though, with the sight of her riding astride and not using the usual sidesaddle which was considered more proper for a woman. When he mentioned this to his lovely, unpredictable wife, he could only smile at her answer.

"Oh, Bradly, please do not be so stuffy. I have never been able to abide riding sidesaddle. It is so uncomfortable and I do enjoy riding astride."

In fact she had all of her riding habits cut at the bottom, so they almost looked like men's britches, except they were so full one could not see the split down the middle unless she were riding.

A moment later she lifted her nose high in the air and added, "I also want to tell you that if some of the men, who constantly try to restrain and keep women in their places, would try to ride sidesaddle themselves they would understand my feelings."

Bradly found himself laughing out loud at her attempt to defend her womanhood. "Madam, I am afraid it would not only be the men who would look upon you with shocked eyes, but most of the women I know would be outraged also."

Katherine's laughter mingled with that of her husband. "I guess that is why my stepmother forbade me to ride when I became a young lady; I imagine she was shocked also at my behavior."

The afternoon was a glorious one for the young lovers. They rode over a portion of the plantation, side by side. Now and then as their legs rubbed against each other, their eyes told of the depths of their feelings.

After a time Bradly led his horse into a small copse of trees, which were grouped so thickly that they almost concealed the sun altogether.

Katherine followed close behind, afraid she would lose sight of him if she dared to take her eyes from his form.

It was not long before Bradly brought his horse to a stop in front of a small stream of water which gently rushed down an embankment and formed a small pond.

There he dismounted and put a blanket, which had been tied on the back of his saddle, under his arm. As he reached up and helped Katherine off her mount, she threw her arms around his neck and cried, "Bradly, this is beautiful; it is as if this whole place came out of a picture book."

"I was hoping you would like it," he replied, his eyes holding hers warmly. He then proceeded to lead her to the edge of the pond and began to spread the blanket on a small grassy section, along its edge. "I used to come here as a boy to dream and fish my days away."

"You must have been a wonderful boy," Katherine said, sitting down on the blanket.

"Not so wonderful, I'm afraid. I was indeed quite a handful for my father and Jezzie."

Katherine lay back upon the blanket and, through the leaves and branches of the trees, watched a small bird who was screeching and whistling at them for having disturbed his quiet and isolated spot.

"I shall admit to you, love," Bradly said softly, as he watched Katherine lie back and gaze into the trees, "never in my dreams as a small boy did I imagine having such a lovely creature here in my arms." He started to unbutton the buttons of her riding habit.

Katherine started to reply, but her words were lost as her mouth was taken by a possessive, yet tender, kiss.

With his lips upon hers, Katherine could feel her senses beginning to reel and her passion starting to build.

Their love-making was made with wild, consuming abandon, there under the trees. Katherine had never thought she could be brought to such peaks of ecstasy and Bradly lost himself and all reason in the softness of her body and the feel of her lying beneath him.

Their passion was brought to an end with a climax that was so devastating that Katherine could only shudder and whisper his name over and over.

Afterward, as they lay contented in each others arms, Bradly began to tell her about Moon Rise and the plans he had made for his plantation.

Katherine listened eagerly, clinging to his every word.

As he began to tell her of his yearly hunting trips and of the cabin he had built in a small valley in the mountains which bordered his property, Katherine was full of questions and curiosity; for she had never been on any kind of hunting trip and she could only envision the fox-hunting trips her father had made twice a year, back in England.

Bradly told her of the game that stayed in this valley and how usually every year he made this hunting trip to bring back venison for the plantation. A few of the Negro men on the plantation hunted during the winter, but Bradly always let them keep their game for their families, so when he went he brought back meat for his own home.

Katherine's mind was coming to a decision and she sat up and started to speak cajolingly. "Bradly may I go along on this trip with you?"

When he cast an apprehensive look toward her, she coaxed. "I promise I would not be in the way and I would try not to be a burden to you. I have never been on such a trip and it all sounds so exciting. Please, Bradly, may I go?"

Bradly looked at her in a serious manner. "I will have to think on the matter. Not many women care to follow their husbands on a hunting trip; but then I can already tell, you are not like most women," he said pulling her back into his strong arms. "I can see one thing for sure, madam; and that is, I shall never stop being surprised at you."

Katherine kissed his lips softly, already knowing she had won and that he would let her go along with him. "Would you rather I were like other women, my lord?" she asked coyly, rubbing her fingers through the thick, black hair that adorned his chest.

The next week flew by quickly for Katherine. She busied herself about the house in the mornings while Bradly attended to his plantation. The afternoons and evenings were spent in Bradly's arms or at his side. Bradly proved to be the most loving and attentive of husbands and Katherine at last thought that she had found the love and security which she had been seeking.

Rachel also seemed to be adjusting more easily now. She took her meals in the dining room with the rest of the household and she did not complain of her headaches any longer.

Bradly had announced to Katherine that at the end of the week they would leave for his hunting cabin, taking with them two pack horses and food to last for two weeks.

He insisted that they leave before daylight, so they would arrive at the cabin a little after dark that same evening.

On the morning of their departure Katherine was shaken out of her peaceful dreams by Bradly's hands upon her body. "Wake up, love; it is time we were off."

"What?" She sat up with a start and looked around at the dark room. "I am so tired, Bradly," she said, lying back down and shutting her eyes once again.

"Oh no, my little wildcat. You wished to go along; now get yourself up and dressed." Bradly pulled her back up into a sitting position.

As Katherine crawled to the side of the bed, Bradly lit a small wick candle on the night table.

With the light from the candle Katherine could see that Bradly had already dressed and was only waiting for her to do likewise. "You look like some backwoodsman!" she exclaimed, taking in his attire: brown leather pants with fringe at the bottom and a heavy pullover shirt of the same cut. He wore a hat made of some fur she did not recognize and had a powder horn strapped over his arm and across his chest.

"You shall understand more of my manner of dress, madam, if and when we can ever leave this house and be on our way."

Katherine scampered into the riding habit she had set out the night before.

Her toilette finally completed, her hair pinned atop her head, and a saucy-looking green hat set upon it and pulled to a jaunty angle, she ventured to speak. "I am afraid, sir, we do not match in our choice of clothing."

Bradly smiled down at her and took her lips greedily. "Perhaps, if you behave yourself, I shall let you wear one of my outfits, love."

"Never!" Katherine recoiled in shock. "Do you honestly think I would be caught alive in something such as that?"

Bradly was laughing as he pulled her out the door. "I was led to believe that you did not care what people thought."

They traveled at a steady pace until noon and then dismounted and shared a lunch Jezzie had packed for them.

"Is it very much farther, Bradly?"

"Why, love, are you tired?"

"A small bit, but I shall be fine."

"It is quite a bit farther; it is over to those

tall mountains that we're headed." He pointed to a group of mountains which Katherine thought could only be a short hour or so ride from where they were.

They rested but a short time and then continued on their way.

It seemed to Katherine as though she had been riding for days, instead of only hours, and as the sun started to lower behind the broad mountain ridge in front of them, she slumped wearily on Golden Girl's back.

Bradly called the horses to a stop, reached over, and gathered her from her mount into his arms.

"I am sorry, Bradly," was all she could say, as she fell back against his chest and resumed her sleep.

Bradly smiled down fondly at his new wife and held her tightly against him.

Katherine slept the rest of the ride and awoke to find the sky dark and Bradly gently rousing her from her slumber.

"We are here, love." He softly kissed the nape of her neck and set her on the ground. "Stand here by the horses, while I go in and start a fire."

Katherine strained her eyes, trying to see about her, but the only things she could make out in the blackness of the night were the shapes of a small cabin and some trees that looked forbidding and menacing in the dark.

Bradly returned shortly, whistling a happy tune. "Ready, sweet? I've got a warm fire going and a pot of coffee on."

Katherine grimaced at the coffee, but the warm fire sounded to her liking. As she started to walk toward the cabin, Bradly swooped her up into his arms. "What is this for?" she murmured, snuggling close against him.

"You might fall and hurt yourself, love; the light is not too good out here."

"Thank you, most gallant sir, but that is really not your only reason, is it?"

"I must confess, no, your beauty blinds these poor eyes of mine and I find I cannot touch and feel enough of your soft body; so I guess forever more I shall be using different excuses to have you in my arms."

"Oh Bradly, you are impossible." Katherine could feel her face deepening in color.

Katherine looked about her as Bradly set her down on the board floor of the cabin. She had never before been in anything as primitive, so when she gazed about her she was surprised to see the cozy and comfortable single room. One wall contained a small fireplace, whose fire was readily warming the room. In the center of the room were a small table and two chairs while two comfortable chairs were placed near the hearth. Katherine's eyes went to the other side of the room and there, to her surprise, was a large bed against the wall.

Bradly saw where her eyes were resting and he rose from tending the coffeepot and took her in his arms. "I sent two of my men here at the beginning of the week with the bed and with orders to tidy up a bit. I hope you're not disappointed with your first hunting trip already?"

"It is wonderful; I hardly expected what I see before me now." She went to the bed and felt the soft fur covers which were neatly folded down. "I must confess, I thought your cabin would be a shambles and very manly." She smiled warmly, sitting down upon the rich furs.

"Quite so. It was just that; that is why I had the boys come here and straighten it out. Clay and I are the only ones who have ever come up here, and I'm afraid we did more hunting than cleaning."

"Oh, does Clay come with you hunting? Perhaps I should have stayed at home." Katherine's brow creased with worry.

Bradly sat beside her and kissed her forehead. "Clay has not come up here since he and Jean got married."

"He does not come hunting anymore?" Katherine asked.

"No, I guess he figures he should stay home with his wife, now that he has one. Not all women are as adventurous as you, my love, and if you had not insisted on coming with me, I myself would have stayed at Moon Rise. I used to tease Clay about not doing the things he used to, but now that I have you, I can understand his reasons."

Katherine snuggled deeper into his embrace

and kissed his lips softly, but with an eagerness for him that she could not hide.

"Would you like something to eat, swee or would you rather get some rest?" Bradly asked with a grin, his own passion building as he held her against him.

"I am afraid I shall have to pass on eating; I find myself so tired I doubt if I shall be abi to undress myself," she replied seductively.

"You just lie back then, love." Bradly gently pushed her back against the furs. "I shall deem it an honor to be your maid this night." His large sun-browned hands started to unbutton and unlace her riding habit.

Katherine did as she was bid, loving every minute of this personal care.

The coffee upon the hearth boiled over and the fire dimmed to only light embers as the night grew on, but the couple upon the bed took no notice of any of this, as their surging passions consumed them.

Katherine awoke the next morning to the smell of bacon cooking, filling the cabin with a delicious aroma. She feigned sleep, her eyes lightly shut, as she peered beneath her dark lashes, and watched her husband cooking breakfast and humming a gay tune. He was so handsome, standing with his back to her, busying himself with his cooking. Katherine felt her breath catch at just the thought of their love-making of the night before; and as she lay abed watching him she felt her eyes mist over. The happiness she had found was almost more than she could bear. Never had she met a man like her husband and she doubted if she would ever meet a man to equal him. Perhaps this is what love meant, she thought to herself. She had never been in love with any man, but she knew what she felt for this man was more than just a passing fancy or mere affection.

Her thoughts were quickly quenched as Bradly moved toward the bed. "Katherine." He spoke softly, leaning down and cupping her face between his hands, and placing a kiss upon her lips.

Katherine played as if she were asleep, but the temptation of his standing over her like this was too much for her to bear. Without warning she clasped her arms about his neck and pulled him on top of her, giggling all the while.

Bradly at first was pulled off guard, but soon he was swept up into the mood of Katherine's playing. "I thought you to be asleep, but I can see you were only lying in wait for a man to come to your bed, you lusty wench." He laughed, rolling upon the bed with her in his arms.

Katherine's laughter filled the tiny cabin as she kissed him on the cheek. "Good morning, Bradly."

"And a good morning to you, my pet," he murmured stroking one of her exposed breasts. "But now you had better be getting up or your breakfast will soon be cold. I can see already there shall not be much hunting done on this trip, if you insist on staying in bed all morning."

Katherine jumped from the bed and out of his arms. "I am sorry; I did not wish to make you late for your hunting," she said, afraid she might have angered him.

Bradly laughed lightly. "I was only teasing; we have all the time in the world to go hunting. I almost have a mind to forget about hunting and stay inside this cabin with you in my arms."

"Oh, no. I came along to hunt, so you get yourself up from that bed and let us eat."

"As you wish, my sweet, but all you have to do is say the word and we shall stay here." He grinned, rising from the bed.

The first day out, Katherine and Bradly walked the trails through the forest, hand in hand, more like lovers than hunters. Katherine was dressed in a forest-green riding habit that trailed to her ankles and snagged upon almost every bush and bramble along their path. By noontime she was a ragged sight to behold. Bradly laughed at her tangled hair; her hat had been pulled from its pin and her hair was tumbling out of its confinement. She sat upon a dead tree stump and watched Bradly laughing at her, as she tried to impose some order on her clothing and hair. Her anger was mounting by the minute. "Will you please quit acting so smug?" she rebuked, irritably.

"I'm sorry, love, but you are a sight. Perhaps now you can see the reason for my manner of dress?"

As he stood there leaning against a tree, cool and composed, Katherine could see quite clearly the comfort and practical use of his clothing. "You could have at least told me what we would be running into!" she exclaimed, looking down at her ruined outfit.

"I believe in learning by one's own mistakes and as you told me quite severely, you would not be caught alive in something I wear." Bradly laughed at her discomfort, finding her even more desirable in her disheveled state.

Katherine started to rebuke him, but he grabbed hold of her hand and pulled her to her feet, taking her lips with his own.

"Come along now, pet." He released her lips, but held to her hand. "I have something I wish to show you."

Katherine followed meekly behind, not knowing what new torment he had in mind for her.

It was some time before Bradly came to a halt in front of her. Pulling her to his side, he said softly, "Behold, your paradise."

Katherine's breath caught in her throat as she looked at the sight before her eyes. Never before had she seen anything as beautiful. It was as though God had lingered at this one special spot, to draw upon the land his one, most special masterpiece.

Katherine's eyes lingered over every detail. Lush green grass grew around a small, crystal-clear pond that lay below a high cliff down which a waterfall was gliding until it showered its sparkling liquid into the pond, she stood transfixed. The sun was shining full upon the falls and the water looked as though diamonds were raining down upon the earth. "This is the most perfect place I have ever seen," she breathed. "I could stay here the rest of my life and be content with the beauty I see before me."

"I also would enjoy nothing more than to stay here with you by my side for the rest of my life, but I'm afraid things are not that simple and we both have other responsibilities. But for the rest of the day we can forget about everything else and spend our hours in leisure here beside the falls."

They spent the rest of the afternoon eating the lunch Bradly had packed for them and swimming naked in the icy water of the falls. To dry their bodies they had made love there in the high, green grass until they were both sated and warmed.

After returning to the cabin and eating a filling supper which Katherine had helped Bradly to prepare, they walked down to a small stream nearby to watch the sun set.

Now, as Katherine sat between Bradly's strong, muscular legs, and he leaned back against an old water oak, she thought back over the afternoon they had just spent. She felt a warm contentment wash over her that she had never felt before. "If I were to die at this moment, Bradly, I would be forever content," she said, laying her head against his chest.

"I'm pleased that you feel that way, love, but I hope you will not leave me for at least another hundred years."

"I shall try to obey your wishes, sir." She snuggled closer against him.

"Katherine, there is something I have wished to ask you," Bradly said in a more serious manner.

"What is it, Bradly?" she asked, turning to look into his gray eyes.

"It is nothing to concern yourself about, love." He stroked her cheek lightly. "I only wished to know if you have ever been in love?"

Katherine looked at him with questioning eyes.

"I know you said that you were not fond of any other gentleman back in England before you left, but I find it hard to believe that a woman of your beauty has not fallen in love at least once in your life."

"I assure you, sir, that besides my mother and father, I have never loved another person," she answered truthfully.

"You do not know how glad I am to hear this, love, for here in my hands"—he held up his strong, sturdy hands, for her to inspect—

"I hold a magical power, which will spin a golden web of love upon your heart and soul and you will forever more be at my mercy." He spoke these words so tenderly that Katherine could feel the emotion coming from his tone.

Katherine raised up and placed a loving kiss upon his lips. "Your web has already been spun, my lord, and my heart and soul will forever, willingly, be at your mercy." As she spoke these words she knew she was being truthful and she knew also that she loved this man with every part of her being.

Bradly rose then and carried her into the cabin, and without another word passing between them they joined as one, their love radiating from one to the other.

They had been at the cabin a little over a week now. Since that night at the stream when Katherine had declared her love to her husband, they both seemed to respond more fully and be more comfortable with each other.

Bradly remained as attentive and gentle as before, but Katherine found a new warmth in his eyes now whenever they met hers.

The hunting trip had become more of a honeymoon for the lovers this first week, than a trip intended for seeking game.

Delighting in the feel of her nearness, as he showed her how to aim and pull the trigger, Bradly, had taught Katherine how to prime and shoot a rifle. Katherine found it hard to concentrate when their bodies were pressed so close together but was eager to please her husband in any and all things.

They walked the forest, holding hands and stopping whenever struck by the mood to make love, out in the open and under the trees.

They visited the waterfall almost every day, swimming and lying in each other's arms the afternoons through.

After a week of this idle life, Bradly declared they would have to go hunting the next day because they would have to be leaving to go back to Moon Rise soon and he did not wish to return empty-handed.

So on a cool, crisp morning, Bradly and Katherine set out in the direction of the small stream by the cabin and followed it in the hope of spying a deer while it was feeding.

Katherine had consented to wear a pair of Bradly's pants and a leather shirt, which she had to cut and trim to fit her slim figure. She rather liked the comfortable fit and the ease with which she could move about without having a full skirt to hinder her. When she had told Bradly of her discovery, he had laughed, saying now he would be finding all of his pants and shirts cut up and on her.

Both had laughed at this joke and then set out to hunt.

They had only gone a short way down the stream when Bradly motioned for Katherine to stop.

She squinted her eyes in the direction he was looking, trying to see what had attracted his sudden attention.

He motioned for her to squat down behind a fallen tree, then he slipped through the trees, like a large panther, stalking his prey.

Katherine felt pride swell in her chest, as she sat and watched his handsome figure disappear.

She sat waiting anxiously, her rifle at the ready. She did not know if she would ever be able to shoot any animal if she were to see one, but Bradly had insisted that she at least try if she had the opportunity.

She was about to give up waiting and start off in search of Bradly when she heard a rustle of branches and then before her eyes a large deer with a head full of antlers came through a thicket.

Now that the opportunity of shooting something had come to her she had no idea what to do. All she could think of was that Bradly would be so proud of her if she were to kill this magnificent beast that was standing in front of her.

She aimed the gun, shut her eyes, and squeezed the trigger. At least she would be able to tell Bradly that she had tried, she thought when she opened her eyes and looked in the direction where the deer had been standing—relieved to see he was no longer there.

Bradly had heard the shot and quickly made his way back to where he had left Katherine. As he made his way back to the stump where he had left her, he stopped short. There, standing off a small distance, was his wife, crying as though she had been hurt. The first thing that went through his mind was that she had shot herself. As quickly as this thought washed over him, he was at Katherine's side and holding her in his arms.

"I killed him, I killed him." She wept hysterically, clinging to Bradly and looking down at the large creature by her feet.

Relief swept over Bradly as he saw that she was not hurt and he also saw the object of her distress. "Love, love," he comforted, gently stroking her head. "We came here to kill a deer. Do not be so upset; the deer are upon the earth to furnish food."

Katherine could not be so easily comforted and her tears coursed down her cheeks uncontrolled. "I but meant to frighten him and to make you proud of me for trying. I never intended to harm him."

"Why, sweet, you have made me the proudest man ever; there are not even many men who can boast of killing such a fine specimen of an animal. Now quiet your tears, love, and let us see to carrying it back to the cabin," Bradly coaxed, trying to bring her back to reason.

It was some time before Bradly could calm Katherine down enough so that she could sit in a soft grassy spot, while he gutted the beast.

It was a good thing that they had not gone too far from the cabin that morning for the large deer taxed even Bradly's powerful strength, and he doubted if he would have been able to carry the whole animal for too far a distance.

The sun was high in the sky when they reached the cabin. Katherine hurried inside and lay down upon the bed.

Why did she feel as she did? she questioned herself. She should feel some measure of pride in herself for killing such a fine beast, and not be lying abed and feeling as though all strength had ebbed from her body. Finally after this brief soul-searching she fell into a troubled slumber.

Bradly left her to her rest until dinner, then roused her from the bed. "You should be proud, love; your deer was an eight-pointer and now for the rest of the week we can just lie around and enjoy ourselves."

Katherine gave him a large smile, feeling somewhat better after her sleep. "Thank you, dearest, but I am sure anyone could have done the same."

Bradly's laughter roared throughout the cabin. "You are an incredible woman, Katherine Deveraux."

The rest of the week was spent leisurely: swimming in the afternoons, talking and laughing, and making love whenever and as often as they wished; then finally when it was time for them to start back to Moon Rise, Katherine felt a terrible sadness.

"I do love this place, Bradly. Promise we shall return here every year."

"Of course, sweet. I shall bring you back each time I come. What other woman do you know who can warm a man's bed when it is cold and also bring a buck home to boot?"

Katherine laughed gaily now, not feeling any qualms about killing her first deer. "It truly was a fine animal, was it not, Bradly?"

"It surely was and I have brought the antlers along to boast of my fine wife to everyone."

The ride back to Moon Rise was as long and tiring as the ride of two weeks ago. But Katherine, this time, had vowed to herself not to be a burden and fall asleep as she had done before.

As the day wore on she relived the past two weeks spent at the hunting cabin. Never before in her life had she had a happier time and she knew that she would always think of these last weeks with the fondest of memories. As she stole a glance at her tall, handsome husband she knew she had at last found the love she had been seeking and she would do everything in her power to keep it.

It was a clear evening and the moon was shining brightly down upon the two-story house at Moon Rise as the two on horseback approached their destination. They were instantly greeted by the sounds of barking dogs. A moment later a large figure, waved fiercely from the veranda—Jezzie.

"You all finally getting yourselves back home," the old Negress shouted, loud enough to wake the whole plantation.

Katherine had not realized how much she had missed this large black woman or the warm friendly old house, until this minute. As soon as she reached the veranda she flung herself down from her saddle and into Jezzie's round, waiting arms. "Oh, Jezzie, it is so good to be home; is everyone well? We had such a marvelous time," she rambled on as Jezzie led her into the house and into the front parlor.

Bradly sat upon his horse watching his wife and his Negro housekeeper until they disappeared inside the house. He smiled to himself and then murmured softly, under his breath. "Yes, it is for sure I have the finest woman God ever created here in my possession. No other would have ever been a fit mistress for Moon Rise or for myself."

As soon as Jezzie had gotten Katherine into the parlor, she began giving her orders. "Now you just sit yourself down in this nice, soft chair and rest yourself for a spell, while I get your dinner on the table. Everyone else has already eaten and gone on to bed, but I had a feeling that you and Master Brad would come a-straggling in tonight. So I been a-keeping your dinner warm and a-sitting by the front window a-watching for you all to get here."

"Jezzie, you are so good," Katherine said warmly as she walked about, stretching her cramped muscles and not heeding Jezzie's orders about sitting. "I am starving and also I need a hot bath and then I would like to sleep for a whole week."

"I don't know about that, honey child, but I do know one thing for sure and that is if'n I don't hussle this fat carcass of mine and get something on the table for Master Brad, he a-going to be like a mad bull when he comes in here from tending to those horses."

"Well, hurry along then, Jezzie." Katherine giggled. "Bradly's been in such a good mood, I would hate for anything to spoil it."

"Yes, ma'am, he sure can show himself when he has a mind to." Jezzie grinned, making her exit.

Katherine threw her arms wide and swung around in gay abandon. It was so good to be back home; she would never have thought she could feel so peaceful and at home in a new house and a strange land, but now she could only pray that nothing would ever change and that she and Bradly would always stay this happy.

Chapter Seven

•

The following morning dawned bright and clear and after a light breakfast in the master bedchamber, Bradly invited Katherine to take a ride with him over to the Johnson plantation.

Katherine was delighted with the idea of meeting Clayton's wife, Jean, and at once accepted.

The Johnsons' plantation house was beautiful, not as large as Moon Rise but lovely with its simple setting and charming structure.

As the couple approached the front of the house, two small Negro boys rushed toward them from around the back; the boys grabbed hold of their reins, in order to take charge of their horses.

Bradly smiled at the youths and called them both by name, which seemed to please the boys, because their faces broke into large grins and they promised faithfully to water and feed their charges.

As Katherine and Bradly stepped onto the front veranda, the door was thrown open wide and Clayton Johnson stood in the entrance with a large grin upon his face. "Well, son-of-a-gun if'n it isn't our long-lost neighbors. So you finally decided to bring your new bride out and show her off, did you, Bradly?"

Bradly gave his friend a large smile. "I'm sorry we haven't been over sooner, Clay, but I wanted Katherine to get settled and then we went up to the cabin hunting for a couple of weeks."

"Well, come on in." Clay motioned them through the door. "What do you mean, Brad? You didn't take this little thing up to that wilderness with you, did you?"

"I certainly did and if you think she is so little and innocent wait until you come over and I show you the rack of horns from the buck she killed," Bradly retorted, pride for his young wife ringing in each word he spoke.

Katherine felt her face start to warm as both men looked upon her: Bradly with a gentle warmth shining from his eyes, and Clay not knowing whether to believe Bradly or not. But to Katherine's relief she was saved from both sets of eyes as a voice was heard coming from the next room.

"Clay, Clay, who's here? I thought I heard voices."

As Katherine looked toward the room from which the soft and pleasant-sounding voice was coming, a strikingly beautiful young woman emerged through the door.

"Why, Brad, we weren't expecting any company and you have brought your wife to visit," the woman said with a soft smile. "Do come into the parlor. Clay would keep you standing here in the foyer all day, if it were left up to him," she added good-naturedly.

"You ladies go along and the two of you get to know each other while Brad and I go into my study to discuss some business, Jean," Clay said, kissing his wife upon the forehead.

Jean led Katherine into a lovely, spacious parlor in which there were a large number of potted plants sitting about, either on tables or in large pots at the corners of the room.

Katherine at once fell in love with this room; it was almost as if one were in a garden within a house.

"Oh, those men," the woman said smiling. "Always excusing themselves by claiming

214

business matters, when in fact they are doing nothing more than having a drink and talking about what their neighbors are doing. Please have a seat, Katherine; I'll have my girl, Millie, bring us something cool to drink."

Katherine took a seat on the sofa and studied this friendly woman, who was busy giving instructions to a young Negro girl. Jean was indeed very beautiful with her auburn hair, a few light freckles scattered across the bridge of her nose and shoulders, and her light-blue eyes. Her complexion was clear and very fair; she was neither tall nor short but what really took Katherine's attention was a fact that she had not noticed earlier. Now that Jean was sitting, one could easily see that she was very far along with child.

"I'm afraid I have not been getting out very much lately, or I would have come over to Moon Rise and greeted you properly. Tell me, how do you like Virginia so far, Katherine?"

"I really must confess I did not expect to fall in love with this strange country so quickly," Katherine stated truthfully. "I have hardly missed England at all."

"I think almost everyone feels the same way. Why I, myself, was born and raised in Georgia and when I met Clay and we married I dreaded the idea of moving from the only home I had ever known; but now I would not leave Virginia for anything in the world."

"How long have you and Clay been married?" Katherine asked, already feeling a close friendship growing between her and this lovely woman.

"It is almost three years now and next month we shall have our first child."

"What are you hoping to have, a boy or girl?"

"Oh, there is no hoping about it. Clay has said from the first it shall be a boy." She laughed. "Why he has already given him a name—Eric Edward, after his great-grandfather."

"That's a lovely name, Jean, and I hope for both of you that it will be a boy."

"It truly does not matter what it turns out to be. Clay will love a girl just as much. It is only that I suppose most men want their first-born to be a son and exactly like them."

Both women laughed at this, while Millie brought lemonade and small cakes on a tray into the room. When the young girl had poured and left the room, Jean resumed her conversation.

"I expect you and Brad will have at least a dozen children running around at Moon Rise one day?"

Katherine was more shocked than she let show by this question. She had not even thought of bearing Bradly's children until this minute. "Why, I-I do not know," she stammered, feeling somewhat embarrassed by the question put to her.

"I know just how you feel, Katherine. I, myself was somewhat shy on the subject of children, but if and when you first become this way," she said, patting her bulging stomach, "you will at once become impatient at having to wait until you see the life you will be bringing forth."

"I am sure you are right, Jean; it is only that I have not even thought on the matter."

"Well, dear, time only will tell if you and Brad will be blessed as Clay and I shall be soon," Jean put in lightly.

Katherine's thoughts wandered to herself as Jean went on about the child she and her husband would soon be having. Would she herself feel the same as Jean if she were round with child? Could it possibly be that she was already in this condition? It was true she had not had her womanly time of the month since she had first lain with Bradly, but she was not overly late and she had been putting this down to her nerves and the excited state she had found herself in since being in Virginia.

Katherine was quickly brought out of her musings by the entrance of Bradly and Clay.

She let her eyes roam over her husband. Would it be so terrible to have this man's child? No, of course not; she loved this man, did she not? Well, what could possibly be her cause of distress? she asked herself. Then, as quickly the thought came to her: Bradly had never mentioned children. What if he did not wish to be saddled with a small babe?

"Katherine, love, we must be on our way." Bradly came to her chair and gave her his hand. "It is getting late and I have some work to do today." He smiled as he helped her from her chair.

"Must you, Brad? Katherine and I have just begun to get to know one another." Jean stood up with a pout.

"I am afraid they are right, honey, and I want you to go and rest for a while. I don't want you to overtire yourself."

"Oh Clay, I'm fine; you would think by the way you treat me that I am the first woman ever to be in this condition," she said, patting her rounded belly. "Please, Brad, can you not stay just awhile longer? I do love company and we hardly ever do receive any, way out here away from everybody."

"You had best do as your husband wishes, Jean. I shall be over often now that I have met you and I promise we shall become great friends," Katherine said warmly, going over and taking one of the other woman's hands.

"Please do hurry and come again, Katherine. I'm afraid my shape is not the most fit for outings, but soon my burden will be gone and I shall be able to visit with you at Moon Rise." Jean smiled, reassured now that she had made a dear friend.

"I shall, do not worry about that." Katherine placed a small kiss upon the other woman's cheek. "Now that I have made a new friend I intend to see you quite frequently."

They rode back to Moon Rise mostly in

silence. When they had first left Jean and Clay, Katherine had asked Bradly why he had not mentioned that Jean was so far along with child.

"I really did not think about it, love. There is not too much to say about a woman who is pregnant; it happens all the time you know." Bradly had spoken absently, with other matters on his mind.

Katherine had kept quiet after this. I wonder if he will be this cold and insensitive if ever I conceive? she kept asking herself.

The next two months seemed to fly by as if on magical wings. Katherine seemed to blossom as the flowers and trees were doing with the first breath of spring air. Her every thought was for her husband and love, Bradly, and the love which she held inside herself for him seemed to radiate throughout the whole of Moon Rise.

Bradly grew more loving and warm toward his young wife with each passing day, and each night he held her as if in wonder at his great fortune in finding such a wonderful treasure.

As time went by Rachel also seemed to mellow and lose some of her sharpness of tongue. Some evenings the three would spend together, talking, or the women would listen while Bradly would read from a book of poems.

To Katherine life at Moon Rise was perfect now; she had strong arms to hold her during the nights and her days were full to bursting.

Most afternoons now, Katherine spent visiting with Jean. The child had been born, and true to the prediction of his father had been a boy and been given the name Eric.

Katherine loved her afternoon visits with Jean and her son. She would sit for hours at a time holding and cuddling the small infant. She thought of him as the most beautiful child she had ever seen. He had a tinge of red through his brown hair, large brown eyes, and a little button of a nose. She could not see how any small child could be more perfect.

One day she had told Bradly of her thoughts about little Eric and Bradly had only grunted and said that to him all babies looked alike when they were small.

Katherine had been hurt at the time by Bradly's crude answer about the small infant who swelled her own heart with love, but now as she sat holding a damp cloth to her head, her whole body was filled with a terrible dread.

It was impossible for her to keep her secret any longer or Bradly would find out for himself and then she would have to meet his anger unexpectedly. She had at first thought the delay in her monthly time had been caused by all the new changes she had had to adjust to, but now she was certain she was with child.

She was actually more scared of Bradly's reaction to this news than she was happy at the thought of having his child to love and hold to her breast.

How would he take it when she told him her

news? Would he be angry that at first he had been forced into marriage and now he was to be a father although he did not even act that fond of children? Would he go into a fit of temper and even perhaps find her undesirable as she rounded out with his child? She questioned herself, not knowing which way to turn.

"Oh, Lord, what shall I do? Am I to lose the love and happiness I have looked for all of my life? What would I be, if not for his love? How could I endure living without his love?" she cried aloud. But as she asked herself these painful questions she knew she had no choice in the matter and the sooner she told Bradly the sooner her torment at not knowing his reaction would be over.

Why was she sitting here worrying about how he would react anyway? she scolded herself. He is just as much to blame as I. Is he not the father of the unborn child? Feeling courage from this thought she jumped to her feet, then wiped her face with the cloth and rushed downstairs to find Jezzie.

"Jezzie, Jezzie!" she shouted, running through the kitchen door.

"Yes, ma'am, what's all your rushing about for?"

"Please, Jezzie, fix me a picnic lunch. Bradly's riding over the south fields today and I want to surprise him and bring him his lunch."

"Yes, ma'am." The old Negress chuckled.

"You young people are always in a dither. I'll have you some fried chicken and salad fixed up in no time at all."

"Thank you, Jezzie. I'll be back down after I change my clothes. Oh, Jezzie, could you send one of the girls down to tell the stableboys to saddle Golden Girl for me?"

"I'll take care of it, honey child; you just do what you need to and everything will be ready when you are."

Katherine rushed back up the stairs, changed into one of her riding habits, and took a few minutes to right her hair; within a few minutes she was rushing back down the stairs.

She was off and galloping down the road with hardly a moment wasted to stop and catch her breath.

As she approached the south fields she let her eyes gaze over the rows and rows of plowed earth until her eyes fell upon Bradly riding his horse toward her.

"Hello, sweet," he shouted and waved as he drew his horse up close to hers.

Katherine's face broke into a large smile as her gaze took in her husband. The weather was growing warmer and already his upper torso was tanned to a dark, golden brown. As he rode up to her his shirt was thrown across his saddle horn and her heart gave a wild beat as she looked at the large muscles expanding on his chest and arms. The first thought which swept through her mind was of those same muscles working as they lay abed each night.

"And what are you about, my little mouse?" Bradly leaned over and placed a small kiss upon the tip of her nose.

"I thought you might be hungry, so I brought a picnic lunch for us to share."

"You are an angel, coming all the way out here to feed your starving husband. Who could ask for a better wife?" he said gayly. "Have I told you lately how much I adore you?"

"Every day," Katherine whispered softly, taking his hand and kissing the back of it.

"Let us find a nice quiet spot, love, and you can feed me what my body is craving," he said with a sly grin.

"I'll race you to the pond, Bradly," she shouted, kicking her horse's sides and starting at a fast gallop.

Soon Katherine found herself standing next to the same pond she and Bradly had visited the first day she had become his.

Bradly placed a blanket on the ground and spread out the food Jezzie had packed for them.

After they had eaten their fill, and Bradly had stretched out with his head resting in Katherine's lap, she ventured to broach the subject which had been plaguing her these many weeks.

"Bradly?" She spoke softly.

"Yes, love?"

"Do you ever wish to have children?" she blurted out.

"Why, one day I suppose so, sweet," he answered, not really listening to what she was saying. His mind could only function upon the soft curves of her body as he let his hands roam freely.

Katherine could feel tears starting to sting her eyes as she said, "Bradly, I truly am sorry, but I am going to have your child."

Bradly lay still, letting his mind fill with her words.

Katherine's tears started to flow in earnest now, for she took his stillness to be anger and she almost expected him to fling her from him at any moment.

Bradly sat up slowly and looked into her tear-stained face. "You did say we are to have a child?" he asked holding his breath, awaiting her answer.

All she could do was to shake her head.

"Are you sure, Katherine?" he asked, taking her face between his hands.

She shook her head again.

"But, love, why the tears? Are you not happy that you will bear a child conceived out of our love?"

Katherine could not answer; she was weeping uncontrollably now.

Bradly pulled her to him and comforted her as if she were a child, until she quieted. "Now tell me, love, why these tears? Are you afraid to have this child?" Then all of a sudden the thought hit him, She thought he would not wish for a child. "Love, tell me, are you weeping because you thought I would not be happy with your news?"

Katherine nodded her head again and whispered softly, "Yes."

"Silly little fool," Bradly rebuked her. "Is your faith in my love so small, sweet? Do you not know that the greatest thing you could ever give to me is a child made from our bodies and our love? I love you more than life, Katherine. I never knew the meaning of the word 'love,' until I saw your face. Do you think for one moment that I would not love and cherish you even more, knowing that you will bring forth my child?"

"Oh, Bradly, I am sorry." She wept, holding tightly to him. "Never again will I doubt your love."

It was some time before either spoke again; each sat holding the other and thinking of their love.

Finally Bradly broke the quiet. "A son, we shall have a mighty son, who will have the beauty and warmth of his mother."

"And if it is to be a daughter?" Katherine asked softly.

"Then I shall pamper and spoil her as I always shall her mother. But I know already that our first child will be a boy, sweet," he shouted, jumping to his feet and twirling Katherine around in his arms.

"Oh, how I love you, Bradly, and I can barely wait to hold your babe in my arms." Katherine laughed gayly.

"Oh indeed, madam, you will be a splendid mother for my son and I shall be as proud a father as ever there was. I should actually be angry with you for thinking I would not be happy with this news, but I guess I cannot blame you for thinking the worst after the way I have talked about children. It is only that I never even expected such a surprise."

"I am glad that you are happy, sir, for I myself have never in my life felt as wonderful as at this moment." She placed her lips over his and drank of the sweet nectar that lay in wait for her.

In the late afternoon when Bradly and Katherine arrived back at Moon Rise and Bradly informed all of the servants in no uncertain terms that their mistress was not to do any kind of work that was any more strenuous than lifting one of her gowns, they all became upset, thinking their mistress had in some way brought harm to herself by the everyday busy routine she had followed. But as he continued on with the news of his heir to Moon Rise, lying in his wife's womb, their faces burst into smiles and Jezzie at once started fussing about and brought all of the house servants to order.

"No, sir, Master Brad, old Jezzie she watch the missus don't be doing anything that's a-going to hurt our new babe. She going to be tak'n care of as though she were a queen."

Katherine started to retort back in anger

that she did not wish to be treated any differently than she had been in the past, but the broad smiles upon Jezzie's face and those of the servants who stood about her stopped her words before she could get them out. She supposed it would be best to wait for a few days and then perhaps things would fall into place as they should. She could not deprive them of the joy they felt at hearing Bradly's news and she was sure she could handle them easily enough.

The one person, who at this happy time went unnoticed toward her room with tears of anger brimming her eyes, was Rachel. She had been on her way downstairs but had stopped short at the top when she had heard Bradly's voice shouting to the servants that his wife was not to do any work. At first Rachel thought her heart would burst with joy at the prospect of Katherine having injured herself in some way, but then as she listened further she could feel the anger and hatred that had been lying in her for the past few years—ever since she had lived in the same house as Katherine— sweep over her body, until she was shaken by a cold fury that seemed to overpower her whole body. "How could the stupid bitch do this?" she fumed, as she leaned against the closed door to her room. "Now I'll have to contend with a sniveling brat underfoot. God, when will Marco come and take me from this terrible fate?" she cried, running her fingers through her hair.

She had only received one letter from her love since she had been at Moon Rise, and that, she had gotten only two weeks ago from a dirty-looking man who had approached her as she was out riding. At first sight of this man, riding his horse at full gallop toward her, she had thought to put as much distance between her and him as she could, but as she had turned her horse's head in the opposite direction he had shouted her name and spurred his horse on faster toward her. Still she had had thoughts of fleeing, but her curiosity overcame her and she sat upon her mount, waiting for him to explain how he knew her name.

"You are Miss Rachel?" he questioned and spat a stream of tobacco juice at the feet of her horse.

"I am and what is that to the likes of you?" she asked in an angry tone of voice, as the stench from the man's soiled clothing and the leer on his face became apparent. "I am sure I have no business with you or you with me," she snapped, slapping her riding quirt against her boot.

"Now, missy, that ain't the way for you to be treating me, after I been riding this dad-blamed nag all over creation today a-looking for you," he sneered, his eyes going over her body in a lecherous way.

Rachel looked anxiously at the old vagrant. "And why have you been searching for me? I can think of no reason for a person of your low degree to be searching for me."

"Ho, ho, perhaps not, missy, but I carry a note right here in me pocket which you might be a-wanting," he said slyly, watching her face for a reaction.

"You say a note? Who ever would send me a note by you?" she asked unbelievingly.

"Now, missy, I ain't that bad you know. Lots of times people trust me with important matters." He spat again.

"Just shut your filthy mouth and give me the note you claim to have, I have not got all day to sit out in this dreadful heat, passing the time with the likes of you," she shouted, her temper flaring to the dangerous side.

"Just hold on there if you're in such a rush, my lady," he mocked her, pulling a piece of paper from his pocket meanwhile.

Rachel grabbed the paper out of his grizzly filthy hand and looked down at the signature. "Marco," the words escaped her.

"That's right, missy, from hisself." The old man grinned.

Rachel had forgotten his presence and when she heard him speak she jerked her head up and glared. "What are you sitting there grinning at? You have done what you were sent to do; now be gone with you, your presence irks me."

"What's your hurry, sweetie? Perhaps you and old Pete here could get to know one another better."

Rachel's eyes blazed with anger and her

riding quirt rose up to strike the filthy braggart full in the face, but just in time he turned his horse and started to ride off.

"You can't blame a soul for trying, can you, now, missy?" he called over his shoulder, in his retreat.

Rachel watched him leave, then turned back to the note in her hand. It was only a very few short lines telling her that she should be patient a bit longer and that soon they would be together. He also wrote that he would soon send another messenger to her, who would take her to meet him.

Rachel's pulse beat to a soaring tempo. "He has not forgotten me," she shouted to herself. He shall come for me soon and I shall be able to leave this place forever.

But all this had passed two long weeks ago, and now as she sat facing her mirror and cursing Katherine under her breath, she felt the strong urge to scream out her hurt and frustration.

She racked her brain, trying to understand why her love did not just come now, claim her for his own, and take her away from this house and the people within these walls. Of course, there must be a good reason for his not coming, but if he felt half of the love she felt for him, she was sure there could be no reason important enough to keep him from her. If only she knew what the reason for his delay could be. Perhaps, she reasoned, any day now, another messenger would come—or even

Marco himself. The thought made her feel somewhat better, but as she pictured herself having to face Katherine every day with her bloated stomach she felt her anger begin anew. Well there was not much she could do about her future at this moment, but soon she would not have such worries as those that were plaguing her now. The next time she received a message from Marco, she would insist on being taken to him or at least on getting word to him.

Chapter Eight

As Katherine's belly grew large with Bradly's child everyone at Moon Rise seemed to lie
in wait in a leisurely way for the new life that
would soon send its wails and gurgles of laughter throughout the old house, which had waited
for the past thirty-odd years for the coming
event.

Katherine herself had only put up with one

day of being treated like a queen, as Jezzie had proclaimed she would be on the day Bradly had proudly proclaimed his news of an heir.

Then she had asserted herself in the same role that she had played in the past; except now she had new tasks to keep her busy throughout her days. She had started right in redecorating one of the upstairs rooms into a nursery. This had taken several weeks of hard work and, with all of the house servants helping, Katherine had repainted and sewed and redone everything within the room.

Bradly had done his best to help during his free time, and he and Katherine took as much pride in the newly done room as they would in the new life that they would be bringing into the world.

This task had been both work and fun for Katherine. Now she had a new task put in front of her. Two days ago she and Bradly had received a letter from an old friend of Bradly's, Jeffery Williams and his wife, Marjorie. It was an invitation to spend two weeks in Richmond with the Williamses and Katherine at once jumped at the idea of the trip; but to her surprise Bradly rejected going and tried to divert her from the subject.

It had taken Katherine these past two days since the note had arrived to convince Bradly that she was in fine condition for a trip and that she would not let the matter rest until he said, in fact, that they could go and that they would leave soon.

Katherine had only two more months until the child would be born and Bradly had to admit she was in the best of health; so reluctantly he had agreed that they could go, but it would take at least a week for him to set things in order at Moon Rise and to arrange for Clay Johnson to come by now and then while they were gone.

Katherine had agreed joyfully with his wishes. Actually, she herself would have wished for a few days more than a week, for now she found herself busy from morning till evening, with the help of Jezzie, trying to let out some of her more elegant gowns to accommodate her shape.

On a warm and sunny day the small carriage made its way over the old dirt-laden roads toward the town of Richmond.

"I hope the ride will not be too much of an ordeal for you." Bradly spoke tenderly, pulling Katherine closer to his large, sturdy frame. "I should have insisted on putting this visit off until after the birth of the babe."

"But Bradly, I am perfectly healthy; even Jezzie says that pregnancy seems to agree with me. You're just getting too fussy, my beloved," she chided softly, placing one of Bradly's large hands upon her protruding belly, as the child within gave a hearty kick.

Bradly had watched over his young wife these past few months as though she were some priceless object. Her gentle beauty overwhelmed him, for he thought her even more beautiful now, if possible, while she carried his child, than he had ever thought a woman could be.

Her eyes always seemed to hold a tender warmness and glow; they radiated love as they looked toward him. And now as he gazed down at her pink cheeks and soft parting lips, he almost wished they were back at Moon Rise in their large four-poster bed. With the world locked out of their bedchamber, he would be able to keep her beauty and tender movements to himself and not have to share one single breath-taking minute of her with another living soul.

Katherine noticed his deep perusal of her and took it to be a look of irritation. "Do not look so angry, my darling. We shall only be staying a short two weeks and then you will be back to your plantation."

"I am not angry, my sweet. I only wish to see that no harm is done to you or the babe. I would move heaven and earth to see that you are safe and out of harm's way." He lightly placed a kiss on her furrowed brow.

"I am fine, Bradly, and shall stay that way. So do not play the doddering old man on my behalf, for I most surely do not wish for any harm to befall the life that quickens within me, and I would be the first to say it if the trip would prove too much for me."

Bradly settled back against the carriage seat,

some of the worry leaving his finely chiseled face as he stroked Katherine's lustrous black hair and she nestled against his chest.

"It was certainly kind of Mr. and Mrs. Williams to extend their invitation to us, Bradly. I am so looking forward to seeing the sights of Richmond. When I arrived there off the ship, I am afraid you rushed me off so swiftly I had no time to see anything except the church and the inn I stayed in."

Bradly gave a loud chuckle and then proceeded to speak. "I'm afraid, love, there are not that many sights to see in the city of Richmond. In fact, you will be staying in one of the sights of the town."

Katherine sat up straight and directed a questioning gaze at him.

"Yes indeed, my pet, the Williamses' house is one of the largest and most lavish in Richmond. And I'm sure Margie will entertain with all kinds of dinners and festivities for our benefit.

"Jeffery Williams, in fact, was a close friend of my father's. I also have business dealings with the gentleman and I must say I admire him more than most men in this day and time. He has done great things for America and particularly Richmond, with his shipping line, and he holds great plans for this country."

"Why, I had no idea we would be staying in such splendor or with such important people." Katherine gasped. "Why on earth did you not mention this earlier?"

"Perhaps I should have mentioned it earlier, but I did not think it of any importance. The Williamses are wonderful people and I'm sure you and Margie will get along just fine. She's the friendly sort, and though Jeffery has his hand in almost every dealing in Richmond, he always has time for kind words to his friends. Besides, my sweet, we are just as rich as they are; only they live a little more expensively."

"I am sure I shall love them, Bradly," Katherine replied, already anxious to meet these people her husband thought of so highly. For in the short time in which she had been this man's wife she had learned one thing; and that was that he did not give his friendship and admiration easily. But when he found a man worthy, the man usually more than deserved it.

Raymond drove the carriage on in silence, trying with all of his wits to keep the carriage at a steady pace and to avoid as many ruts as possible.

Finally, with the penetrating glare of the sun directly over head, Raymond pulled the carriage to a slow halt on the side of the dirt road, next to a small copse of trees.

Bradly handed Katherine out of the carriage and steered her toward the shade of a great, ancient oak tree. "Here is the perfect spot to idle away an hour and eat the lunch Jezzie packed," Bradly said lightly, as he spread a quilt upon the soft, green grass and laid out the contents of the picnic basket.

"You, dear sir, are too kind," Katherine rejoined in as light a voice as his own. "But I must confess, it is a thoroughly delightful pleasure to sit here in the cool shade, instead of bouncing in that old carriage."

Bradly helped her to sit upon the quilt, his brow once again creased in a worried frown. "Has the ride already been too much, my sweet? Are you sure you are not ailing?"

Katherine's light laughter filled the peaceful quiet. "I was only teasing, my beloved. I am fine; now do wipe that worried frown from your face and sit down. I fear your worrying is going to starve me to death."

Bradly laughed loudly and sat down next to his beautiful wife. "I should scold you harshly for the worry you cause me, but each time I look upon your sweet face I think of but one thing." He placed a lingering kiss upon her soft parted lips.

"Bradly, I am hungry." Katherine smiled, pushing against his chest.

"As you wish, my sweet, but I could think of a much pleasanter way in which to spend the next hour instead of eating food."

"Oh, Bradly, you are wicked," Katherine mocked in horror.

"And you, my sweet—now confess—you love every minute of it. Now, do you not?"

Katherine could not suppress the peals of laughter that welled out of her mouth. "Let us eat, Bradly, or Raymond will be down looking for us soon and I doubt if I will have the strength to walk back to the carriage without some food to sustain me."

Bradly agreed reluctantly and then set himself to tackling the food in front of him.

They both ate the packed lunch with delight, talking and laughing in between mouthfuls of fried chicken and salad, and sitting as close as possible while enjoying the cool breeze which stirred beneath the large tree.

After the meal was consumed and each was revived for the ride ahead they clambered back into the carriage and were on the road once again.

"It will not be but a couple of more hours now, my pet, and we will be there," Bradly said, laying Katherine's head upon his shoulder.

"Thank you, Bradly," Katherine murmured softly, as she shut her eyes and fell into a light sleep.

Bradly sat watching his wife sleep, his arms wrapped around her and one hand lightly placed upon her rounded stomach.

He smiled to himself as the tiny being within lightly moved against his hand. What would it be like—he questioned himself—to hold that tiny presence in his arms? He had changed greatly in the past months, since this small slip of a woman had come into his life, and not for one minute could he imagine himself living the same life he had lived before her.

He could never again be satisfied with the bachelor way of life. Not to have this beautiful creature here beside him to protect and love would prove the end of him.

As he sat gazing at her dark head, his chest swelled with a bursting pride. And as he thought of the child nestled deep within her womb, he could hardly believe that he would indeed be a father soon. But what did the word "father" mean? Did the word mean to love, to teach, to raise a boy to his manhood knowing that he would be strong and proud in his dealings with his fellow-man? Was this the meaning of being a father?

He let out a deep sigh; it should not prove too hard a task, though, with Katherine's love to give him the strength he would need.

The carriage pulled into the city of Richmond just as the sun was going down, and Katherine stirred at her husband's side.

"Are we there yet, Bradly?" she asked languidly, stretching her stiffened limbs.

"Why yes, we are, sweet, but it will be a few more minutes before we reach the Williamses' house."

Katherine gazed out of the carriage window at the same dirt road she had only months ago ridden over with a man who had become her husband overnight, and who had frightened her more than any man she had ever met. It all seemed like some faraway dream now, as she sat beside this kind and gentle man, whom she had learned to love and adore. Her whole world seemed to hold nothing but happiness and love. Her life before had almost vanished from her mind.

"There it is." Bradly was pointing toward a large, three-story frame house, with huge, white brick columns towering in the front.

"Why, this must be the largest house here in Richmond!" Katherine exclaimed, stretching her neck to take in the majestic beauty of the home they were approaching, and the beautifully cared-for grounds that surrounded it.

As the carriage drew up in front of this residence, a small, dark-haired woman in a beautiful, blue satin dress ran down the front steps; and when Bradly opened the carriage door and stepped down she threw herself into his arms.

"Oh, Bradly, Bradly, it has been so long. I am so happy you could come for a visit," she cried, kissing him full on the lips.

Bradly chuckled gayly and twirled her around happily in his arms. "You look as lovely as ever, Margie; but now if you will allow it, I will introduce you to my wife."

"But of course, Bradly. This is terrible of me; I forgot all about the new Mrs. Deveraux in my excitement at seeing you once again."

Katherine felt her first stabs of jealousy as she watched this other woman in her husband's arms; kissing the mouth that she had believed to be hers and no other's. But as she was helped out of the carriage and the woman

241

showed as much happiness at meeting her as she had shown her husband, Katherine felt a great relief fill her body.

She soon found that Margie Williams was one of those women who just naturally showed their affection to those they care about. But as fond as she was of Bradly and a number of other gentlemen, to her there was no other man who could match her husband.

The Williamses' house was even more impressive on the inside, and as soon as they entered the door, Margie at once took Katherine in hand and led her up the stairs and into a guest room.

Katherine herself felt very weary from the long ride from Moon Rise and the dust from the road seemed to cling to her clothing.

"Here, my dear; let me help you remove your gown and you will be able to bathe," Margie said, unhooking the catches at the back of Katherine's dress and indicating a small screen divider, behind which waited a large steaming tub of water.

Katherine smiled her thanks and let the kindly lady help her out of her dress.

"Now take your time, Katherine. My husband has not yet arrived home and dinner will not be for a time. So just relax in the water and ring this small bell when you wish for help with your dressing. I'll send Bradly up shortly to you, but I would enjoy a small talk with him first. It seems like ages since he has been a guest at our home."

"Thank you for everything, Margie. You are so kind and I confess a long, hot bath will be wonderful."

Before Margie left the room she took Katherine's hands and clasped them tightly in her own. "Anything you wish for, dear, you will have. I am so glad Bradly found himself a woman such as you. I can tell by the way his eyes rested upon you downstairs that he is deeply in love, and that in itself shows what kind of woman you must be. Never in all the years I have known him have I ever seen him with that look of love in his eyes for any other woman; and I assure you he has been besieged by women ever since he became a young man."

Katherine's face flushed deeply but she listened intently while the other woman talked on.

"I am sorry if I am embarrassing you with my frank manner of speaking, but I have hopes that you and I will become close friends. I wanted you to understand how fond Jeffery and I both are of Bradly and I also wish you to know that we are quite happy over the events that have happened since you have come into his life." She patted Katherine's bulging stomach lightly, her eyes twinkling warmly. "I imagine Bradly will be the proudest father in all of Virginia."

Katherine's blush deepened a shade brighter, but she could not help but like this woman who spoke so boldly.

"Well, I do not wish to keep you any longer from your bath." Margie squeezed her hands for a second, then let them go, and turned to the door. "I'll see you later, Katherine, and I am so glad you came," she added before shutting the door.

Katherine sat languidly, relaxing in the brass tub, her mind going over the events of the months since she had arrived in Richmond.

To think she had been so set on not marrying a man she had never met and to think of the many times she had cursed her stepmother, Joann, in her mind, for arranging her marriage. As she thought of Joann's hatred for her, a slow, lazy smile crossed her face. If only Joann knew of the happiness, love, and security she was feeling this minute, her stepmother would be damning herself for ever talking John Rafferty into sending his daughter to America to marry.

"Just think," Katherine sighed out loud, "I have a husband who is the man of my dreams; strong and gentle, at the same time caring for my mind and my feelings, and who, above all else, loves me so much that other people can read it in his eyes."

Jeffery Williams was a man of some importance in the new America and Katherine was swept off her feet by the feeling of authority and power which seemed to radiate from his very presence.

When Katherine came down the stairs to have dinner with Bradly and their host her eyes at once fell on the man who stood by the fireplace in the small sitting room.

He was as tall as Bradly, and although his build was not as large and sturdy as her husband's, he held himself in the manner of one who is assured of his strength and ability. His hair was a golden blond with touches of white at the temples. But the most compelling feature of all were his eyes. Never before had Katherine seen such light-blue eyes; they looked like the sky on a clean, bright day.

"You must be Katherine." He spoke deeply, his face crinkling at the corners of his eyes and mouth as he smiled and walked toward her, extending his hand. "I have heard quite a bit about you, young lady, and I can see now those who spoke of your beauty were not exaggerating. Bradly, you are a lucky man." He looked at Bradly who stood at Katherine's side.

"Thank you, Jeffery, I shall not argue with you on that score. I myself can hardly believe my good fortune." He gave Katherine a loving look that warmed her whole body and left her cheeks a rosy red.

"Come sit here on the sofa by me, Katherine." Margie patted the soft, velvet sofa and smiled invitingly. "Dinner should be ready soon and perhaps you will fill me in somewhat on what is going on back home in England. It has been almost ten years since last we visited there. Jeffery hardly has the time for anything except his business."

The men stood by the door talking in low tones and the women spoke of the latest fashions and the latest gossip which Katherine had learned before leaving England.

When dinner was finished, the small group retired for the evening, with Margie assuring Katherine that she would be needing her rest, for the following days would be full of activity.

Katherine found Richmond to be gay and alive, after the lazy months at Moon Rise. Margie was one of Richmond's most prominent wives and the head of all manner of social functions.

Their days were full of teas, luncheons, and shopping sprees and Katherine, now a new member of the group of ladies who led the social life in this city, was treated with affection and admiration.

At first she was accepted as Bradly Deveraux's wife and the good friend of Margie Williams, but as the good ladies of the town got to know her for herself they instantly fell in love with her. Her innocence and good breeding helped somewhat, but her kindness and generosity were her key features.

Daily invitations arrived at the Williamses' house for dinners and parties. Katherine was swept off her feet by all the excitement. She was the belle of the ball at all the social parties and Bradly protectively stayed by her side.

When at such an affair he was dragged away by one gentleman or another, her eyes never left his tall, broad frame.

The women of the town were charmed by her adoration of her husband and one of the ladies even remarked to her husband, "It would be absolutely scandalous, the way she watches her husband with her heart in her eyes, if not for the fact that they are married."

Bradly himself was of no different nature; when not by his wife's elbow his eyes glanced her way constantly. To him she glowed and became more beautiful with each passing day. Her dresses were cut full to hide her burdened stomach, and from the tips of her tiny slippers to the dark, lustrous curls atop her head, he thought her perfection itself—and many of the gallant young men who attended the parties given, were of the same mind.

And although she was approached by such young men and started into conversation, she would answer in kind, laugh gayly at their witty jests, but in a few seconds her husband would again be at her side, scowling darkly at her companion of the moment.

Katherine never noticed Bradly's jealousy or the quick departure of the gentleman to whom she had only seconds ago been talking, for she dismissed every other man as nothing compared to her love.

If she had ever guessed the extent of her husband's jealousy, she would have been shocked out of her wits. For his were more than mere jealous thoughts; they were thoughts of rage at any other man flirting with and eying his wife. He was constantly having to hold himself in control so as not to hit a youth or gentleman too much in his drinks to know whose wife he was tampering with.

On one such occasion a rake, as Bradly thought him, by the name of Owen Lammon, had arrived late to one of the Williamses' balls; and as soon as he entered the room, his eyes fell on Katherine, sitting by herself across the room. He immediately made his way to her and with a bow introduced himself.

Bradly had been in conversation with a group of men and out of the corner of his eye, had glanced his wife's way.

Owen Lammon, not knowing to whom this temptress belonged and thinking her fair game, had at once taken the seat beside her and commenced to charm her.

Katherine, not knowing anything was amiss, was laughing freely at his gallant talk and never noticed the young man's arm slip easily about the top of her chair. But Bradly noticed and quick and lithe as a panther he strode from the group of men and—with only one thought on his mind, to break Owen Lammon's arm—appeared in front of the two.

"You will extract yourself at once from my wife's side," he drawled, menacingly and in a deathly tone.

Owen Lammon's face turned to ash as he grasped the situation in which he had placed himself. He knew Bradly Deveraux for what he was: a dangerous and fearsome enemy, if one were to cross him. He had no wish either to be beaten by the large powerful fists which loomed above him or to be challenged to a duel, which he would have no way of winning. He quickly rose to his feet, his face now turning a deep red as he made his apology and left Katherine's side and the Williamses' house, thanking his good fortune that he was leaving with his body intact.

Katherine was perplexed by Bradly's manners, but when she made mention of it to him, he only kissed her on the forehead and said lightly that it was his turn to sit beside her and admire her beauty.

His rages were always quickly spent as soon as he looked into her violet eyes and innocent face; and also he did not wish his wife to know of his deep jealousy and the fury that swept over him when she was near any other man.

To Bradly, the time could not come soon enough to leave this town and get back to the country and Moon Rise, where his eyes alone could feast on his lovely bride.

As usual Katherine and Margie went in a carriage to teas in the afternoons; groups of four or five ladies held them at one or another's homes. Katherine enjoyed these visits and the quiet talk of the women. There was always the latest gossip and talk of children and at times these talks would turn to childbearing. This last subject was most enlightening to Katherine, for she had not known exactly of what the process of bearing a child would consist.

The women would talk of their own children and the pain they had endured bearing them, but Katherine, in her mind, did not fear bringing Bradly's child into the world. The only time these talks upset her, was when eventually one or more of the women would talk of one of their own children who had died at birth, or of a friend or some unfortunate woman who had died while trying to bear a child. Whenever the talks dwelled on these subjects, Katherine would dig her nails into the palms of her hands, while she smiled and acted as though it were terrible but not something for herself to worry over.

She knew these kind ladies were not trying to frighten her, but unintentionally a fear deep inside her began to grow. She tried throwing it off, by bolstering herself up and thinking of how happy she was going to be to sit and hold and cuddle the small bundle that would be Bradly's. But again and again thoughts assailed her of a baby lying dead near her side—or worse still, she being dead and never again to have Bradly's strong arms to hold her.

It was after a rather long and tiring day during which Katherine had attended one of these long teas at which the talk had been of childbearing that she and Bradly went to bed. As they lay side by side Bradly placed his large palm gently upon Katherine's stomach. Katherine could not contain herself any longer and burst into a gush of tears.

"What is it, love, are you in pain?" Bradly leaned over her, beside himself with worry.

"No." She could only sob; she had no wish for him to know of the terrible fears which had been attacking her.

Bradly took her in his arms as though she were a child and rocked her gently; her tears streamed onto the black mat of hair on his chest.

"There, there, sweet. Tell me what is ailing you; I do not like to see you like this. It tears at my heart to see you weeping so."

"Bradly, Bradly, hold me tight. I am so afraid." She wept.

Bradly tightened his arms about her and gently, but firmly tried to persuade her to talk. "Tell me, my pet, what is it, the baby? Is that what you are afraid f?" He could only fathom that she had heard of the terrible pain that came with having a child.

Katherine lay quiet for a time, secure in his strong arms. Then, between sobs, she talked to him. "I love you so, Bradly, and I shall bear any pain to have our child, but what frightens me so is that our baby could be born dead or I could die and I could not bear to be away from your love and gentle touch. I should be ashamed to feel this way, but I have heard so

251

many stories of babies dying and mothers dying and I just cannot stand the thought."

Anger flashed over Bradly momentarily. Stories, she said. Damn this town; stupid women sitting around and telling his dear, sweet Katherine frightening tales. Then, all of a sudden, his anger turned into fright. His own mother had died in childbearing. No! He swore to himself, he would keep his wife with him and nothing would happen to her.

"Katherine, listen to me," he said, tilting her damp, tear-stained face up to his own. "We shall have a fine, healthy son, and you will be fine. I promise you this; nothing will ever take you from me. Your pain to bring our child into the world will be my pain, and I shall be there beside you and bear it every minute with you. I told you once before you did not have enough faith in my love. I tell you now you must forget this fear and have faith in me, for I shall never let anything happen to you." His light, silver eyes pleaded for her to believe in him, as he looked deep into the liquid, violet pools before him.

Katherine sighed as if a huge burden had been lifted from her shoulders. She could not do anything but believe him; no harm would come to her or her babe as long as Bradly took care of her. Her earlier fright seemed to vanish with his words and look. "Thank you, darling," she whispered, closed her eyes gently, and fell asleep. He held her throughout the rest of the night.

*   *   *

The first week in Richmond had gone by quickly and the second was almost over. Katherine had mixed feelings about leaving the city, for she had many close friends now; most of all, Margie. She almost thought of her as a sister. She knew, though, that for the past few days she had been longing for the peace and serenity of Moon Rise and was starting to miss Jezzie terribly.

Bradly had no mixed emotions. When he had lived a single life he had enjoyed visiting the city—for the excitement, drink, and women—but now with Katherine as his wife, and the baby soon to come, he could hardly bear to wait the two extra days until they could go home.

Margie gave a last dinner party for her close friends on the last evening of their stay in town. There were only two other couples invited, and Katherine thought this to be one of Jeffery's ideas. She imagined he would mix a little business with pleasure, since this would be Bradly's last night in his home and Bradly and all the other male guests owned shares in Jeffery's shipping line. Just exactly what amount Bradly owned or to what extent he participated in this shipping line, Katherine did not know and she found she really was not interested, as long as it did not take her husband from her side for long intervals.

The guests arrived early for dinner that evening and Katherine was delighted, for she

253

was especially fond of Cindy Wells and she and her husband, James, were the first to arrive.

The other couple, Nancy and Warren Godfrey, arrived only minutes after the Wellses.

The small gathering was happy and light-hearted tonight. In the parlor and on the sofa the women sipped sherry, while the gentlemen, seated in chairs, drank snifters of brandy and talked business until dinner was served.

Dinner was a delight; every course as delicious as the next and Katherine, who had eaten very little during the day, put her full attention on her food. Therefore, she did not notice the tension in the men's speech or that Jeffery was eating less and drinking liberally of his wine.

Katherine's attention was drawn, though, when she heard Jeffery say in a voice he was trying to control, "Damn it, Bradly, we must do something about these rogues or all of us will be losing money!"

Margie was shocked that her husband would use such language in front of their female guests—and especially at the dinner table—and she started to protest. "Jeffery, please, can this not wait until after dinner when you men can retire to the library?"

"By hell, no!" he shouted, looking directly at Bradly.

Katherine's own face turned red with embarrassment for Margie, who now sat with her face turned down toward her plate of food.

Bradly stared at Jeffery eye to eye and then finally spoke. "Do as you think best, Jeffery. We have talked about this matter before and I have told you the reasons why I cannot at this time take off and go chasing the seas. You will have to do whatever you think best." Bradly's voice was soft, but by the sound of it, one could tell there was no changing his mind or getting around him.

"By God, if it were your father sitting there instead of yourself, my boy, he would be out this minute with me chasing down that Marco Radford and his band of cutthroats," Jeffery shouted across the table; the words came out almost in a drunken slur.

At the mention of Marco Radford's name, Katherine dropped her fork on her plate, her face turning as white as porcelain. Her thoughts left the table and those around her. All she could think of were piercing black eyes coming toward her and the words screamed over and over again in her head: You shall be mine one day.

The conversation at the dinner table stopped abruptly, as all eyes turned toward a shaken, white-faced Katherine.

Bradly was kneeling beside her chair in an instant. "Katherine!" he cried, anguish written on his face, "for God's sake, what is the matter?"

At once Margie was on her feet and sent a servant to bring smelling salts and a glass of brandy; then she turned and started her attack on her husband. "Do you see how you have upset the poor child, with your vile talk at our dinner table?"

Jeffery hung his head low, afraid he indeed was the cause of whatever was ailing the poor child; she looked as if she had seen a ghost and she was shaking as though she were packed in ice.

Bradly picked her up from her chair and carried her to the sofa in the parlor. After he had calmed her somewhat and made her drink a few sips of the brandy, he excused himself to his host and their guests and gently carried Katherine to their bedchamber.

He tenderly laid her upon the bed and then without a word spoken started to undress his wife.

"I can do that, Bradly. I honestly do not know what came over me; it must be my pregnancy. I have never acted like this in my whole life." She spoke weakly, trying to rise so she would not have to burden him with undressing her. She would not tell him her cause of distress because she didn't want to place any more burdens on him.

Bradly lightly pushed her back down upon the bed. "I'll undress you tonight, sweet. You need to rest. I fear this visit has been too much for you and I will be glad to get you back home where you belong."

Katherine was relieved he was not going to question her or try to find out what had caused her collapse. She only wanted to wipe out of her mind that dark, swarthy face and the words that Marco had told her on his pirate ship. Though, for the life of her, she could not figure out why now Marco's name would cause such a fearsome feeling in her, after all of this time.

Bradly also could not understand why Katherine would be so upset by Marco's name. He knew what had upset her. The minute Jeffery had spoken that hateful name, he had glanced at his wife and seen the turmoil she was experiencing. He did not wish to upset her more; so he decided against asking any questions. Perhaps her upset was due only to her pregnancy.

The following morning after a farewell breakfast and profound apologies from Jeffery, Bradly and Katherine were back in their carriage and on their way back to Moon Rise.

Katherine slept most of the way on Bradly's shoulder, for she had barely slept the night before. Her dreams had been full of the black, piercing eyes of a man who must have been the devil himself, chasing her; and she would run and run but find no escape until finally she would awake and Bradly would be holding her closely and whispering over and over, "It is all right, my love. I am here, no one will harm you."

Bradly's thoughts were tormented all the way back to Moon Rise. Three times during the night he had been awakened by Katherine calling his name and crying out loud, "Do not let him catch me." He held no doubt of who the "he" in her dreams was and Bradly swore over and over during the night that the first chance he got he would rid the earth of Marco Radford for what he had done to his wife.

As far as Bradly knew, though, Marco had done nothing except hold his wife a prisoner for a few days and then release her. Had she not been a virgin when they wed? And she had not acted distressed when he had met her that first day in Richmond. He just could not figure out what could have happened; and all the way to Moon Rise he turned these thoughts over and over in his mind.

Chapter Nine

Home again at Moon Rise and around those she loved the most, Katherine's dreams did not return and Bradly, ever watchful for any movement of her body in slumber, was relieved and happy that she was once more her old self.

Katherine had only one more month left of her time to carry Bradly's child, and, happy as a bird, she sewed tiny clothes and made ready for her new babe. Her only constant irritation was Rachel, who was always about nowadays and it seemed to Katherine that she was forever looking at her stomach or wrinkling up her nose in distaste as Katherine waddled across the floor or tried to pull her bulk out of a chair.

Bradly and Jezzie would always chuckle or smile fondly at her attempts, but Rachel acted as though Katherine were some kind of monster and she could barely stand the sight of her.

One bright, sunny afternoon, while Katherine was sitting on the front porch doing some sewing, she felt the hair rise on the nape of her neck, as though someone or something was staring a hole through her.

She turned quickly and saw Rachel standing off to the side of the veranda, just watching her belly. Suddenly Katherine had a thought: perhaps Rachel was only wishing that she herself were in a like condition, with a husband, and a child in her belly. She knew that was the wish most women had and she felt sorry for the girl, standing there and just staring.

"Rachel," Katherine said softly. "Would you care to talk awhile?"

Rachel, who had been so intently watching Katherine's belly, jumped at the mention of her name. "What would you like to talk about, Katherine? I cannot see what we could have to say to each other," she replied cautiously, walking up the veranda steps.

"Well," Katherine began. "I was thinking that perhaps you would like to go back to England or to take a trip into Richmond."

"Why what for?" Rachel asked indignantly. "If you are wanting to be rid of me just say so."

Katherine *did* want to be rid of the girl. She was forever making her feel uncomfortable lately. It was as though she were waiting for the baby to pop out of her stomach. Katherine could not fathom her reasons and she was too well brought up to speak her feelings to the woman in front of her. She replied in an even tone of voice, "Rachel, you know I did not mean anything like that. I just thought that if you could get away from Moon Rise you might find someone you could care about. I have watched the way you have looked at my shape and I thought that perhaps you would like to find someone to marry and to have babies and a house of your own." Katherine smiled sweetly, trying to draw the girl into a conversation.

"I am sorry to inform you, Katherine, but I would not for the life of me want to be bloated or look as you do now. And as for marrying and having a home of my own, that may be sooner than you think; but it is definitely none of your business." Rachel all but shouted these last words as she stomped into the house.

Katherine looked after the girl's retreating back and only shook her head. She was used to Rachel's rude manners and all she could hope for now was that perhaps she had met some gentleman and would be leaving soon.

With only two weeks left until Katherine would be at the end of her pregnancy, she found that with each day she became more tired and irritated. On one such morning, Katherine awoke feeling a nagging backache and when Bradly asked how she was feeling this fine morning, she all but snapped off his head before she burst into tears. "I am sorry; I have been so cruel to you," she cried. "I am such a bother recently and I know I have not been very nice lately."

Bradly never lost his patience with her and today was no exception. "Are you not feeling well, sweet? Why do you not just stay abed today?"

"I have a nagging backache and I cannot seem to find any way to ease it," she sobbed.

"Here, my pet, lie on your side and I will rub it for you." His gentle hands rubbed and soothed and almost instantly Katherine was sleeping once again.

Bradly kissed her on the nape of the neck, spread a soft coverlet over her, and tiptoed out of the room.

Downstairs he told Jezzie and Lucy he would be gone only a short time to look over the fields and that they were to let their mistress rest and not to disturb her.

Lord, he thought wearily, as he left the house. I hope it will not be too much longer before the babe arrives. I don't think I can take much more of this waiting.

When he came home shortly before lunch, Bradly found that his waiting had about come to its end. As usual, he sought out Katherine. Jezzie told him she had not heard her up yet so they had let her sleep.

"Good," Bradly replied. "She needs all the rest she can get."

"Yes, sir, she sure do, that young'un going to be coming most any day now." Jezzie chuckled, as Bradly left the kitchen.

He made his way to his bedchamber and peered across at his wife. When his eyes fell on her form on the bed he felt his guts draw up into a tight ball.

Katherine's face and the coverlet he had lain across her were drenched in sweat. Her hands were gripping her bulging stomach.

Bradly's face was death white as he rushed to the bed. "Katherine, is—is it the baby?" he questioned, hardly able to get the words out and knowing what her answer would be before she spoke it.

She nodded her head yes, and gritted her teeth as pain consumed her body.

"I'll fetch Jezzie; I'll not be but a minute, love." He rushed to the door. "Jezzie, Jezzie," he bellowed at the top of his voice, rushing down the stairs three steps at a time.

"Where the hell are you? Katherine's time has come and she's in pain; hurry your fat carcass up here."

"There ain't a thing can be done for the pain, Master Brad," she panted, rushing out of the kitchen and up the stairs.

"Well hurry, something must be done to help her," Bradly shouted, bounding back up the flight of stairs.

"I'm a-coming just as fast as these two old legs of mine will carry me," she yelled at him. Then she shouted for the kitchen girls to bring up hot water and for Lucy to get clean towels and linen.

"Now, Master Brad, you just calm yourself down or you a-going to scare that poor child worse than what she already is," the old Negress admonished her master, before they entered the bedroom.

Jezzie swept in, placed a bowl of cool water by the bed, and started to wipe her mistress's face. "There, there child, you just save your strength and with each one of them pains you just push and bear down. Try to relax between each pain, sugar, for it might be awhile before that young'un comes."

Bradly had made an attempt to get hold of himself, and now he sat holding one of Katherine's small hands to his lips and wiping her brow with the damp cloth.

Katherine, looking into his eyes, saw the worry and concern written in their depths. "I shall be fine, darling," she whispered, between contractions.

Bradly leaned over and kissed her soft, pale lips. "I'll be right here beside you, love; just try to resy easy when you can."

As she was about to answer him a tremor shook her body; she was pulled along with another almost unbearable pain. Jezzie coaxed her to bear down with the pain and shortly it was over and another began. This went on into the late afternoon.

Bradly broke out in a cold sweat, not knowing what to do or which way to turn as he sat and watched his wife valiantly bearing down, the silent tears running down her cheeks. His mind filled with thoughts of his own mother's death, going through this same torture, trying to bring him into the world—and his whole body shook. What would he do? his insides screamed. How would he be able to live without this ray of sunshine whom he had found so late in life? What if his love died bearing his child? Could he do as his father had done and raise his child alone or what if—worse still—she and the child were to die. Then he would not even have a part of her to love.

"Master Brad." Jezzie brought him out of his black thoughts. "I don't think it's a-going to be much longer."

Bradly, coming to his senses, knew that he had to be the one to help his wife and to bring their child from its nest of love. Had he not promised her that he would see no harm befell her or their babe?

"Here, Jezzie, get out of the way. I'll do it," he said soberly as he positioned himself between Katherine's legs. "You just get everything ready," he told the old Negress, who had once done this same thing for his mother and him.

"I ain't never heard of such a thing, Master Brad," Jezzie said in a huff. "This here's women's work and you ain't got no business a-doing this to Miss Katherine."

Bradly shook his head. "Just do as you're told, Jezzie," he said gruffly.

Katherine let out a scream, as another pain struck.

"Push down, love," her husband coaxed. "The head is making its way out. That's the girl; just bear down," he added, watching his child being pushed out of its mother's body, with the help of his hands.

Bradly reached down and scooped up the small frame in his large hands.

The babe gave a large wail as it drew its first breath of air, and Katherine's and Bradly's eyes locked in a more passionate and tender look than any word of love could descsribe.

Finally Bradly looked down at the infant in his hands. "It's a boy," he breathed, hardly believing his own eyes. "We have a man-child, sweet, and he shall be the strongest child in all of Richmond."

Katherine rose up feebly. Looking at her

husband's happy face and glowing eyes, she knew in that moment that all the pain and the months of waiting had been worthwhile.

After gently giving his son into Jezzie's waiting arms, Bradly rinsed his wife's body. With loving hands he wiped her clean and changed her night clothing.

Before Katherine fell into an exhausted sleep, Jezzie had cleaned up the new little master of Moon Rise and placed him in the crook of his mother's arm.

Katherine looked him over carefully, taking in his dark, downy hair and his very light eyes. "He is perfect, Bradly." She marveled at his tiny features, and his likeness to his father. "His eyes will be the same silver as yours. See, they are light, not like my dark blue."

"I agree completely with you, love, he is perfect in every way and you, my angel, are the most wonderful woman I have ever known." His eyes misted over as he watched his wife and small son.

Katherine fell into a sound sleep instantly, holding Bradly's hand and looking down at their child.

Bradly easily disengaged his hand, slipped his son from his mother's arm, and carried him to his small cradle. He stood a few minutes looking down in wonder at the small bundle.

This child was a part of himself and the woman he loved. To think, his love could create something this small and helpless.

He felt a pride grow inside himself, until he felt he would burst. Only a year ago he would not have thought that he could feel so deeply about a woman and a baby. Katherine had shown him the meaning of love and now this small innocent child, lying asleep in his cradle, held his heart in his tiny fists.

He decided then and there, staring down at the tiny little boy, that he would name him Charles William. It was a good name and one that would be a credit to the Deveraux family.

The first rays of the morning light were starting above the treetops when Bradly went down to his study and poured himself a large glass of brandy as a toast to himself for the fine son he had acquired during the night, and the wonderful wife he had and would always treasure.

The next morning Katherine awoke to the sound of her hearty son screaming his lungs out for his breakfast. She lay there listening while Jezzie and Lucy cooed and fussed over the tiny infant and started making him ready for his first feeding.

"This here's got to be the most rowdy young'un I ever did see," Jezzie said, bringing the tiny bundle over and placing it in Katherine's arms. "He thinks he's starving half to death."

Bradly entered the room with a warm smile on his face for his wife and son. "I heard our son all the way from downstairs, love, and thought perhaps I should see what was troubling him."

Katherine looked at her husband, her eyes holding in their depths all the love she felt for him. "I was just going to feed him his breakfast, Bradly." She spoke nervously, unbuttoning her gown.

Bradly took a seat beside the bed, waiting expectantly for the scene to come.

Katherine placed her son's mouth next to her breast, her face blushing at the feel of his tiny lips trying to secure the nourishment that he knew was waiting for him. But she pulled back in surprise and almost dropped the infant when his greedy mouth actually overtook and latched onto her nipple.

As he took in the eagerness of his tiny son and the confusion and surprise on Katherine's face, Bradly's deep-throated laughter filled the room.

Jezzie whirled around when she heard her master and Katherine's face blushed profusely because she felt all eyes were upon her.

But when she took in what had just taken place, Jezzie's own face broke out into a large smile. Instead of speaking, she took hold of Lucy's arm and together they left her master and his young wife, to be alone at this tender moment.

"Hearty little rascal, isn't he, sweet?" Bradly laughed, patting his son's little rump.

"Oh, Bradly, it is all so new to me." She sighed, gazing down at the tiny head snuggled upon her breast.

"I know, love, but I could not imagine my son in the arms of any other."

Katherine became accustomed to the newness of the baby suckling at her breast and relaxed back against the pillow.

Bradly reached over and rubbed the black fuzz that adorned his son's head; his fingers also lightly caressed Katherine's bosom.

She felt a shiver of delight course over her body and looking up, her warm blue eyes locked together with his somber, silver-gray gaze.

They stayed thus, the tiny infant between them, drinking in all of the warmth and love they shared for each other, until Bradly spoke softly.

"I did not get the chance to tell you last night about all the love I possess here in my heart for you."

Katherine gazed softly at him, her own heart feeling as though it would melt at any moment from all the love she herself held for this giant of a man.

"I can hardly put into words the happiness you have brought into my life. You have opened a whole new world for me, one which now I have tasted, I could not bear to part with. You have brought to me a son, made from our love. I shall forever be grateful to you for this wondrous life, that we shall watch grow into manhood." He spoke, his voice almost choking from the tenderness he felt

270

inside himself.

"Oh, Bradly, to know your happiness with me and your pride in our son, I would in a minute do it all over again. I never thought I would know a love such as yours and I would die now before parting with one fraction of the love which you have shown me," Katherine whispered softly, tears coming easily to her eyes.

"Love, never will you lose any of my love; my heart runs over with the love and adoration I feel inside for you," he said, bringing his lips to hers and taking them in a burning, passionate kiss.

It was as though time stopped for Katherine and she had to pull herself back to reality with an effort and concentrate on the babe at her breast. "You shall have your son crying again, sir." She tried to sound gay and not show how his burning lips had shaken her.

Bradly gave her a sly grin, as if reading her mind. "Is it the babe you worry for, madam, or yourself?" He took her lips again, this time with more hunger.

Katherine had to push against him with her free hand. "Please, Bradly," she groaned, wanting to feel his lips, but not wishing for the sensations that those lips awakened in her body when she was powerless to do anything about them.

"As you wish, my love," he murmured. "But heal quickly, for I am not a patient man and already I can barely wait to feel the pleasures of your body."

Katherine's face blushed deeply at his words.

"I am only jesting, love. I shall not push you on the matter until I am sure I shall only bring you joy and pleasure and not pain."

There was a slight knock on the door, interrupting the loving moment of the couple.

Following the knock Rachel entered, wearing a dove-gray riding outfit, her eyes icy chips as she took in the tender scene before her.

Bradly rose from his chair near the bed, annoyed to be disturbed at this time.

"I am sorry if I am interrupting anything. I only came in to offer Katherine and the child my best wishes."

Katherine clasped Bradly's hand tightly to her own.

"I won't be long, love, but there are matters to which I must attend." He placed a fleeting kiss on the tip of her small nose and patted his son's behind. "Take care of our son, madam," he added as he left the room.

"I appreciate your coming, Rachel. Would you care to sit and perhaps talk for a while?" Katherine questioned.

"No, thank you," the girl answered, the sight of a baby nursing at the breast sickening her. "For heaven's sake, why on earth do you not get a wet nurse to do that dreadful job? You will ruin your figure if you insist upon doing it yourself."

"Rachel, I enjoy my child against my

breast; I am his mother!"

Rachel started to comment, but Katherine spoke before the other girl could.

"I had hopes that we could be on friendlier terms and that you would soften somewhat with a child now in the house."

"Now come, Katherine, I only came in here to pay my respects, because I felt it my duty, since I am a guest in your house and have no place else to go at this time. But if you think for one minute that I shall forget the way I have been treated in the past, simply because you now have a child, you are very much mistaken. I loathe children and their crying and the mess they make."

"Well, since you have made your feelings clear, I do not believe there is anything else we have to say to one another. And if you cannot abide watching my son have his breakfast, you may leave." Katherine spoke in a low, meaningful voice and put one hand protectively around her baby, but the other shook from her aggravation.

"You do not have to get so uppity about it; you have known how I have felt since we left England and I hope it will not be too long before I shall be out of your house." With this, she turned on her heels and left the room, leaving the door ajar.

Katherine's anger soon abated as she sat and pondered Rachel's words. Was she misreading her meaning now, or could there possibly be someone Rachel cared about? She had thought this once before but when Rachel had made no more mention of leaving Moon Rise she had let it slip her mind. If this was the other woman's intention, Katherine would be more than glad to let her leave. She truly doubted she could take much more of her ill-bred manners, and she certainly would not put up with her snide remarks about her son.

Rachel left the house in a furious rage. "Who did the little bitch think she was?" she stormed as she mounted her horse and whipped it to a faster pace. She'd be damned if she were going to start being friendly now to that little snob; not when so soon she would have her revenge on her and her darling Marco would be beside her.

At the thought of Marco her blood rushed fiercely through her veins and she pushed her steed even harder, in order to get to her destination faster.

As her mount neared a large thicket of trees her eyes scanned the area until they finally spied a horse tied to a small pine.

It was dark and eerie here under the boughs of the trees, but Rachel felt no fear as she leaped from the back of her horse. Her senses kept pounding, over and over, that soon, soon, she would be lying in her lover's arms again.

And there, leaning against a large oak tree, stood her one and only—Marco Radford.

"Marco!" she cried, her brown hair flying as she ran and threw her arms about his neck.

"It has been almost a month now since you last met me." She snuggled her face close against his neck.

"I'm sorry I could not come sooner, but a pirate's life is not his own," he murmured with a twisted grin on his face.

"I know, I know; it is only that I have been so miserable without you, and when I sit in my room all alone, my whole body yearns for the feel of you close beside me."

"It will not be for much longer now, Rachel; perhaps only a few more weeks."

"But why do we have to wait? Why can we not just leave now?" Rachel pleaded, raising her head to look into Marco's dark eyes.

"Now, Rachel, we have been through all of this before. We shall need all the money we can get our hands on, so I can treat you as the queen you are."

"I do not care!" she pouted, her bottom lip trembling slightly.

"I do!" Marco replied in an angry voice, setting Rachel from his arms. "Now, tell me what has been happening, since last I have seen you?"

Rachel, her face flushed from her hurried ride and her eyes showing the hurt she felt from his harsh words, spoke in a strained voice. "There really is not too much to tell. The bitch had her brat last night and I do not think I can bear much more."

"So, little blue eyes had her whelp, did she?" he asked with a faraway look in his eyes.

His mind was going back to the day he had promised Katherine aboard his pirate ship, that he would make her his. Yes, soon now, he told himself, he would have that blue-eyed vixen, who had haunted his dreams for these past months, in his power.

"And what did the arrogant Bradly Deveraux sire?"

"A boy, a little red-faced, wretched monster, that will scream the walls down at Moon Rise."

"Now, my flower, don't bare your claws; it does not suit you." He spoke kindly, taking Rachel back into his arms and guiding her to the ground.

"It will not be long now. We but have to wait for the right minute and we shall be leaving Richmond for good."

Rachel did not know the meaning of his words, or what he meant by waiting for the right minute. All she knew was that she loved this man with every fiber of her being and that he loved and wanted her also. Why else was he holding her in this manner and why would he risk his life coming to meet her, if it were not for love?

But as Marco hoisted her riding outfit up about her hips and proceeded to take her in a cruel, brutal manner, his thoughts were not of Rachel. With each thrust he made into her body, his mind went over and over another woman, who had the bluest eyes and the softest features he had ever seen in his life. He swore in his mind that soon he would have Lady Katherine Deveraux lying in his arms. Then perhaps he would be able to put his mind on something else and not be plagued night and day by visions of that beautiful, blue-eyed temptress.

The warm spring days swept by in a radiance of color and peacefulness. And for Katherine this was just the beginning of her life.

Her son, Charles William, was growing healthy and happy and promised to be as strong and hearty as his father. It was still a wonder to her at times—when she would sit and watch her small child discover something new and chuckle—how she could have produced something so perfect. Her whole life now seemed to have a special meaning. It had been two months since she had had her son, and Bradly, since the time of his birth, had treated Katherine with a new and special tenderness.

He constantly was at hand and offered her any service of which she might be in need. And now, with a masquerade ball going to be held at Moon Rise in only two more days, Katherine found herself often seeking Bradly out for his help and advice.

There were so many things to arrange for a ball and this would be the first one Katherine herself would be giving, so she insisted on everything being perfect. Everything inside the house was polished to a brilliant sheen and the outside grounds never had looked as neat and trim as they did at this time.

Everyone throughout Richmond had been invited and Katherine promised herself no one would find any fault with the new mistress of Moon Rise.

Even Rachel seemed to be looking forward to the affair. Katherine had noticed the glint in the other woman's eyes each time the subject of the ball was brought up.

Now, as Katherine sat in the small rose garden, she made a mental note to remind the boys who worked about the yard to carefully cut roses to place inside the house.

Yes, indeed, she sighed to herself, the masquerade party would be a huge affair. Several of their guests would be staying for the weekend and others would have to be put up for the night.

But as the time grew closer for the affair, Katherine found herself growing nervous and apprehensive. She had a feeling of impending catastrophe, but Bradly soothed her fears by saying they were due to her wanting to make a good impression with her first party.

Dear, sweet Bradly, she thought; what would she be without his kindness and love? She could imagine no other man for her husband.

Since their son's birth, Bradly had not yet approached her to reconsummate the marriage bed. But just the thought of their wonderful love-play now sent shivers through Katherine's body and she could feel a fire begin to grow at the depths of her belly.

Oh, he had best do so soon, she thought, or I shall die from the want of him. She never would have believed she could have such strong feelings toward a man, but just the slightest touch from him and her senses would reel; and his kiss would send her mind soaring to gigantic heights. Perhaps tonight, she hoped, she could lure him to her bed. He must know that she was healed from the birth of their son and fine now. Well, if he did not make the first move, she would just have to force the matter upon him and bring them back to the way they had been before the babe.

The rest of the day went by in a flurry of activity. Katherine, with the help of Jezzie, went over the entire house again, to be sure that nothing had gone unnoticed and everything would be ready for the ball.

Katherine wore one of her most seductive gowns to dinner that night, in the hope of bringing Bradly's blood to a boil. And when she made her way to the dining room her hopes were answered.

Rachel was already sitting at the table. Bradly, his back turned from the room, was looking out the front bay windows. He whirled around when he heard her footsteps. His eyes devoured Katherine's face and when they went farther down to fasten on her breasts, Katherine felt her own intake of breath. His eyes felt like twin flames of passion, searing her flesh with their hungry greed.

Finally Bradly's eyes rose and locked with hers, and as if his eyes spoke the words, Katherine felt him say, "Tonight, my love, tonight I shall make you mine once again."

Bradly regained his composure, strode to his wife's side, and took her arm. "You are ravishing tonight, sweet. I hope you know what your beauty does to my simple mind?" he murmured softly, not wishing for Rachel's ears to hear.

"I hoped you would notice, darling, for tonight I had hopes of tempting the beast," Katherine whispered pointedly before she walked saucily over and took her place at the table.

Bradly stood looking after her, the full meaning of her words reaching him.

Jezzie's delicious dinner was eaten hurriedly. There was little conversation but Katherine stole covert glances at her handsome husband; she wished for the time to fly, so they could make their way to their room.

Bradly quietly ate his meal, wondering if he could have read more into his wife's words than she had intended. Could it be, he wondered, that she wanted him as much as he wanted her? God, he had bided his time, waiting for the right time to approach her. Could she be just as anxious as he? Or perhaps he thought she had meant more than she had intended with her short reply. Damn! he thought to himself, if Rachel were not sitting at the table he would come right out and ask the little temptress.

Rachel was the first to rise and excuse herself.

So when they were left alone, Bradly attempted to break the silence. "And how is our son this evening, love? I did not get a chance to go to see him before dinner."

"Little Charles is fine, Bradly. He was sleeping peacefully and Lucy was sitting with him when I came downstairs," Katherine replied, a bit nervously, now that she was alone with him. Her thoughts kept going over his love-making.

"He is getting to be quite a lad," Bradly said, barely realizing he had spoken; his eyes and thoughts were entranced by her beauty.

"I agree. Charles will grow, I am sure, to be a replica of his father," Katherine added, her eyes clouding with the love she felt for this man.

Bradly rose from his chair and went to her side. "And will it be so terrible, my love, if our son is like his father?" He kissed the nape of her neck.

"No, Bradly. I only hope he will be half as kind and good as you." She turned and rose, her eyes holding his.

Bradly lost himself in those deep blue eyes and bent his head to take the soft pink lips which rose to meet his own.

He raised Katherine from her chair and held

her tenderly in his arms, his lips and tongue exploring and tantalizing her mouth, until she leaned against him breathlessly.

Bradly could feel Katherine's slight trembling and could sense the passion he had awakened within her. "Perhaps we should retire to the bedchamber, madam. I would hate for Jezzie or one of the other servants to accidentally come in here and catch us taking stolen kisses here in the dining room."

Katherine could only nod her head and let him lead her by the arm out of the room and up the stairs. Her whole body was aquiver with sensations she had almost forgotten existed.

In the privacy of their bedchamber, Bradly took Katherine once again into his arms. As he took her lips again in a possessive but gentle kiss, Katherine's pulse seemed to burst into a feverish tempo.

Bradly took the pins, one at a time, out of her hair, until it was flowing free and its glossy curls fell about his hands. "Oh, sweet, I have been waiting for this moment for so many weeks now."

Katherine could feel his manhood grow large and hard against her clothing and she could hardly wait to be lying naked against him.

As if reading her mind Bradly spoke softly against her ear. "Let me help you out of this dress, pet. Your body's much too lovely to keep hidden under all these garments."

Katherine turned her back to him, in order

to allow him to unbutton her gown.

Bradly's hands were strong and sturdy as they sought and undid each of the tiny rhinestone buttons. He had to hold himself in check, so as not to let his eagerness overrule his actions; he wanted to tear the clothing off his beautiful wife's body and have an end to his waiting.

As he finally unfastened the last button and Katherine stepped free of the gown, Bradly's breath stuck in his throat. His wife was even more beautiful now after having given birth to his son.

As she walked over to the dressing table the light from the candles made her skin shine with a golden hue. Her black, shining hair cascaded to her waist; it looked as if she were wearing the crown of the night draped upon her. But slivers of moonlight shone through her dark curls. Bradly found himself rendered almost senseless as he stood across the room, passion and desire pouring from his eyes and from every pore of his body.

Yes, he thought, as he tried to clear his mind to fully appreciate the tempting picture that his young wife was presenting to him. Childbearing had not hurt her figure in the slightest; in fact, she was even more beautiful, if that were at all possible. Her breasts were more rounded and fuller, but as firm and high as before; her stomach was as flat as ever, but now there was a more mature and womanly look to her body. As all these thoughts coursed through his mind his body shook with a spasm, caused by his desire for her and his memory of that graceful body lying supple and responsive beneath his own.

He walked up behind her as though he were a panther stalking his prey; his eyes devoured her as his lips bent down and nibbled the sweetness of her satiny shoulder; his senses swirled in the rose-scented perfume which seemed to cling to her hair and body. "Oh, sweet, you are tormenting my very soul. Come, take mercy on this lowly man and let me once again feel the warmth and sweetness of your body's joys."

She turned in a single motion and her body molded perfectly against his. "As you wish, my lord; my only wish is to please you," she whispered softly, rising on her toes, her lips meeting his as her arms wound around his neck.

Their love that night was like no love before or after. Their bodies molded as though they were one. Each touch given by the other was that of fire, burning in its intensity, scorching in its desire to be closer, to reach in and to feel the other's soul. Their kisses, like molten liquid, seemed to devour, to ravish, to draw out all of the secret and hidden love that seemed to be in the depths of their bodies.

Never before had their love been so complete; never had either one of them seemed to feel so much a part of the other.

Katherine knew it with a certainty the

moment Bradly raised above her and gazed deep into her passion-filled face to see if she also were feeling the same fierce and overwhelming feelings as he; she knew then as shudder after shudder coursed over her body, that at this minute if some quirk of fate were to happen and the bowels of the earth were to open and devour them in darkness, neither would notice. Their minds, bodies, and souls were so consumed with each other there was no room for anything that could possibly affect them.

Chapter Ten

The day of the masquerade party arrived. Katherine's nerves were on edge, but her eyes were shining and full of anticipation. The great house and lawns of Moon Rise were immaculate. The servants rushed about humming and singing, grins spread across their faces—grins that no sharp words would or could take away. But not a sharp word had been spoken and with the feel of a party in the air none would.

Even Jezzie, usually stern and demanding with the lower servants, was in a high and carefree mood. There had not been a party in the large house at Moon Rise since before the last mistress, Bradly's mother, had passed on. The thought of the compliments that this evening would be paid her cooking and planning brought a huge grin across the large, black woman's face. But suddenly aware of eyes upon her, she turned.

"What are you a-grinning like a big, dumb possum, you fool of a black man?" Jezzie shot the question out as she looked up from placing several pies in the oven. Her brows furrowed, her eyes glared at the end of the long worktable, where Raymond was casually lounging, his long legs stretched out and a big smile on his dark face, as he sat watching the ample-bodied woman going about her duties.

"Answer me, you hear? Ain't you got nothing better to do than sit about getting underfoot of people who a-got plenty to do?"

Raymond's eyes were shining with merriment as he watched Jezzie getting riled up. "Now, Miss Jezzie, you be knowing I ain't got nothing to be a-doing right this here minute, and as for getting in the way, why I be just a-sitting here out of the way of everyone."

Jezzie gave a loud snort as she stirred pots, boiling upon the large, wood-burning stove.

"Miss Jezzie, ma'am, I don't recollect ever

seeing you in such a fine mood." Raymond spoke sweetly, trying to placate this fiery, black woman.

"Don't you be a-trying any of that sweet talk on me, you old fool." Jezzie's lips started to turn up in a grin, nothing able to darken her good mood. "You just be a-saving that kind of talking and the likes, for someone who be a-wanting to hear its likes."

"Now Jezzie, honey, you be a-knowing there ain't never been another, I be wanting to say sweet words to. You just say the word and after these white folks' party tonight, you and me we can get ourselves together and I be a-telling you all the sweet words I ever did hear."

"Why I ain't never in all my born days heard the likes of your foolish mouth." Jezzie rounded in shock, trying hard to hide the race of her heart and the blush of flattery she felt. That this man would truly wish to romance her! She had never thought that much about Raymond's hanging around, always about and underfoot. The truth of the matter was, and she knew it to be, that she had never thought too much of any man as a possible mate. Her life had always been wrapped up in the masters of Moon Rise and the running of their home, and for her to do her best she had always put her all into it. Now, though, with the mistress helping out in every way she could and taking care of Master Brad, Jezzie realized with a start that she had all the time in the world for romancing and even marrying if'n she felt like it. But still it was hard for her to show these feelings after all this time.

"I ain't got no time for your nonsense now, you old black devil, and if'n you don't get your lazy tail off'n that chair and get out of my kitchen I'm a-going to show you how to be a-moving with this here rolling pin aside your old black head."

Raymond eyed the rolling pin she waved in the air menacingly, and rose to his feet. "Well, I guess I be a-going but if'n you change your mind, just give me a word."

"Well, you just get yourself away from here," Jezzie said, going back to her cooking. Then, as though as an afterthought, she put in as Raymond reached the door, "Maybe I be a-needing a big, strong man like you, to be a-helping with some chores after the party. If you got the time you can stop by and see; it don't make no never mind though to me if'n you do or you don't."

Raymond winked broadly as he opened the door. "I sure be a-stopping by then, Miss Jezzie, and I be a-ready to do any of them chores you be a-needing done."

Jezzie chuckled deeply to herself, when he was gone. "Chores indeed, the old fool." Life sure was picking up here at Moon Rise; it surely was.

Katherine stepped back from the mirror, to admire the costume which, with the help of

Jezzie and Lucy, had taken her over two weeks to make.

She would be Aphrodite, a Greek goddess, for the evening and Bradly would be Adonis, her lifelong love.

Her gown, which was made of white satin, clung seductively to her body. It was held together at one shoulder with a pearl clasp; the other shoulder was bare to the top of her swelling bosom, which strained against the satin material. Her feet were encased in sandals made of leather, and indeed as she surveyed herself she felt something of the luxury the fabled Greek god and goddess must have enjoyed.

Lucy had taken great time and attention with her mistress's hair. She had woven lengths of pearls throughout braids; these created the effect of a crown upon Katherine's head. Indeed her costume was overwhelmingly beautiful in its entirety.

One more quick glance in the mirror, and then Katherine was out of the room and headed to the den, to find Bradly.

She had as yet not seen him in his costume and she had to admit her impatience was prodding her.

At first, she had thought that Bradly, upon seeing the costume he was expected to wear, would refuse. Katherine could still hear his words in her head. "You do jest with me, my beauty?" He had looked at the scant material with a frown on his features. "I do not care to

290

expose all of my body to half of Virginia."

Finally, after an afternoon of pleading and also an afternoon of soaring love-making, Bradly had good-naturedly given in, his last words on the matter being, "If I find that yours is of the same style as mine, I am afraid your guests will be missing their hostess, for I shall without reservations lock you in your room."

Katherine had quickly reassured him about her costume and promised to show him her attire before the first guests arrived.

And now, the moment to fulfill that promise had come. Katherine could not wait for Bradly to see her in her outfit and to watch his eyes come alight. She was sure that her doting husband this evening would not stray too far from her side. Her only real fear was that he might just make her go back upstairs and change into something less revealing than this costume. But this thought she pushed to the back of her mind, knowing that with a little persuasion she could get her way in almost all things when it came to her husband.

Bradly was leaving his study, a goblet of brandy clasped in his hand, when Katherine descended the staircase.

At first he thought his eyes were playing him false or that the light from the candle sconces along the stairway was casting an image that could not possibly be reality. His breath held for a full minute before his brain registered what he truly was seeing before him. This was his wife, his beloved, not an image conjured up from his imagination.

Katherine herself could not conceal her utter pride and astonishment in her husband. Bradly did indeed look like a Greek god, standing there looking up at her. She could see the costume, which she had painstakingly made, fit him to perfection. His, like her own, was of the same material, but only reached to his muscular thighs. The top was robelike, but open from chest to waist so that his dark tan and dark hair made a striking contrast to the snow-white material.

To Katherine's own astonishment she felt small stabs of jealousy shoot through her body. She would have to be the one to watch over her property this night.

"God, you are lovely," Bradly lightly said, reaching up for her hand, his gray eyes never leaving her face.

"I am afraid those were my own thoughts of you, my Adonis. I never imagined you could look so beautiful."

Bradly's laughter lightly fell on her ears. "I'm afraid those are not quite the words for a woman to put on a man, love, but coming from you I am grateful. I am afraid, though, that you are indeed the image of a goddess tonight and that every man here will be fighting for your attentions."

"I myself had in mind the same thought about you as I saw you standing there, so do not forget that you are *my* Adonis this evening and I, Aphrodite, will not share you for one minute with any mere mortal woman."

Bradly smiled. "Never fear, my sweet; no other woman could penetrate this cloud of magic with which you have covered my mind. But right now, my love, I have in mind one last taste of those delicious lips of yours, before our guests start arriving."

Katherine's body molded against her lover's, her lips rose up to offer freely that which he desired. It still amazed Katherine that her body and lips could so willingly overcome her mind, even after all the time she had been married to this man. It seemed as though each time he looked at her, with desire in his eyes, her body would yearn to have him close; and when his lips sought hers, her own would respond with a fierce, possessive will of their own, trying to devour and pull out his very soul, so that she herself would have it in her own keeping.

Bradly released her lips, and almost as though knowing her thoughts, murmured softly, "My love, my sweet, no man alive would think to look at such a genteel and lovely woman as you, that you could be so responsive, so demanding, and so loving. You have made me the happiest man on earth by being mine, and I cannot but feel sorry for the rest of the men roaming the earth for they will never know what good fortune I have found in you."

Katherine's eyes misted over at these tender

words, but before she had time to reply a carriage was heard pulling up at the front of the house.

Carriage after carriage followed to the front door of Moon Rise. The large house was packed with people, and the sound of laughter and friendly talk filled each downstairs room.

The dining room was lined with tables laden with fragrant food. Every kind of meat for which one could wish was set amidst bowl upon bowl of steaming vegetables and there were desserts which made one's stomach growl just to look upon them. Jezzie had decided that they would not serve, but would let the guests, whenever they wished or whenever their stomachs called, go to the dining room and pile their plates with anything they desired.

The large ballroom was crowded to its fullest with brightly costumed guests. The music flowed through the house and couples swept the dance floor or stood drinking and talking freely.

To Katherine everything was going along perfectly. She had danced the first dance with Bradly and as the music came to an end she was swept once again onto the floor by another of their guests. As the evening progressed, Katherine was claimed by gentleman after gentleman, often not knowing her partner until he would speak. Then she would smile softly, but would not let on that his costume had not concealed his identity.

Katherine tried to make it a game, attempting to guess who her partner was without revealing her own identity. To her the game was marvelous, as everything that evening was. Her spirits were soaring, yet already she could not wait for the end to come, so she could be alone with her husband.

After the first dance with Bradly, Katherine hardly saw him again except to glimpse him talking comfortably with a neighbor or dancing with one of their wives. So now, as she cast her eyes about trying to spot her husband, a slow smile crossed her features.

Her eyes had fallen upon Rachel, who had outfitted herself in a Marie Antoinette costume. She actually looked pretty in her pink satin gown, set off by a white, powdered wig piled high atop her head and a beauty patch and half-mask on her face.

Katherine had glimpsed the girl several times dancing on the arm of a tall man who wore a black domino and a half-mask. She thought Rachel looked happier than she had ever seen her since knowing her. A fleeting look of unhappiness crossed Katherine's face as she thought that if only things had been different, she and Rachel could have been friends. But then the distressed look left her. Hadn't she tried to be friends with the girl? It was not her fault that Rachel refused her friendship. Perhaps if she could attend more affairs and visit more often she would change. Tonight she did not in any way look like the old Rachel.

The evening wore on gayly; everyone was having a marvelous time and no mishaps had as yet occurred, for which Katherine was very thankful. She had, for the last weeks, thought of nothing but something going wrong on this evening, but her fears had not as yet proven true.

When Bradly finally found his way back to his wife, he found her drinking champagne with a gentleman dressed in a sultan's costume who turned out to be Clay Johnson. As Bradly approached, Clay graciously turned Katherine over to him and left in search of Jean.

"I'll be damned if I'll ever get used to these kinds of parties, Brad. I have already approached at least three different ladies, thinking them to be Jean. I think half of the Richmond women here tonight must be dressed as Gypsies, and if I'm not careful I'll wind up having to fight one of these fine gentlemen for thinking his wife is my own."

"I hope not, Clay; I would not want anything to interfere with Katherine's party," Bradly answered laughing, as Clay made his way through the crowded room.

"Are you having a good time, sweet?"

"Just a wonderful time, Bradly. I could go on all night like this," she breathed, looking around at all the costumed figures.

"I'm glad you are having a good time, love.

And now, if you will do me the honor, I would at least like one more dance with the most beautiful woman in the room."

"I would be deeply honored to comply with your wishes, sir." She gave him a small curtsy and then laughed softly as he took her in his arms. "I love you with all my heart, Bradly."

They danced this dance quietly, neither speaking; their eyes held and locked, speaking of their love; their hands tenderly touching, showed the strength and foreverness of their union. They were bonded together this evening more closely than ever before.

As the music drew to an ending another man made an approach toward Katherine, and she with all her might willed him to be gone. She did not wish to be taken from Bradly's arms; she did not want to be held there on the dance floor by any other.

But Bradly, not knowing her mood, gallantly gave his wife up for the next dance and placed her in the hands of the other gentleman, who wore a black domino costume and a half-mask.

This man, who was now holding her, glided her across the floor as though she were as light as a feather and they were dancing upon a cloud.

Katherine searchingly looked at her new partner, trying to seek out his identity. He was attired in a black domino, the hood pulled down closely about his face. The only part of his face which could be seen was his mouth and chin. Of a sudden it came to Katherine; this must be the same gentleman who earlier had been dancing and flirting with Rachel.

As the dance progressed the gentleman's mood seemed to change. His arms seemed to hold Katherine much too closely and when Katherine felt his one hand lightly caress the small of her back, she tried to pull away.

"Sir, I am afraid I must beg you to release me at once. I do not take kindly to being mauled upon the dance floor."

The man holding her did not seem to be aware of her plea, for still he held her in his uncomfortable embrace.

Katherine tried to keep her temper under control and once more started in a quiet voice, to ask for her release, but as she looked up into his face his lips drew back into a sly, crooked smile.

"Uh, little blue eyes has a temper to match her beauty. Do not be so reluctant."

Katherine's eyes bore more intently upon his face. Where had she heard that voice before? She felt shivers of cold fear seep into every portion of her body. "Sir?" she finally got out, wishing to hear his voice again and perhaps to find out his identity. Then another part of her warned her to run, to escape from this man who could put such fear into her by merely saying those few words.

Before she could hear his voice again the music came to a stop and he left her side, losing himself in the mass of couples throughout the room.

Katherine stood frozen there on the dance floor, her hands trembling and her mind racing in a whirlwind, as she tried to sort out the reason for the sudden and overpowering fear which had overtaken her.

Those words he had spoken; that was it: little blue eyes. Who had said those same words before? Who had looked down at her with those same piercing black eyes before? Who could this man be? she racked her brain.

"I must get out of here and find a place where I can collect my wits," she mumbled aloud to herself.

On wobbly legs, she made her way out of the ballroom and started up the stairs, to seek out the privacy of her bedchamber.

"Where are you off to, love?" Bradly asked softly as he came out of his study, where he had been leisurely talking with a group of men.

"I-I thought to go up and check in on little Charles, Bradly," she murmured, clutching her trembling hands together in order to steady them.

"Is anything amiss, Katherine? Do you not feel well?" he questioned her with concern, having taken in her shaky composure.

"I am fine, Bradly. I do feel a small headache, but it will be well after I reach our chambers and rest for a few minutes." She smiled, not wishing him to know the real reason for her distress. It could well be that

with all the excitement of the ball her mind
had been carried away and she was unduly
worried over nothing. That must be it, she
reasoned with herself. Everyone here tonight
was a guest and she—or at least Bradly—knew
them all.

"Would you like me to come up with you
for a time?" Bradly asked, pulling her from
her thoughts.

"Nay, my love, we mustn't both leave our
guests. I will be fine; I shall see to Charles and
then lie down for a few minutes to clear my
head. I shan't be gone long." She lightly
placed a kiss upon his chin. "Do not look so
concerned; I shall be gone such a short time
you will hardly notice."

"Any time I am not with you I notice, but I
shall do as you request and entertain our
guests until your return."

"Thank you, Bradly." She sighed, again
starting up the stairs.

Bradly stood watching his wife's retreating
back, a worried frown upon his features.
Perhaps the party was proving too much for
her. If she was not downstairs again shortly he
would go to their chambers and see if he could
be of any assistance to her. What were mere
guests where his wife was concerned?

As Katherine entered her chambers, Lucy
trailed in behind her carrying little Charles.

"I was a-going to come down to fetch you,
ma'am. Little Master Charles has been a-

fretting for his meal for the longest time now. I do reckon all this noise be a-botherin' him," the black girl said, bouncing the bundle in her arms, in order to quiet him.

"Here, Lucy, let me take him for a while and put an end to his great hunger." Katherine took her son and tenderly placed him in the crook of her arm.

"I do swear he grows more like his father every day." Katherine smiled, softly caressing his dark curls.

"Yes, ma'am, he sure is his papa's image," Lucy replied, leaving her charge to the care of his mother, as she silently went into the nursery, adjoining the master chamber.

Katherine sat upon the bed and unclasped the pin holding the strap to her gown, so as to free her breast in order to feed her babe.

She had calmed some, now that she was in her room and holding her child. Whatever could have come over me? she scolded herself. She could almost look back and laugh at herself for acting like such a frightened ninny.

The babe had quieted and lay nursing at her breast and now Katherine actually felt embarrassment over the way she had reacted to one of her guests, who had probably only had a bit too much to drink and had thought to make her one of his conquests.

It was only a short time later that Charles with his belly full fell peacefully to sleep, and Katherine on hearing the door being gently pushed open did not look up, thinking it to be

Lucy, coming to take the babe back to his own bed. But as she heard a sharp intake of breath and a low moan coming from a man's throat, her eyes raised from her son's face.

There was but one small tallow candle to light the room and at first Katherine could not make out the dark form, standing with his back against the door.

"What is the meaning of this? You must have wandered up to this room by mistake." She gasped, as she clutched Charles tightly to her bosom, realizing that the intruder was the man in the black domino.

"Nay, whatever else, this is no mistake, my fair lady. I promised one day that I would have you, and now I have come to make that promise good." The man before her spoke, but the whole while those piercing, black orbs seared her breasts.

Of a sudden and as if lightning had struck her, Katherine knew who her tormentor was. He was none other than the one who had tormented her dreams upon occasion—the one man in all the world whom she feared the most, Marco Radford, the despised pirate . . . who killed and destroyed without showing mercy to his victims. "You, what do you want here? If Bradly should catch you here he will kill you," she got out.

"Do not fear on my account, my little blue eyes, he shall not find us here." His gaze still greedily feasted upon her.

"Get out of my chambers!" she shouted,

seeing where his eyes were resting, and started pulling her gown up to fasten the arm strap.

Lucy, who had been about to go to retrieve Charles from her mistress, heard the noise from the other room and entered, thinking to be of help to her mistress.

At the same time the master bedchamber door opened and Rachel entered the room.

Lucy stood wide-eyed staring at the man in the long, black robe, standing over her mistress. "Miss Katherine," she ventured. "Is something wrong?" She swallowed.

Katherine looked to the black girl as if she were her salvation. "Lucy, quickly, run and get Bradly."

"Hold!" Rachel shouted, as the black girl started to the door.

Katherine looked in Rachel's direction in some surprise. "Rachel, what are you saying? Do you know who this man is?" As Katherine said these words she realized with a start that the other girl was no longer dressed in her costume, but had changed into a dark, somber dress; and a dark cloak was draped upon her shoulders.

"Of course, I know who he is, you stupid little fool. I told you that one day I would get my revenge for the way I have been treated by you and now it is going to be your turn. We shall see how you feel having to beg and to plead."

Katherine could not believe the hatred and fury that shone in Rachel's eyes; could the girl have gone crazy or mad?

"Cease your bickering," Marco leashed out. "We have not the time now for your fighting." He directed his words in Rachel's direction. "Now, my flower, get yourself up and ready, for you are coming with me."

"You have to be insane to think that I will willingly go with you," Katherine shouted, looking at the pair in front of her and clutching Charles tighter to her breasts.

"Insane? Nay, my lovely, we are far from that and I assure you I do intend to take you along," he grated, stepping to her and reaching to take hold of her child.

"If you dare to lay one finger upon my child, I shall kill you," Katherine spat with venom, moving Charles out of his reach. "I shall shout these walls down until every man downstairs makes his way up to this chamber, if you try to lay hold of my son."

Marco looked into her angry face, her eyes shooting daggers of anger at him. For a moment he was reminded of an angry lioness protecting her cub and he knew that to take the child from her arms would be no easy task. "Very well, bring the child along then if you must. But I warn you now, if you so much as try to call out for help, I shall cut the brat's throat." He pulled back his robe, revealing two large pistols and a long sharp-edged knife, secured at the top of his trousers.

Katherine had no doubt that he would do so and though she could not bear the thought of being separated from her infant she knew she could not endanger his life by taking him with her. "No, I shall leave the babe here with Lucy," she said at last, laying him down on the soft bed.

"I said bring the brat; he may come in handy. Bradly will think more cautiously about following us and I think the pair of you should bring a much higher ransom."

Rachel looked in horror. "You cannot mean to take that squalling monster with us? He will only hinder us, dear one."

"I said he shall come along, and his maid also. Now let us hear no more about it. I am ready to be gone; we have already spent too much time with this ceaseless prattle."

Rachel did not argue further. Though she thought taking the child a mistake, she held her tongue, not wishing for Marco to unleash his anger on her.

The group made their way quietly down the back servants' stairs and into the dark night, where a carriage awaited them.

Katherine held her son, still sleeping, in her arms. And Lucy walked beside her on wobbly legs, her large brown eyes circles of fright. Rachel was in the lead and Marco brought up the rear of the small group.

Just as they were in reach of the carriage, a voice brought them to a halt. "What for you all back here? Ain't no one suppose to be a-parking their carriage here in the back yard. Is that you I be a-seeing, Lucy girl? Where at the missus be?" It was Raymond, straining his eyes in the dark to see what was going on.

As he advanced closer, Marco drew his pistol from his belt. Katherine smothered a cry with her hand, as Raymond came closer still and Marco jumped and hit him full blast with the butt of the gun.

"Get into the carriage," Marco snarled, as Raymond fell to the ground in a heap.

Two rough-looking men were atop the carriage, their capes billowing behind them as they shouted and cursed, whipping the team of horses to a reckless speed in order to arrive at their destination in a short time.

Inside the carriage, little Charles awoke with a whimper, not being used to the lurching of the carriage.

"Shut that brat up, before I do it for you!" Marco sneered, watching through the window to the rear of the carriage to see if anyone followed them.

Katherine, frightened that this madman would do harm to her child, comforted him gently at her breast and soon he fell gratefully back to sleep.

The ride wore on through the night, ever at a fast pace, with occasional sounds of cursing and shouting from the drivers above.

Rachel sat within quietly beside her lover. At last her dreaming would be at an end and she would have the man she loved at her side and be the mistress of her own future.

Marco's mind's wanderings were far from

what Rachel would have expected, as he sat in the darkness of the carriage, intently watching Katherine's fine beauty.

His mind was already made up about the child she held clasped in her arms. He would let her keep him for a time and then would let the fine Bradly Deveraux have the brat back for a tidy sum of money. After he got Katherine back to his own home there would not be any chance for her to escape or for her spouse to rescue her. Aye, he thought, his plans would indeed work out better with the babe with them. He could use the child as a threat to Katherine and then when they reached his home he would send the Negro girl along with the child back to Bradly, thereby keeping the lovely Katherine at his side and also gaining a tidy sum to boot.

Never once did his thoughts touch on Rachel. She was beyond his thoughts now that Katherine was before him.

Katherine could barely believe what had been happening to her for the past few hours. Never once did she doubt that Bradly would soon be following them and save her and her child, but she knew she would have to keep Charles quiet until that time because Marco left no doubt as to his means of silencing her child. To do this deed, she knew for a certainty, he also would kill her, for there would never be any other way for him to get to her babe.

More upsetting to her than any other of the

events of this evening was the revelation of Rachel's betrayal of the people who had taken her in and cared for her. There was no doubt that the girl was indeed in love with the pirate, but that she was a part of this cruel trick of abduction rankled sourly with Katherine.

It was almost daybreak when the carriage was brought to an abrupt halt amidst a group of trees that lay next to a strip of water, which led out to the sea.

The carriage was quickly emptied of its passengers and Katherine and Lucy were shoved into a small boat which had been awaiting their arrival.

The same two men, who had been driving the carriage, silently and with sure strokes began to row the lesser boat out into the sea and toward the large pirate ship which had been lying in wait for its captain's return.

For the first time since leaving the carriage, Marco spoke to Katherine. "Aye, little blue eyes, it is the same ship that you were on before and it will be your new home for a time again. I hope, though, that you will enjoy yourself a little more this time. I'm afraid the last time I was not expecting you, but this time, my flower, I had the foresight to have your cabin done over."

Rachel felt the hair on her neck rise and her temper flared at his words. "Must you talk so sweetly to the bitch, my love? Is it not better now to show her that she is no more than a prisoner and will be treated as such?"

"Shut your mouth, bitch. I shall talk how I please and not have any simpering slut telling me otherwise," Marco hissed and his eyes bore upon Rachel as though she were nothing more than a common whore.

"Why do you talk to me in such a manner as this? Have I not shown you how much I love you? Why do you dishonor my love by looking so at her and talking as though she in fact were your love and not I?" Rachel whimpered, her eyes filling with tears.

"I find your mouth too much to bear, woman! Shut it now, before I am moved to slap it shut for you," he shouted at her, raising his hand, as if to get the job done with.

Rachel sat back, hanging her tear-stained face. How could he be so cruel to her after all she had given him? It had to be that bitch Katherine's fault. She must have bewitched him, and the sooner they were rid of her and her brat the better off they would all be, she thought.

Bradly remained for a time in his study, but his thoughts kept going back to his wife. She had seemed unduly upset and this thought kept preying on his mind.

Soon he left the men in his study in order to circulate among his guests, his mind ever watchful for her descent back down the stairs.

A good hour had passed before Bradly

finally started to make his way to his chambers and to find out the reason for Katherine's delay.

Upon opening his chamber door, he knew at first glance that the room was empty so he went to find Katherine in the adjoining nursery room. But as he reached for the door a sudden pang of fear turned his stomach. "Katherine," he called softly, entering the room.

Within, the room was as quiet as the last; a small candle was lit, showing the room in emptiness.

"Katherine, Lucy," he called more loudly and stepped to the cradle, to find that it, too, was bare.

Fear, for no apparent reason gripped his heart as he whirled about. "Katherine," he shouted, this time his head filling with irrational fears.

Where were she and Lucy and Charles? What matter of madness was being played, that they were not to be found here in their chambers?

He began shouting earnestly now, running through the chambers and out into the hall.

He ran down the stairs, his thoughts taking flight. Jezzie, she would know his wife's whereabouts; but as he reached the bottom steps, a panting and distraught Jezzie met him head on.

"They done took her, Master Brad, they done gone and took our missus and our young'un right from us," she cried, her eyes pouring tears down her large black face.

"What?" Bradly shouted, feeling his body going numb. "What are you talking about Jezzie; who took my wife?" He almost screamed the last word.

"They done come and took Miss Katherine and little Master Charles and they took that Lucy girl, too, Master Brad. You gots to go and get them back, Master Brad; you just gots to," she wailed like a banshee.

"Who, Jezzie, who took them?" He grabbed her by her massive shoulders and shook her until she thought her neck would snap.

"I dunno, Master Brad; they come and took them and then they go and hit old Raymond atop the head when he be trying to help the missus."

"Raymond? Where is he, Jezzie?"

"He be in the kitchen, Master Brad, resting his poor cut head; they done lay him open good."

Bradly did not wait to hear more, but pushed his way through the mass of people who had congregated at the foot of the stairs to listen to the old black woman's rantings with disbelief on their faces.

When Bradly burst through the door like a mad bull, Raymond was sitting at the kitchen table holding a wet cloth to the side of his head.

"Raymond, where are my wife and son? What happened to them?" he bellowed, a

311

snarl pulling back his lips, his hands rolled into fists.

"I tried, Master Brad; I done tried to save the missus, but that there man he comes out of the dark and hits me a bad lick, right on the side of the head and knocks me right out." The old black man whimpered, rocking his body back and forth in the chair.

"Who took them, Raymond? Did you see who it was?"

"I dunno, Master Brad. I was just a-sitting out in the back by the steps when I sees them a-coming down the back stairs. Miss Rachel, she be with them too, but she be a-talking to the man as if'n they be friends. She even called him by his name. That's about all, Master Brad; that's about all there was to it."

"His name, you say? Think, man, what did Miss Rachel call the man?" Bradly coaxed, knowing that to frighten him would only confuse him more.

"I sure done heard it clear, Master Brad. Miss Rachel, she be calling that man by the name of Marco, but Master Brad I ain't never heard that name before."

Bradly's face turned to ash as the name Marco pounded into his brain. "Marco," he said the name as softly as a deathly caress. "The bastard dares to lay hand to my wife and child. I shall find him," he said with a finality, which left no questioning. "If it takes searching the world over, turning every loose stone upon the earth upside down, I shall find him

312

and cut his very heart out of his black soul."
Bradly spoke as though vowing these words to
himself.

Raymond felt cold chills coursing down his
spine, as he looked into his master's face. He
had indeed seen his master mad before, but
never had he seen him in such a deadly temper
as this. The man standing before him now was
like some stranger with the promise of death
glaring from his eyes. Raymond had a fleeting
regret for the man called Marco, but that
regret was gone in an instant. Any man who
could dare such a thing as to take his master's
wife, deserved death or anything else his
master gave him.

Bradly stomped about the kitchen, shouting
out orders to have his horse saddled and for
Jezzie to go and fetch Clay Johnson to him.

Jezzie hurried from the kitchen to do her
master's bidding. She was only gone a short
few minutes, when she came rushing back
with Clay and Jean fast behind her.

"What is it, Brad; what's going on? Almost
all your guests are out there whispering
something about Katherine's having been
taken off by someone." A worried frown
creasing his forehead as Clay questioned his
friend.

"Aye, Clay, she has been kidnapped—and
my son also. I have not much time to explain,
but, Clay, I would greatly appreciate it if you
could send someone you trust to oversee
things here while I'm gone. I do not know how

313

long I will be away, but it was Marco Radford who did this foul deed and I'll be gone until I find the knave and get my wife and son out of his hands."

On hearing this news, Jean burst into tears. "Oh my God, Katherine and Charles kidnapped. What are you going to do, Bradly?" she sobbed.

"Do? I shall track them down and kill that mangy pirate and then I shall bring my wife and son, God willing, back to Moon Rise." He spoke calmly now, but the silver-gray eyes could not belie the anger that filled his body.

"Of course, Brad, I shall do what needs to be done here, but are you sure that you would not rather I come with you? You may be in need of help."

"No, Clay, this is something I should have done long ago and now I shall see it to its finish. I need your services much more here, seeing to my people and caring for Moon Rise."

"Anything you say, Brad," Clay said, extending his hand which was received in a firm clasp by Bradly.

"Thank you, Clay." Bradly started to the door and out into the night.

As Bradly mounted the large black beast that was saddled and waiting out back, he was filled with an anger so deep, a hatred so vast that he was overcome by a tremendous power to kill. He could envision his hands clutched around Marco's throat, squeezing and squeezing until his opponent's eyes were popping from their sockets and his tongue was turning a dark shade of blue.

Never before in his years had he felt this cold deathly presence inside himself and he knew with a certainty that no matter how long and how far his search would go, in the end he would draw the very life out of the man he now pursued.

Bradly's great stallion felt some of the tension and rage that flowed from his rider's body and man and beast were as one, racing through the dark night.

The moon was high in the sky and Bradly's pace never slowed except now and then to spot the tracks which he followed.

He had no idea how much of a head start Marco had over him, but he knew that he had to be upon them before Marco could reach his ship.

He pulled his thoughts away from the idea of Marco ever reaching the safety of his ship. He would not think of Katherine, defenseless against a band of cutthroat pirates, aboard that ship again.

The night grew long and endless for Bradly, his gray, cold eyes scanned the countryside and his hand lay ever ready on the butt of his pistol; his body and mind were ready and eager to face his adversary.

But it was past dawn and the sun was beginning to rise and melt the morning dew, before Bradly spied a dark carriage sitting quietly in a small group of trees that were near a slight stretch of beach.

He rode straight away in the direction of the carriage, his gun in hand and his heart beating at a tremulous rhythm. But even before he pulled abreast of the silent vehicle he knew it would prove to be empty.

He reined in his horse and dismounted, looking about the area for any traces of his wife and son. But the only sign he could see were tracks leading down to the vast sea, and search as he did over the endless amount of blue-green water the pirate ship was not to be seen.

Bradly's mind was in a rage. He cursed and condemned Marco to every kind of torture that hell had to offer, as he pulled the door to the carriage open.

On first looking into the empty interior his breath caught in his throat. There, lying on the floor, was a soft, white lace handkerchief. He tenderly plucked it up in his large hands and drew it to his lips. At first glance he knew it to belong to his beloved and now as Katherine's fragrant perfume seemed to fill his very soul, tears coursed down his face, flowing from tormented, pain-filled gray eyes. Tears for a love so strong and so fulfilling that life without that love was meaningless and beyond comprehending.

It was impossible, he knew at that moment, to go on without that small white face looking up into his own with adoring eyes; impossible to live without her warm body held tightly against his own, moaning in ecstasy or being protected and cherished and depending upon him with her complete trust.

As visions of Katherine in all her many different ways tormented his soul, he tenderly smoothed the small handkerchief inside his shirt next to his heart. "I shall get you back, my love," he whispered, almost as though he were saying a prayer. Then he turned and faced the sea.

"Revenge!" he shouted to the empty seas. "Hear me well, Marco Radford. I shall get my revenge upon you for this foul act, and I curse you for the rest of your days upon this earth. You shall not know a moment's peace, for I shall hunt you down until I have not a breath of life left in my body and then if need be I shall follow you into the very pits of hell; but I swear to you here and now that I shall have my revenge upon you." He stood shouting at the sea, his fists raised and his slate-gray eyes holding a promise of doom.

Chapter Eleven

The weather held fair and the winds blew softly out over the blue seas, bringing joy and hope to the crews who manned the many vessels that roamed the seas. Foremost in the thoughts of all these men was the hope that fair weather would prevail until they reached their home ports.

But for one woman at sea there was no joy

in the weather or much of anything else. There was only hope, anguish, and fear. Katherine had been aboard the pirate ship now for over two weeks. The time had gone slowly, almost at a crawl.

She paced the floor of her cabin and tended her son; then, nothing else to do, she paced again, going over and over the course of events which had shattered her life.

The only other person, besides Lucy and Charles, whom she had seen in the course of her imprisonment, had been the young cabin boy who brought their meals and daily brought water for them to wash.

She had not seen Marco—or Rachel for that matter—since they had been brought aboard ship that horrible morning.

Katherine once more went over that morning in her mind, as she gave her breast to her son to nurse.

When finally the small boat had pulled aside the larger pirate ship and they had boarded, her last glimpse of Rachel had only revealed the girl's hatred for her and it had also seemed to Katherine that she also had seen a look of triumph in Rachel's eyes.

Almost as soon as their feet had touched the deck of the ship, Marco had given the order to hoist the sails and then he had gone to Rachel and whispered in her ear. That was the last Katherine had seen of her; for after turning and looking in Katherine's direction for a matter of seconds, Rachel had turned and disappeared down a passageway, leading to where, Katherine had no idea.

After Rachel was out of sight Marco had turned to Katherine. "Now, my fine flower, let me show you to your cabin." He took a firm grip on her arm.

Katherine surged away from that hateful grip upon her person. Earlier her only thought had been of her son, but now the whole scene of what stood before her made her want to fight and scream her fury at this madman who had dared to take her and her son from their home. "I can walk to my prison without you putting your filthy hands upon me," she ground between clenched teeth.

Marco looked at her as though her words had cut him deeply. "Nay, my flower, I insist. You had better start getting used to my hands upon you, for from this day forth you are mine and no other shall ever have the right except myself to hold you." His words were a deep, husky promise which sent cold shivers coursing over Katherine's body.

Once again his hand took hold of Katherine's arm, as he led her grudgingly to her cabin. Lucy, fear written on her dark face, followed close behind carrying Charles, who had been fitfully sleeping.

Marco led his captives to the same cabin that Katherine had shared before with Rachel, but as he opened the door, Katherine froze stiff, as she viewed the interior.

She looked about her, not believing this to

be the same room which she and Rachel had shared a year ago. There was a thick white Persian carpet on the floor and yards and yards of white satin cloth hung from the walls; the middle of the room held a massive bed and scattered about were statues and ceramic figurines that could have at one time been residing in a sultan's castle.

"Your royal barge, my lady." Marco made a deep bow. "I hope you find everything to your liking. Every feature was placed here with you in mind."

Katherine ignored his words, her chin rising a notch higher in the air. "You are a cad if you think for one moment I shall enjoy a fancy prison more than the filthy one I occupied before. You, sir, are very much mistaken. I despise the very sight of you and your evil ship," she sneered into Marco's face.

"You will learn, my little wildcat, and you will also submit. I think I shall enjoy every moment of breaking you to my will, for I swear to you that you will bend to my every whim." He said this menacingly, his dark, piercing eyes watching her face for the reaction he was sure would come.

Katherine glared back at him, looking into his eyes with her own cold stare. "You tame me? Never, do you hear? For never shall you tame my spirit and, yes, my hatred also. Bradly will search you down and one day soon he will kill you for the filthy bastard you are."

"And why would he wish to track me down,

madam?" he demanded, his lips drawing back into a sneer. He had not expected these heated words of hate from her. He had hoped to see fear written on her face and perhaps to see her beg for mercy. "Let me tell you something, my pretty, in the first place Bradly has no idea of your whereabouts, and in the second, do you think that a proud man such as Bradly Deveraux, who has been forced into a marriage, would not gladly await its ending? I know Bradly, and he has no concern for anyone but himself and his fancy plantation. But if by chance," he added in a low growl, "if he should be stupid enough to chase the seas over for you and the boy, I shall be awaiting his coming with cutlass in hand and I assure you I shall be done with him as I should have a few years ago."

Katherine's voice could not conceal the sarcasm as she replied, "Have a care, sir; if I were in your place I would not be too overconfident of the outcome of your meeting with my husband for I vow to you and every other person aboard your scurvy ship that Bradly will come for me and his son."

Marco stood admiring her fine anger and had to squelch the thought of taking her this moment to show her how easily he could shatter her fierce pride. "Then, my pretty, we shall see in due time the outcome of this folly and whoever will be the victor will be able to enjoy the spoils." He gloated and caressed her with his eyes as if he were already the victor.

Katherine felt a cold fear grip the pit of her stomach. What if Bradly were to find them and be killed by this terrible pirate? She knew with a certainty, if Marco could help it, it would not be a fair fight. What then would happen to her and her son?

"I'm sorry I cannot spare more time now, little blue eyes. I must go topside and see to my ship," he said strolling toward the door. "Perhaps soon we shall see things to their ending."

Katherine did not wish to beg or grovel at this horrid man's feet, but she had to persuade him to release them. For her son's sake, she felt she had to make a try. "I shall ask of you one more time to release us and go on your way with Rachel, if that is what she wishes."

Marco turned about at her words and softly chuckled. "Do you think I would let you out of my hands now? After these many months of nothing else on my mind except your fair beauty?"

"But what of Rachel? She loves you and would gladly go anywhere you want."

"She is nothing compared to you." He walked over and lightly caressed a tendril of hair which had escaped her coiffure. "She is the type of woman who only wishes to rob a man of his manhood and in return give nothing but her scrawny body and her cease-less bickering."

"But why—why have you used her in such a manner?" gasped Katherine, jerking her hair

323

out of his reach.

"To get to you, lovely Katherine; need I explain more?"

"You must be mad!" Katherine stammered, not believing any man, no matter how foul, could be this inhuman to another person.

"I truly am mad, my flower, but only for you."

"Then you are doubly mad, sir, if you think I shall ever willingly let you put your hands upon me."

"Oh, but you shall, little blue eyes, for when we reach our destination you will be treated with all the honor and splendor with which my mistress should be treated. You will live in my home and will also treat me with all the respect that I shall insist upon," he said sternly. "But for now, my flower, I must see about my ship and men." He walked to the door, slammed it shut, and locked it behind him.

Katherine stood stupefied watching his leaving. She must pull herself together. What was she going to do if Bradly did not come soon? Could she possibly give herself to that vile creature? She doubted it; even at the risk of Charles's life, she doubted she could do that desperate act.

Lucy's whimpering brought Katherine from her horrible thoughts. She made her way to the girl and took her son. "Do not weep so, Lucy. Bradly will rescue us any time now."

And now with the passage of time, two

weeks since the day of her abduction, Katherine still did not know what was to become of herself or her infant. Each day seemed to dash to pieces the small hopes which she held in her heart. She never doubted that Bradly would find them and rescue them, but now the fear that he would arrive too late filled her with constant dread.

She had no idea where they were headed. Marco had talked of his home, but he had not spoken the name of the place where that home was. If she knew where they were going perhaps she could start planning some sort of escape for them all. Without knowing there was little sense in making any kind of plan. She had hoped, at first, when Marco had not visited her cabin, that perhaps he had had a change of heart and would settle for a woman who was in love with him; but as soon as this hope rose it fell. Did she not already know what kind of man held her captive? He seemed to feed off people who did not care for him. Did he not say he would enjoy breaking her and bending her to his will? This was the type of man who would never be satisfied with a girl like Rachel who gladly would do his bidding. He was the type who thrived on conquest and would not willingly take that which was offered, preferring to indulge his power to take.

Constantly the hope of Rachel visiting, if only to try to vex her, was close to Katherine's thoughts. Perhaps she could persuade the girl to see what Marco had planned and then the two would be able to make some form of plan. Rachel, most probably, would know of their destination and would have some idea when they would arrive there. But she had not seen the other girl since that first morning and Katherine thought that Marco had probably had the same thoughts as she, and did not allow the girl to come to visit his prisoners.

Most frightening of all Katherine's considerations was the fact that her son's and Lucy's lives depended upon her. At any time, Marco could order some kind of harm to them and she would be powerless to do anything about it. She had no doubt that he would use her son's life as an instrument to bend her to his will and she knew that if her son's life were to be put at stake she would have to comply to every whim of the black-hearted man who held their lives in his hands.

It seemed to Katherine that in the past two weeks not a minute had gone by without her thoughts being full of a black dread. Lucy still grew terrified every time the cabin boy brought in their meals, thinking the opening of the door would bring in either Marco or one of the other pirates, intent on doing her some harm.

Katherine could not count the number of times in the past two weeks in which she had had to go to the black girl, who sat whimpering in a corner, when she would hear footsteps outside of their cabin door. Katherine would go to the girl, almost glad for the diversion and thankful to the Lord that Lucy was here with her. If she had not had to show a brave face for Lucy, Katherine knew that she herself would have been reduced long ago to a trembling mass of tears.

Indeed, the only bright spot in Katherine's life now was her son, who did not notice the fear and sorrow about him. Little Charles's only thought was of his stomach and, occasionally, of playing with his mother or Lucy.

But this small happiness was also her undoing. Each time now that she looked upon her child he seemed to be growing more into the image of his father. His black, raven hair had the same curl and shape as Bradly's and when his light, silver eyes looked into Katherine's with a trust and love that was shattering, Katherine could feel the tears come to her eyes. Each time she looked upon her child she yearned desperately for Bradly to be at her side and to find herself safe and warm at Moon Rise just waking from some terrible nightmare of pirates and death.

The air became stifling; hardly a breath of a breeze could be felt as the men labored, meanwhile glancing constantly at the large, ominous-looking clouds overhead. A storm was brewing and by the looks of it the heavens would open up and unleash their mighty fury at any moment.

Marco stood in the midst of his men,

shouting out orders to secure his ship and hoping with all of his might that the rain would wait until everything was in order. The sky had darkened so quickly they had been taken by surprise and now Marco cursed himself for a fool, for being lulled into the sense of security he had felt for the past few days.

Only a matter of two more days of the fair winds they had been having and they would have reached Grand Terre and been safe in port. He should have known better than to trust the sea. She was as fickle as any woman ever was, and could change from calm, serene depths into a ravaging, deadly opponent.

He held no doubt about any of his men and knew that they each would give his best in any kind of storm to keep the ship from being swallowed by that great lady, the sea. If not, each crewman knew he would in time answer to him.

Marco smiled as he looked about. Aye, his men would rather face the storms at sea any day than to be left defenseless in front of him.

Marco himself loved the changeable sea, as he had never loved any other thing. He had known even as a small boy that one day he would sail in a ship of his own and be the law and master over his own fate. He could remember as a lad sitting in a corner of the small squalid shack that served as a home for him and his mother and listening to every detail of the tales that the men his mother brought home told of the sea. His small dark eyes envisioned himself standing at the rail of a fine ship, the wind and water taking the very breath from his lungs; but all the time his young heart soared with the joy of being free and sailing across the oceans.

By the time he was nine, though, he was not allowed to sit and listen to the stories told by these strange men. The day of his ninth birthday his mother, who from the moment he had started talking had insisted he call her Meg, had told him that it was time for him to start helping out with the making of their meager existence.

She had been a schemer, his mother had been, so now with her son old enough she had thought out a plan to add a few more pounds to her purse.

That first night Marco was as frightened as a newborn kitten, but with the thought of the beating he was sure to get if he did not follow through with Meg's idea, he forced himself to be brave. He had waited outside the small wooden, rat-infested structure that was their home, freezing in the cold for over an hour, until he heard his mother's signal, a loud tinkling laugh. To this day, sometimes late at night he would wake from his sleep thinking he heard the sound of her laughter filling his ears. Marco, small, filthy and frightened had silently entered the front door.

The moon had cast an eerie glow into the room and at first Marco had held his breath and looked fascinated at the couple upon the straw pallet against the wall, on the floor of the one solid room. There, lying on the floor, was Meg, completely nude, her large breasts pumping with every movement of her body and her high-pitched laughter grating off the walls of the room. The man atop her, his skinny long frame seeming to Marco to be trying to beat his mother into the floor, was so involved with his pumping up and down and his increasing groaning that he never noticed the small, ragged figure. Finally, remembering his mother's orders, he moved silently toward the single chair in the room and quickly searched his mother's guest's pockets. So quickly did Marco search the contents of the pockets and leave the small hut, that the couple were still going at each other for a time, which seemed like hours to Marco, while he sat in the shadows in order to conceal himself and await his mother's loud voice.

Once Meg had finished with her partner of the night and he was dressed again, she would become enraged over the fact that he could not seem to find any of his possessions in his pockets.

"You never did intend to pay, you scum; you thought to topple me good and then be on your merry way, did ya?" Marco heard his mother's screams from his hiding place outside.

"I swear I had me possessions about me when I left the pub with ye this night," the man shouted in disbelief, searching frantically through his clothes for his few pounds and his watch.

"Be ya calling Meg Radford a thief, ya scurvy bounder?" she shouted, reaching for a long pipe she had hid under the pallet for just such an emergency.

"I ain't be a-saying that now, but sure I did think I had me things."

"Well, I tell ye this sure, you loafer, ye got yer tumble fer free and that will be all ye be a-getting from me, excepting if ye don't get out of me sight this minute, I'll be a-givin' ya a split head." She threateningly waved the pipe about in the air.

The man quickly left the shack, Marco watching him still searching his pockets as he disappeared from sight. Marco smiled to himself; old Meg sure knew how to get the upper hand where money was concerned and he himself liked the thought of outsmarting a man years older than himself.

Marco's mother was as proud of herself and her son as she was of the coins that they had gained this night and for the next three years this ploy was used as often as possible.

The men whom Meg took up with were mostly a poor lot, either working on the docks or poor men who put out to sea and when on shore spent their money on whiskey and women. So never did the pair of thieves gain too much on these adventures, but it proved enough to buy more whiskey for Meg and to buy a little more food than they'd had previously. At least when Meg was not too drunk and could make her way to the market streets.

But alas one evening Meg's foolproof plan did not work out as usual. Marco had lain in wait until he'd heard Meg's high-pitched laughter; then he crept into the hut, viewing the same scene he had witnessed over a hundred times in the past few years, and silently went over to the chair and started going over the man's clothing. As his fingers came into contact with the coins lying in the bottom of the pants pocket the man's voice boomed across the room.

"What the hell? What's going on here?"

Marco froze stiff, sensing danger with his instincts that were bred out of the fear which lived with him and every other child who was forced to live a life of theft and drudgery.

The large man atop his mother stilled and squinted in Marco's direction. "What be that and what be you doing with my things?" he shouted, raising up off Meg.

Meg, her heart thudding hard, knowing something was amiss, started to pull her lover back atop of her. "They ain't nothing over there; ye be seeing things."

"Nay, I be having eyes in my head, you slut." He smacked her hard across the face. "What kind of game do you think yer a-playing with old Tom Shane, bitch? I know what I be a-seeing."

As soon as Marco heard the man's voice and the slap given to Meg he dropped to the floor the few coins he had held in his grubby hand and ran, fast as a cat, out the front door. Listening to the loud shouts and screams coming from the hut, Marco had hidden next to the building, his heart beating wildly.

"Get ye'self out of me home," he heard Meg shout.

"You think to steal all of my coins and then threaten me with that little old piece of pipe, do you, you old hussy? I'll teach you a lesson you won't soon be a-forgetting."

Then the dark night echoed with Meg's screams, while the large man in the cabin, without letup, smashed his large fists into her puffy white body.

Marco silently hid and waited, listening to Meg's pitiful pleas for mercy and her screams of pain, too frightened to try to give her aid. In this section of town no one much cared that another of their kind was being tormented as long as it was someone else.

After a time the hut had become quiet and Marco watched for the large man to take his leave. As soon as he left the cabin, Marco cautiously made his way back into the room. He knew without doubt that Meg would blame the man's beatings on him, and he had no doubt that he would be the next to get clubbed.

Within the shack Meg lay quietly upon the straw pallet, her body's limbs bent in a number of odd directions. Marco at first thought her to be sleeping, but on closer inspection he saw that her swollen and bruised face was lying straight up, her eyes looking hard at the ceiling; and no breath seemed to come from her mouth. He slowly bent over her and called her name, but the only answer was the quietness of death.

Marco, on looking at Meg's form, did not feel any sense of loss, even though he realized that this woman lying in a broken heap was his mother. To be perfectly honest with himself, the only emotion he was feeling was one of relief. Meg's death meant the end of his having to look upon her too soft and puffy body as she plied her trade upon unsuspecting men. And never again would he be the one who received the pipe when he did not please her.

So on that same night, with his mother's body growing cold on the straw pallet, Marco put his few meager belongings into a pack and left their small shack in the hope of finding some way in which to keep himself alive.

The next morning found him roaming the waterfront, looking for something to come his way; he did not have too long to wait. As the dirty, ragged boy ducked between two crates, two rough, foreign-speaking men walked by. Marco could not understand their words, but he did understand the heat and anger that poured from their mouths.

About a minute after he had heard them arguing, there was a low grunt and a thump as though someone had fallen.

Slowly he raised his eyes a bit and looked over the crates. There, lying only a few yards from him, was the body of one of the men and running away and disappearing around a group of buildings was the other man.

Slowly creeping from the shelter of the crates, Marco went over to the fallen man and searched his pockets as deftly as though this were an everyday occurrence.

But Marco's head rose quickly when he heard footsteps behind him, running down the wharf. "Ha, you, what you doing over there?" a voice yelled at him, getting closer with each second that passed.

Quick as a flash of lightning Marco was on his feet and running from the steps pursuing him.

The man behind him was now shouting out an alarm. "Thief, murderer, help thief, murder."

Marco ran and ran, his lungs aching with every step, his mind screaming for him to find a place to hide. Soon he knew that the shouts from the man behind him would bring others in pursuit.

Thanks to Marco's luck, it still was early morning and most of the people who worked and lived near the waterfront were still abed; and thanks to his size and agility, before long he found his way to an old abandoned building and hid his small frame in the dark shadows of its doorway.

With a large sigh Marco heard his assailant's steps running past the doorway in which he had hidden.

His eyes growing accustomed to the dark, Marco sought out a place in which to rest for a while. There, in a dark corner, he found what he sought, laid his frame down on a pile of old rags, and immediately fell asleep.

He awoke hours later, hungry and not knowing which way to turn next. Cautiously he left the building. It was dark now and he realized that he had slept the day through.

On cautious feet the young, ragged street waif made his way back to where he had been that morning when he had hidden between the two crates.

The waterfront now was alive with excitement: men and women laughing and fighting, drunkenly stumbling along the sidewalks, going to some isolated place to cool their lust-filled passions or heading to a pub to quench their thirsts. As a woman in a faded, torn, violet dress, drunkenly staggered by, Marco, for the first time since leaving the hovel he had known as home, thought of his mother.

But Meg's face vanished quickly from his mind as his eyes constantly moved about the streets. While he had lain sleeping on that pile of filthy rags, he had dreamed of being on a great, sleek ship. He could feel the motion as it rolled with each toss of the sea.

So he walked the streets listening to the

drunken talk of the sailors, roaming about. It wasn't long before he heard the name of a ship called the *Golden Eagle*, which would be leaving England and heading for the China coast at dawn. As sly and crafty as a fox he found the ship and stowed away, hiding himself below decks, under a large pile of canvas.

It was almost a week before he was found early one morning, as he ventured out from his hiding place in order to find some food. Immediately he had been turned over to Captain Bently, a short, angular man, who constantly wore a frown and snapped out orders with a barking, sharp voice.

Marco had not let himself be intimidated by the dour man and easily answered the captain's questions.

The ship's captain had been furious to find a stowaway aboard his ship and especially one as filthy and unkempt as the boy who stood before him acting as proud and as noble as if he were some kind of lord. He ranted at Marco as if he were possessed and cursed and swore that at the next port he would have him put off his ship. Then he told the boy, with an evil smile on his face, that he would regret the mistake of boarding this ship, for he would have to work and work hard, from morning to night to pay for his passage.

Work on board the *Golden Eagle* was just as the captain had warned. Marco was awakened by the cook before dawn and set to swabbing decks, scrubbing pots and pans, and cleaning the captain's cabin. Every foul job which came along the cook pushed toward Marco and if it was not done quickly and as efficiently as ordered he would be cuffed on the head or flogged with a large rolling pin that the cook kept hanging from a short string.

Marco took all of the abuse handed him in his stride. Life had never been easy for him and this was no different from the beatings Meg had inflicted upon him. He knew he would be treated the same at any other job that he would have been able to find in England—if he could have found a job. But here on the ocean, lying on the deck of the ship at night and looking up at the stars and feeling at one with the great motion of the ship, he knew that this was the type of life he had always wanted to live. This was a start to the fulfillment of his long-ago dreams.

Life for Marco Radford held many different kinds of twists which fate deigned to offer. It was fate that before Captain Bently's ship ever came near the China coast it was attacked by pirates and at this point his fortune changed in Marco's favor. The pirates themselves treated him no better than Captain Bently or his men, but from the moment he had seen the pirate ship giving pursuit to the *Golden Eagle*, Marco knew that come what may he for one would survive.

Survive he did, by hiding under the canvas below deck. Then after the pirates had boarded the *Golden Eagle* and killed and maimed her crew, Marco had silently gone above deck and stood in front of the pirate captain. "I am Marco Radford and I wish to join you and your men." He spoke loudly, pulling himself up to his full measure of height.

The bearded, one-eyed man before him looked at this boy in wonder. "What's that you say, boy?" His laughter flowed over the ship and out over the sea. "Where the hell did you come from, mite? And ain't you got the nerve for being me captive?"

Marco's features never wavered; he looked this man in the eye as the crew's laughter filled his ears. "I ask for nothing more than to become one of you," he said, holding his anger.

The pirate captain's yellowed, rotten teeth showed large in his face. "If'n you ain't got the nerve, you scamp, but I'll tell ye true, lad, this life of a pirate is a harder one than you could ever imagine and if'n you're really wanting to become one of us, you had better do everything you're told, boy. If'n that's what you be a-wanting, you get yourself started right now by going down and getting me and my men some grub."

Marco had hoped for a more romantic job, but if this was what he had to do to survive, he would do it. That same day Marco made a vow that one day he would be master of his own ship and would live his own way by laws that he would make and all would obey.

So now as the torrents of rain lashed down upon Marco and his vessel, the *Black Hawk*, he knew again the power in his hands as the captain of his ship. He had survived being a small ragamuffin, a frightened child, who stood up to a rough pirate captain, and he had become himself one of the most feared and hated men upon the seas.

Winds as crushing as a battering ram hammered at the *Black Hawk*. The ship rolled and shuddered under the force of the storm, valiantly holding its head up, above the sea which greedily strove to bring its prey into its bowels.

The mighty storm lasted for two days but finally it had diminished to a light drizzle and occasional gusts of wind.

Damage was minimal to the *Black Hawk*. Only one sail was badly torn. If they had had to be out at sea for a longer length of time, the *Black Hawk* might have suffered losses of life, for the sea water had covered the ship and gone into the galley, spoiling most of the rations stored there. But as it was, Marco hoped to be reaching home port in one day's time, so his spirits and those of his crew were high and a bit joyous.

Pulling the covers up tighter under Lucy's chin, Katherine finally sat back and rested against the back of a chair.

With Charles and Lucy sleeping, she at last had a few minutes to herself, for the first time since the storm had started.

Due to the shattering force of the rain and wind, Lucy had been taken with seasickness and, until now Katherine had about given up hope of the storm ever ceasing and the black girl ever resting. Charles had not minded the motion of the ship; in fact he seemed rather to enjoy being jostled about.

Katherine herself had had no thought during the storm other than how close they were to death. She knew it as she held her child clasped tightly in her arms and tried to walk steadily, as she was thrown about the cabin, or as she tried to go back and forth to tend to Lucy—to bring a bucket for her to relieve her stomach or to wipe her forehead with a wet cloth when the girl mumbled and groaned in her delirium. Katherine had felt with a certainty that they would all be killed and become sunken prisoners of the sea.

She seemed to have aged years in the past few weeks and a part of her wanted nothing more than to give up. Just give up; lie down and sleep and perhaps never wake again. The stronger part of herself fought against such weakness. She had her child to think of and Bradly's face was constantly in her mind. "Oh, Bradly," she breathed aloud. Hurry, my love. I do not know how much longer I can last, she silently prayed and then burst into racking, tormenting, soul-shattering sobs.

"Land ho, straight ahead, Captain," came the shout from above. And there in the distance a bright, green patch of earth rose from the depths of the dark-blue ocean.

Katherine also had heard the shout and rushed to the porthole, but, strain her eyes as she did, she was not able to see anything more than the sea. As she looked out over the water she glimpsed something in the air. At first it appeared to be a small dot, but soon she was able to make out the features of a sea gull. She clutched her throat as she watched the bird swoop down low to the sea.

A sea gull meant land and perhaps a chance to get off this accursed ship and to find someone to help her. Perhaps the storm had blown them off their course and they would be putting into a port where she would be able to obtain help.

Directly, the cabin door was jerked open. Lucy, who felt much better now with the calmer weather, sat clutching Charles to her bosom but her eyes went to the door as Marco Radford entered.

Katherine spun about at the opening of the door and with her first glance at her captor, her hopes of finding help at a strange port came to an end. "What—what is happening?" she stammered, clutching the folds of her gown.

"Why, madam, we are arriving at your new home, Grand Terre. We are in sight of her now and in a matter of a few short hours you will be on dry land once again."

"Home. Grand Terre!" she gasped. Where

on earth had she heard that name? she asked herself.

"Yes, my little wildcat, Grand Terre, the most famous pirate stronghold there ever was. And you, my flower, will be the envy of every man there. Even Jean Lafitte himself will turn green when he sets his eyes upon your lovely face. But do not be frightened, my flower, for no man on this island will dare to touch what is mine, unless I bid them to."

"You cannot think to force me to live here?" she asked incredulously. Of course she had heard of this notorious island and the cutthroat Lafitte, and at the memory of the horrid stories she had heard, she felt her body begin to tremble.

"You are mistaken, little blue eyes, for I *can* keep you here. You will have a large, beautiful house and everything you wish."

"Except my freedom," she murmured.

"Aye, you are mine now and shall ever more be," came her answer. "Now come along, Katherine. I would like you to view our arrival." He took hold of her arm.

"My son," she gasped, breaking loose his hold and running to her child and Lucy.

Marco followed and grabbed her by the shoulders. "Your son will be carried by the black girl, when I order it. You will not be so hindered as you walk by my side, as my lady."

Katherine started to protest, pushing at his hands.

"If you do not abide by my wishes,

343

Katherine, I shall fix it here and now so you have no son to concern yourself about. I hope you take my meaning and will do as you are told, madam."

Katherine took his meaning all too well and slowly nodded her head.

As they left the cabin she looked about for Rachel, but her searching was futile. The girl was nowhere to be seen. "Where is Rachel?" she ventured to ask.

"Do not worry yourself on her account; she is of no concern to us," he replied, dismissing the subject as if Rachel were nothing better than an old cast-off shoe.

"What have you done with her? I would wish to have a few words with her," Katherine said angrily.

"I do not wish to speak of her." Marco's own anger flared and the subject was dropped. Katherine was frightened for her son's life and had not forgotten what this man had said only minutes ago in the cabin, so she did not mention Rachel again.

Katherine's first glimpse of Grand Terre, from the rail of the *Black Hawk*, revealed a white beach of considerable width and backed by green grasses. From a distance the island looked beautiful, even lovely. Small wooden structures were gathered along the white sand and behind them were a number of larger homes that blended in with the jutting rocks and mountains, which made up most of the interior of the island. These houses, to her mind, looked like fortresses, able to stand off any attack or foe.

As the ship neared her destination, two loud cannon booms heralded its arrival and soon every man, woman, and child who resided there, appeared on the beach.

Small boats were lowered from the *Black Hawk* and sat awaiting the passengers to take ashore.

Katherine felt a lump of fearful anticipation grip the pit of her stomach as she, her child, and Lucy were placed in the first boat and rowed toward the mass of people shouting and waving on the beach. As they were brought closer, Katherine could see the women were mostly a filthy lot, with ragged clothing, unkempt hair. The men seemed no better; most were even worse than the women about them. And the stares, which were directed toward Katherine by this band of brutes, made her flesh feel as though it were alive with crawling vermin.

When their small boat touched shore the mass of people swarmed toward Marco, shouting out happy greetings and wishing news of the cargo he had brought on his ship.

Marco himself seemed to pay little heed to these people, but silently helped Katherine from the boat. Katherine was repulsed by the filthy hands which reached out to help her and also by the vile talk which spewed out of not only the men's mouths but also the women's.

She shunned the offered hands and stepped out of the boat with only Marco's hand at her elbow. As soon as her feet were on dry land she turned and helped Lucy out of the boat, not wanting to let the girl or her babe out of her sight with these dangerous-looking people nearby.

Leading a pirate's life, none of the men in this crowd had ever seen a woman as beautiful as Katherine. Greed and lust showed on their faces but none dared to take hold of the woman Marco Radford had brought to their island. All of them had seen Marco's cruel temper at one time or another; they knew him to be a man without mercy and one of the most savage of their kind.

The women of the island, as they laughed and shouted out obscenities along with the men, only felt regret for the beautiful woman Marco had brought to Grand Terre. It was better, they thought, as they looked upon her lovely features, to be dirty and unkempt than to attract the attentions of Marco Radford. They all knew about the other women Marco had brought to the island. Young women, some even beautiful, but all had ended their lives either in torment from his cruelty or roaming the island of Grand Terre, their beauty lost, trying to survive. No one could envy this girl her status as Marco's mistress, but in each of their minds was the glad thought: better she than me.

Marco led the women away from the boat

and toward the houses, which were barely shacks, set back from the water. Katherine stared at these hovels, wondering if her fate was going to be to live in one of these wooden structures.

As they walked past the first house, another smaller group of men could be seen walking in their direction, coming down the sandy road. They came closer and Marco cleared his throat and called out to them.

"So you finally found your way back to us, did you Marco? We had about given you up for lost." A rather tall, slim man with dark-brown hair and the same colored eyes spoke first.

Marco acknowledged his words with a slight smile and clasped hands with the man. "It is good to be back after being gone so long, Jean."

"I just bet it is," he said with a grin, looking at Katherine. "And who is this you have gone and found and brought back with you?"

"Aha, Jean you do have an eye for beauty, but you had better not let Lillian hear you talking so or you may find your throat being cut one fine night."

Another of the men in the small group laughed as his eyes roamed over Katherine's face and bosom. "But say, man, where on earth did a rake such as yourself come across something as pretty as this standing before us?"

"Let me introduce you to her, gentlemen,"

Marco said, caressing Katherine's back. "This is Katherine; she shall stay here as my guest." He stressed the words "my guest," so there would be no misunderstandings. "And this, my lady, is Jean Lafitte, and his brothers, Pierre and Dominque."

Katherine looked upon the three men in front of her, her body as stiff and unyielding as a mountain of pure stone. Only her eyes told of the turmoil going on within her body.

"It is an honor, Mademoiselle Katherine," Jean Lafitte stated, taking her hand and kissing the tips of her fingers.

The other two brothers only gave her a slight bow and smiled their deep appreciation of her beauty.

Katherine for a moment had a fleeting hope that perhaps this pirate lord would help her in her distress and perhaps bring about her release. He seemed the most mannered and well-dressed man on the island and she thought that maybe he could show some kind of sympathy.

"Sir," she ventured, directing her words to Jean Lafitte, "I beg your help. I, my maid, and my son have been taken by force from my husband's house and have been brought here to your island."

Jean Lafitte looked at her with interest in his eyes.

"I beg of you, please help us to get back to Richmond and to my husband?"

"Abducted you say?" he questioned, as

though pondering the situation. "Well, I have but one thing to say. Marco, you are a man after my own heart and if it had been I who had first set eyes on this beauty she would be sharing my bed this evening instead of your own."

When these words were thrown in her face and as she listened to the other men's laughter at this cruel joke, Katherine let go of all her pent-up anger. Jean Lafitte was standing a few short steps away from her so when she brought up the hand that his lips had kissed only a few short minutes before and slapped his arrogant, handsome face, all laughter quieted.

Jean's face paled visibly for a second but then was broken by a huge grin. "I'll say one thing for her Marco, your lady here is a bit of a hellcat. You had better warn her, old friend, that in the future she had best be more careful where she puts that dainty hand or she may find herself in a worse position than she does now."

Katherine's body quaked with fear. What had she done? One did not slap the face of a man like this Jean Lafitte—a man who killed without a second thought, a man who pirated and ravaged the seas for his livelihood.

The men at once started to talk and laugh as though none of the last few minutes had taken place. Jean told Marco to come to his house for a conference within the next hour, then the three men took their leave. Jean Lafitte gave a small bow in Katherine's direction, "It has been a pleasure, Mademoiselle, I hope to have the honor again soon." He lightly traced his face where she had laid her hand.

Katherine ignored his jibe, knowing this man for what he was.

Marco immediately grabbed hold of Katherine and pulled her after him down the dusty road; Lucy followed close behind until finally they reached a large, stone house, set back and away to itself.

The house was much larger on the inside than it appeared from the outside. It was furnished beautifully with all kinds of splendid tapestries and paintings hanging upon the walls. Each room held deep cushioned carpeting and exquisite pieces of furniture. This shocked Katherine for she had expected Marco to live in a hovel, such as those along the beaches, not in anything as grand as this.

A small, almost fragile, elderly woman rushed up to them as they entered the house.

Marco greeted the gray-haired woman harshly and abruptly. Katherine had never seen a black person being treated in such a manner as he was treating this poor woman in front of them.

"Emily, I hope to find everything in order, for our coming."

"Yes, sir," she curtsied, keeping her eyes to the floor.

Katherine could sense the woman's fear and her heart went out to her.

"I hope you're right Emily, I should not want to find that in my absence you have not been doing your duties. Now you can show this girl a room for herself and the child she carries."

"My son shall stay with me," Katherine stated firmly.

The old woman called Emily looked at this beautiful young woman as though she had taken leave of her senses. No one ever disputed her master's orders. She had seen them try before and always it had led to the same ending, Marco Radford always got his own way.

Marco's own face clouded with anger. "You are going to have to control that waspish tongue of yours madam, or I shall have to tend to the matter for you. You shall do as you're told and not question my orders again. I hope you understand me. Now, Emily, do as I told you and you girl"—he pointed to Lucy—"follow her up to your room."

"Yes, sir." Emily jumped to do his bidding, and started through the main room and up the stairs, with Lucy, holding Charles, following behind.

Again taking hold of Katherine's arm, Marco followed them up the staircase. He led her into a large, lovely appointed bedchamber and then let go of her arm. "I sent word ahead of the *Black Hawk* for Emily to have everything prepared for you, my beauty. I knew when I first laid eyes upon you that one day I would bring you here to my house and that you would be sleeping here in this room."

He walked over to the closets along one wall and threw the doors back wide.

Surprise was written on Katherine's face as she viewed the treasure of gowns within.

"Yes, my flower, I have prepared well for your arrival. I have even had dresses ordered for you. You, Katherine, shall have all the luxuries you could desire. You shall be waited on hand and foot. I shall make one thing clear to you, though, do not try to escape me, for if you do I shall retrieve you. There is no way off this island for you and when I have you back, I shall not think twice about sharing you with the other men on Grand Terre, who will be more than glad to help look for you."

She did not doubt the truth of his words. Katherine would not put any foul act beyond his doing. But she knew as she lived and breathed that if the chance presented itself, she would in a moment take up her son and flee no matter what the outcome.

"I'm afraid for now, I must leave you for a time. Jean wishes to speak with me on important matters but when I return I expect to find you bathed and wearing one of these gowns that I have had made ready for you." He left her side and started to the door. "We shall have plenty of time to get to know each other better when I return, my flower."

Katherine did not respond to his words of promise, her body stood stiff, her eyes focusing on a flowered design in the carpet.

Marco slowly walked to her, brought her chin up with two fingers, and kissed her soft, tender mouth with a deep, burning force.

Nausea rose in the pit of her stomach, and an overpowering revulsion stole over her. In the grip of panic she pushed with every ounce of strength she possessed.

Laughter filled the room. "You shall be a pleasure to tame, my little wildcat, but right now I have not the time to show you what thrills you shall receive by being my mistress."

"Never!" came her angry reply.

"Shortly, my vixen, I shall be back to show you. I shall send Emily to you to help with your bath," he murmured as he went out the door.

Going over to the bed Katherine fell upon it and dissolved into tears. What was she to do? What could she do when he came back? "Oh, Bradly," she wailed, how could she bear to have this vile monster touch her where no other except her love had ever ventured? If only Bradly had found them before they had arrived on this accursed island, her mind thought frantically, but now even if he did find their whereabouts, would he be able to reach her?

It was only a short matter of time after Marco had left before there was a soft rap on the door.

"Come in," Katherine answered, sitting up

and wiping the tears from her eyes with the backs of her hands.

Emily entered the room, embarrassment written on her face at having found this young girl in tears. She could well imagine what had brought the girl's tears about and the thought of Marco playing his cruel tricks on this lovely girl tore at her heart. "Ma'am, would you like me to prepare your bath now? The master said I should attend to your needs."

Katherine tried to put a strong grip on herself, hating to show her tears in front of Marco's servants. "That will be fine, I feel so dirty, it shall be a pleasure to be rid of the grime."

"I'll be back in a few minutes then with hot water and perhaps you would care for some tea or something cool to drink?"

Katherine gave the small woman a warm smile. "Tea will be fine, Emily, it is kind of you to be so charitable." There was no reason not to be kind to this friendly woman, Katherine thought; the woman herself did not act too fond of her master and perhaps this Emily was in a like circumstance as she herself.

"Yes, ma'am, master Marco said to get you anything you will be wanting." She left the room, quietly shutting the door behind her.

Katherine wandered about the room for a time, until Emily came back carrying a large tub and leading two girls carrying large buckets of steaming hot water.

She lingered in the bath, scrubbing and

rinsing her skin to a dark pink color and then doing the same process over again. After having to endure Marco's hands and mouth upon her, she felt as filthy and grimy as the people down at the beach. But after the water had turned cold she forced herself to climb out of the tub and to choose a dark green gown, which fit to perfection, out of the closet. Thus, having completed her dressing, on Emily's return she asked to be taken to her son and Lucy.

She was grateful that the old woman had given them the next room down the hall from her own. It was smaller than the one to which Marco had shown her, but it was nicely furnished and quite comfortable, as was the rest of the house.

Lucy seemed more nervous now in Marco's house than she had been earlier on the *Black Hawk*. When Katherine entered the room she ran to her with tears brimming in her eyes. "Are we a-going to stay here from now on Missus? Ain't Master Brad a-going to come and take us back home and away from that pirate?"

"Don't worry, Lucy, you have nothing to fear." She was the only one who had anything to fear at the hands of Marco Radford, she thought to herself as she walked through the room and picked up her son in her arms.

Emily had been standing at the door and as she looked at Lucy's tear-streaked face and then at Katherine holding her baby tenderly in her arms, she ventured to speak. "I beg your pardon ma'am."

"Yes, what is it, Emily?" Katherine glanced up at the old woman.

"I just thought I might ought to tell you that you probably will not have anything to fear from master Marco this night. When he goes over to visit with the Lafittes, he doesn't usually get back till all hours of the morning and then he doesn't never know what he is about anyhow. Why all the men on this island probably will be drinking until they can hardly walk tonight, since master Marco brought a large cargo back with him today."

Relief flooded Katherine's features as she thanked Emily for this bit of information. Perhaps she would not be forced to become Marco's mistress as soon as she had thought. And any amount of time, no matter how small, could be to her advantage and she could still hope for a way to escape.

Before Emily left the room she informed Katherine that she would bring dinner to her room in about an hour.

Katherine spent the time before dinner nursing Charles and trying to console Lucy. She had no idea what was going to happen to them or how she would go about planning for their escape. She did know that it would be up to her to do it and that she would have to use all of her strength in order to protect Lucy and her son against Marco's madness.

Dinner was served to Katherine in her room

and she found some small pleasure in the fact that she was alone. She barely could summon any appetite for her meal, for her whole body waited in fearful anticipation for Marco to come barging through the door at any moment.

But Marco did not break away from his friends and make his way back to his house until the early hours of the morning. Katherine jumped to her feet with a start when she heard a large noise, as if someone had fallen, and the curses outside of her door seared her very soul with the certainty that Marco had at last come to make good his threats of this afternoon. After hardly picking at her food, Katherine had curled herself in a chair and started to read a book and now with a growing fear she realized that she must have fallen asleep.

The door was flung wide and Marco came stumbling into the bedchamber. There was a glazed look in his eyes as he tried focusing them upon his lovely captive and his mouth twisted into an ugly grimace as he approached her, walking unsteadily upon his feet.

Katherine, her heart hammering, backed around the chair, her mind flying over thoughts of saving herself from this drunken fiend.

"Do not be shy my beauty, I have returned to take that which I have been dreaming of for over a year now," he mumbled, his words slurring together.

"No!" Katherine gasped, her hands clutched

to her throat.

"Now come to me. Let us not fight, for I assure you I shall prove out the winner." He rounded the chair and grabbed hold of her arm, as she started to make a run for the door.

"Let me go, you scum," she screamed, pulling at her arm and pushing against his chest.

"Oh my little wildcat, I can hardly wait to get between your soft, white thighs. It shall be the most pleasurable conquest I have ever made."

He was drunker than Katherine had first thought and the smell of liquor and cheap perfume clung to him. But try as she might she could not break his grip upon her. His fingers crushed into her tender flesh, which already showed large red welts that brought hated tears of pain to her eyes.

"I shall squelch that temper out of you and bring you to your knees this very night," he roared, dragging her to the bed and throwing her in its center, before he proceeded to undress in a wobbly fashion.

Katherine saw her chance and took it when he was pulling his pants down to his knees. She flung herself to the other side of the bed, looking about for an object with which to try to fight him off.

Marco's roar of laughter filled the room and grated on Katherine's nerves. "You think to escape me do you?" He pulled his pants the rest of the way off his legs and fell flat on his back upon the bed. "You shall not get away, my little blue eyes," he murmured softly, barely loud enough for her to hear.

Katherine stood, bracing herself for his next attack. She dared not leave the side of her bed until he made another attempt to get her, but as she stared down at his still body, she could not make up her mind about what to do. He appeared to have fallen into drunken unconsciousness but Katherine could not see his face so she could not tell if he were only trying to take her off guard or if he were in fact truly sleeping.

She stood as still as possible, hardly daring to breathe as she watched Marco's prone figure for the next few minutes; to her it seemed as though hours had gone by while she stood there. Finally she braced her courage together and stepped around to the other side of the bed in order to see his face.

Marco lay as still as death, with his eyes shut and a cruel grin on his face. Katherine let out a long sigh, as if she had been holding her breath for the past frightful minutes.

She then threw a quilt over his naked body, not wishing to be forced to look at that nude figure. This completed she went back to the chair she had earlier occupied and tried to still her shaking hands and thumping heart.

What would she do if he awoke again? How could she protect herself from such a man as this? She sat as alert as a cat and as frightened as a little mouse, waiting for him to make a movement.

*   *   *

It was late into the morning when there was a banging at the bedchamber door. Katherine jumped to her feet, her face pale and her hands tightly clenched together, as Marco stirred on the bed.

"What?" Marco rose on his elbows, adjusting his eyes to the light in the room.

Katherine started to the door, relieved now that Marco was awake, to allow someone else into the room.

"What are you doing already dressed and out of bed, my pet? You will have to learn that being my mistress means that you shall stay on your back unless otherwise bid." Marco sat up, his bloodshot eyes traveling over Katherine's form.

Katherine halted in her tracks, her mind whirling in a frenzy. What was he talking about; did he not remember what had happened? Or had he been so drunk last night that he had forgotten what had occurred and thought now that he had indeed lain with her? Well, she was not about to correct his memory and she could only pray that when his next attack came she would be able to find some other means to save herself.

The knocking sounded again so Katherine was saved from having to explain her dress and being up and about.

"Come in, damn you!" Marco shouted, holding his head. "Can not a man find any rest in his own house?"

Katherine started back and sat down in the chair as the door was opened and a young man entered the room.

"What the hell do you want, man?" Marco questioned, rising naked from the bed.

"Mr. Lafitte sent me to inform you that his ship will sail within the half hour and he wished to be sure that you would not be late," the young, well-dressed man said.

"Well, you just get your ass on back to Jean and tell him I'm on my way. You would think Jean would at least give me a few days before I have to take to the sea again," he added, mumbling to himself.

Katherine had not bothered to look up at the man who had come into the room, but, having digested the bit of information he had arrived to tell Marco, she looked at the young man's back with interest. She could not have hoped for better news, Marco would be going back to the sea and this very day. Her heart beat with a tremendous joy as she listened to their conversation.

"Well, get the hell out of my room, man. You brought your orders and I'll be there shortly," Marco shouted as he started pulling on his breeches.

"Yes, sir, I shall tell Mr. Lafitte that you shall be there shortly," the young man said, turning about and starting to the door, then stopping in mid-stride as he glimpsed the woman sitting across the room.

My God, it could not be, Katherine thought as she looked into the man's face. But even as she thought this she knew it was he— Mark Prescot—she could not be mistaken, it was him.

The young man stood looking, mouth agape at the woman he had once loved with all his heart. He had heard yesterday of the beautiful woman that Marco had brought as his captive to Grand Terre. But never would he have imagined it to be Katherine Rafferty.

"What are you staring at?" Marco demanded as he watched Mark Prescot gaping at Katherine. "I thought I told you to be gone?"

Mark Prescot did not speak but went out the door, his mind going frantically over the past events. He would have to find a way to speak to Katherine alone. How could she possibly be in the hands of someone like Marco Radford and where was the man she had come to America to wed? He would have to try to help her if he could and perhaps he now had a chance to win her himself. His hopes rose a notch.

Marco was in a foul mood as he went about dressing. Katherine sat silently by, while he stomped about, cursing and ranting at Jean Lafitte and his brothers.

Finally his murmuring stopped as his eyes fell upon Katherine, who sat primly in her chair. "You heard I gather, that I shall be going back to sea?"

Katherine nodded her head, feeling uneasy under his penetrating gaze.

"Those damn Lafittes are going to capture a Spanish ship that is carrying gold and silver. It should be but a short trip, so if you have any thoughts in that lovely head of yours about escaping, let me tell you now to forget it, for I have already posted guards about the house and you shall not be allowed outside the doors."

Katherine did not answer but sat clutching her hands in her lap.

"I hope you shall heed my warnings, my little flower, but enough of this," he said, placing his hands on either side of her shoulders and raising her from her chair. "Let me taste the sweetness of those soft lips of yours to take their memory along with me." He pressed his mouth over hers while she pushed against him trying to free herself.

"I would think you would not be as reluctant after last night." He chuckled. "But I swear I could if time would allow it, again take you and make you mine once more. You are a witch Katherine, even though I know I possessed you last night my manhood cries out again for you beneath me." He released her and started toward the door. "But for now I have not the time, though you cannot imagine how I wish I did, but be sure that upon my return I will stay locked in this room for a month with you lying beside me, until I have had my fill of your soft, sweet body. I will tell Emily to tend to your needs and do not try to fly from me or you shall come to regret it, my little blue eyes." With this final warning he left the room slamming the door after him.

Chapter Twelve

On the day of Marco's leave-taking Katherine had spent her time tending Charles and worrying about whether Mark Prescot had recognized her and if he also were going to sea or if he would be staying on the island and perhaps try to get in touch with her.

With Marco's departure, a great burden had been taken off her mind, but still she felt the confines of her prison. Emily had informed her that Marco had indeed been true to his word and had posted four, burly looking men around the house. Katherine was fast winning the loyalty of the old woman and she felt some comfort in the fact that Emily was on her side and if the need arose she would be able to secure her help if it was needed to make her escape.

Laying awake that evening Katherine prayed that Bradly might come before Marco's return to save her from the fate that would surely be hers if she remained on the island.

She clutched the hope that Mark Prescot would come to try to help her out of her prison. Perhaps he would help her to escape but what if he himself had become like these pirates, she thought. Then would he still help her and betray his friendship with his new mates.

Tomorrow, she promised herself, she would look about and perhaps she would be able to think more clearly and start to form a plan for her escape.

The next morning found Katherine, after she had fed Charles, eating her own breakfast out on the small garden patio, when Emily announced that a man was waiting at the door and wished to have a word with her.

"Show him in Emily and bring another cup for tea." She held no doubt who the man was. It could only be Mark Prescot.

"What a fetching sight you make sitting

there with this lovely background." Mark Prescot walked to her and bent and took her hand.

"Mark." She cried, clutching his hand tightly in her own. "I never thought to see you here in the midst of these terrible people." Tears stung her eyes as she looked into his familiar face.

"Katherine, Katherine." He kissed her hand softly. "How be it that you are here? I thought you were to be wedded to a man from the colonies. Does your father know what has happened to you? Is no one trying to find you?" He piled the questions on her, not giving her a chance to answer.

Katherine felt tears stream down her face at the kindness of his words and at seeing an old friend in her time of need.

"I am sorry, Katherine, for going on like this," he murmured as he saw the sorrow on her face. "You could not imagine the shock I had when I saw you in Marco Radford's bedchamber. Please, Katherine, tell me what has brought you to these circumstances?" He softly patted her hand, trying to give her strength.

Katherine commenced to tell him, hardly knowing where to start, about what had happened in her life since last she had seen him.

Mark Prescot quietly listened throughout her long story until she finally told of how Marco had taken her and her child from her husband's house. He could see the love and the hurt that filled her whole face when she told him of her husband. His own hopes of ever gaining her for himself were quickly dashed. He was not the type of man to take a woman who did not want him, no matter how much he desired her.

When at last she sat quietly, looking into his face with trusting eyes, he spoke, "I shall try to see you out of this, Katherine, but if I may be so bold as to ask, I wish to know if you were happy with this Bradly Deveraux, this man you were forced to marry?" He already knew his answer but he told himself he had to take this one last chance to gain her if it were at all possible.

"Mark," Katherine said softly, rubbing the back of his hand. "Never have I known such a man as my husband. My whole life has changed since knowing him, he is my only hope for love and for the future and I do not think I would wish to live if he were taken permanently from me. The only thing that has kept me going so far is his son, who is his image, and his own loving face which is constantly in my thoughts."

Mark Prescot felt his old wound opening anew at her heartfelt declaration of love for her husband. But he did not let his features give way to the hurt and distress he felt at those words. He knew that he would wish to his dying day that it was he of whom she had spoken of with such affection, but at the same time he knew that he would still give his life to save the only woman he had ever loved.

"I understand, Katherine, and I am glad you have found so much happiness, I only wish that it could have been I who brought you so much love."

Katherine had almost forgotten the love he had held for her back in England and now she felt shame for having hurt him again. "I am sorry, Mark," she said softly. "If I could have loved anyone else besides Bradly I am sure it would have been you."

He tried to stop her flow of words by telling her that there was no need to explain, but Katherine would not be put off and added, "I love my husband with all my heart Mark and I long to be by his side once again; he is as much a part of me as I am of him. After knowing his love I could never love another." She wanted him to know how deep her love for Bradly was so that if he did help her to get away from this island, he would not have the slightest thought of her staying with him.

Mark stood and walked about the patio for a minute, trying to get his feelings under control. "I shall help you all I can, Katherine. I promise you, I shall not rest until I see you safe and off of Grand Terre." He stopped and stood in front of her.

"I cannot express my thanks for your friendship, Mark, but here I have run on and on about myself and have not even asked you how you came to be mixed up with these men and living on this island?" She gave him a warm smile, knowing he was telling the truth and would help her as much as possible.

He explained in short order to her how he had left England shortly after she had, to go to America, to see a plantation in which his father had only recently invested. His ship had been captured by some of Lafitte's men and he had been taken prisoner along with the rest of the passengers and some of the crew. But since he had not cared to go back to England or for that matter to go to America, after losing her, he had fast become well liked by Jean Lafitte and had become his personal secretary.

Katherine was amazed at the turn of fate they had both received since only a little over a year ago. It seemed like yesterday that they had been standing in front of a dress shop on a London street and now here they both sat on an island which housed some of the most dangerous men in the world.

"I had better leave now, Katherine," Mark said, rising to his feet. "I had to bribe my way in here, through your guards, and I do not wish Marco to know that I knew you before in England, so it is best if I do not visit too long. And also there is Jean, he has a bit of a temper, when kept waiting."

"But I thought he had left yesterday with his other men," she said, rising to her feet to show him to the door.

"No, no. I think he is planning to go into New Orleans soon though. I may have to go with him, Katherine, but never fear I will find a way in which to help you get back to your husband."

"I do not know how I shall ever be able to repay you, Mark." She placed a light kiss upon his cheek, before he went through the door.

With Marco gone time seemed to pass at a swifter pace for those living in the large stone house on Grand Terre. The weeks turned into a month and still Katherine was held prisoner, without any further word from Mark Prescot. Her nerves were shattered due to the oppressive heat of the island and the constant plague of mosquitoes. They all retired early, thankful to get under the mosquito netting affixed to their beds, and, thereby, keep away the small, painful insects.

The fear that Marco's ship would be sighted lived with Katherine night and day, until the slightest unexpected noise would have her trembling like a child.

It had been almost two months now, she thought as she nursed Charles, since she had seen Mark. What could have happened to him? He had promised to help her but so far she had not been given any word or sign. Perhaps he had been harmed in some way or even killed. Oh Lord, she prayed not. He was her only hope for leaving this terrible island. She was still sure that Bradly was searching for her and his son and she never once gave up the hope that he would appear any day to take her from this miserable existence, which had been forced upon her.

She herself had tried a means of escape and had failed miserably. She had one day gone to the back door, and begged the guard standing at his post, to help take her and her son to New Orleans. She had promised to give him any amount of money he would wish, after she was brought to safety, but the guard had only grunted and proceeded to tell her in a rough, low voice that he would not rouse Marco's anger for any amount of money. Then he had walked away laughing, and saying that if he did as she wished Marco would only find him and cut his throat before he had the chance to spend a pound of it. Katherine had tried to call him back and to plead with him at least to ask about to see if anyone else would take the chance. But the guard, thinking her somewhat of a madwoman had only roared with laughter, until she had slammed the door and burst into tears.

Several days after this sorry attempt to gain her freedom Katherine had thought of Rachel. Perhaps the girl was still alive and living on the island. If she could get word to her mayhap she could come up with some means by which to help her. Quickly she had called Emily to her, Emily being the only one allowed to go out of the house to gather food or any other supplies that might be needed.

The news Emily brought back to Katherine was hopeless. Rachel, on hearing who Emily was and who had sent her, had refused to talk with her.

Indeed, Rachel had been thrown into a fit of temper when the old woman had stood knocking at the wooden door of the shack in which she now lived, and had yelled at the old hag to get away before she came out and beat her away.

Once the old woman's retreating back could be seen walking back down the beach, Rachel had burst into a shower of tears.

"The bitch," she screeched. "If it were not for Katherine I would be the one living up there in that fancy house, awaiting my lover's return." Instead all she could look forward to now was the nightly return of the pig with whom she shared this cabin.

"Lord, that slut has nerve," she cursed. If not for that blue-eyed whore, Marco would never have given her over to his men. Oh, she knew the way of it; her love had been bewitched. On that first morning aboard the *Black Hawk* he had ordered three of his men to forcefully take her out of his cabin and to put her into the bowels of the ship. Screaming and kicking at the men and calling out for Marco, knowing that some terrible mistake had been made, Rachel had been taken out of her lover's life.

But being moved out of his cabin and locked in a small, dingy room, was only the first of her degradations. That evening Marco had told his men that being good and deserving men they could have her for their own and take turns with her as they saw fit.

By the time the *Black Hawk* reached the island of Grand Terre, Rachel's mind was in a state of numbness. At first she had kept the thought that Katherine had somehow bewitched her lover, but as more time passed and her body was continually mistreated, she tried to stop thinking all together.

On Grand Terre Rachel had survived by the use of her body alone. She had found a man to take her in. He had only a stump for a right arm; his breath was foul and he reeked of uncleanliness. And though the man was cruel and harsh—when drunk he beat her mercilessly—she knew that she would have been treated the same way by any of the animals on this island except her love. So she lived, if one could call it that, with only one thought constantly in the back of her mind, Marco, her love, and that one day she would have him back.

Katherine had been deeply hurt at the vehemence of Rachel's hate, which Emily had reported back to her. She still could not understand the girl. Did she not know that the only thing Katherine wanted was to be away from Marco and back at Moon Rise with her husband and son? Did she think that she had deliberately set out to take Marco from her? How could the girl be so mistaken?

Katherine had begun to rely on Emily as she had years ago on her old nurse Biddy. The older woman seemed to possess a simple understanding that comforted Katherine in her times of need.

Katherine had been correct in her estimation that Emily's circumstances were close to her own. They had begun to have long talks in the afternoons, sitting out on the patio, and Katherine now placed complete trust in the woman.

She had found that Emily once had been a governess in France, and that almost fifteen years ago she and her three charges had been traveling to Spain on a holiday visit, to their charge's grandparents' home, when their ship had been attacked and all aboard, save she and the young girls in her care, had been killed.

Emily had sat weeping softly, as she told Katherine about the fates of the young girls and herself. She had always been thin and plain to look upon so she had not been forced constantly to submit to the pirate men. But the other girls with their mother's dark Spanish looks, had been violated unceasingly by the vile men's lust. Two of the girls had died on that depraved ship and the other had only lasted a few short weeks once she had been brought to Grand Terre. Emily herself had nursed the girl day and night, but the young woman had given up on life and eventually died.

No one had paid much attention to Emily at

first and this mere stroke of luck had, she was certain, saved her from sure death. She had only survived by becoming, soon after reaching the island, the friend of the mother of the girl called Lillian. Lillian herself was now Jean Lafitte's mistress; her mother had been born here on Grand Terre. It was the mother who, years ago, had arranged for her to become the housekeeper of this house.

Katherine had listened in a daze to the woman's story. "Did you never try to go back to France and leave this island?"

"No, child, the day they brought me here I knew I would never leave this place. I was ravaged by a pack of degrading men, who sealed my fate for me. All was lost with the death of Maria Eliane, the last of the daughters who were entrusted to my care."

Katherine kissed the old leathered cheek of the woman, who sat telling her this sad tale. "If ever we get away, Emily, I promise you, you shall always have a place with me at Moon Rise." But she knew even as she saw the tender smile turned to her by this old woman, that she would never leave Grand Terre. She had punished herself over the years for the fate of the girls and she would forever do the same until the time of her death.

Katherine rubbed the black curls atop her child's head. How like his father he was, she thought. He was growing so big that he promised to be as large and handsome as his sire. Bradly would be proud if he could see the size of his son now, she thought, feeling a terrible hopelessness wash over her. With Rachel not willing to help and no word from Mark, her fate would be sealed by the return of Marco Radford.

Bradly Deveraux had indeed not given his wife and child up for lost. After finding the carriage that morning, he had gone directly to Richmond, forced his way into Jeffery William's office and demanded a ship be ready to set sail immediately.

Jeffery, not wishing to argue with this anger-filled Bradly who stood before him, and not having the right to tell him nay, since Bradly owned half of his shipping line, tried to find out what had brought the young man here in such an uproar.

After Bradly quickly outlined for him what had taken place at Moon Rise, the night before, Jeffery, his features having turned even whiter than his hair, at once jumped to his feet, went to the door, and called for the clerk in the outer office.

A ship was made ready that same day and Bradly, chafing at any delay, was aboard and starting on his search late that night.

No rest came to him as he prowled the ship night and day. His orders to the crew were abrupt and given only when necessary, and his eyes constantly were turned to the sea, searching for a sail in the distance.

At every port where his ship docked, he

questioned every seaman who could be seen. Did anyone know the whereabouts of Marco Radford and his men? Always the replies were the same; some knew Marco, but none had seen him. What did this large man, who looked as though there were devils riding on his back, want with a man such as Marco Radford? they would ask themselves.

After weeks of searching Bradly had hardly eaten or slept; his thoughts were continuously tormented night and day by the faces of Katherine and his small son.

His temper became nothing short of an angry lion's and his crew avoided him whenever possible. Those who did not recognize the signs of his unleashed anger were berated for any wrong word said or wrong move made.

In one of the ports where Bradly docked, a familiar play was unfolded for his crew in a waterfront tavern.

Upon docking, Bradly would roam the waterfront taverns until the morning hours, trying to pick up a word or a clue as to the whereabouts of Marco.

In one such tavern Bradly approached and questioned a large sultry man, who was leaning against the bar. The large man, in no mood to talk after losing his last months wages in a card game, turned his back on this oppressive intruder.

"I asked you a question, man." Bradly took the reluctant fellow by the shoulder and spun him about.

The man pushed Bradly's hand away and spat at his feet. "Get away ye bloke," came his answer.

Losing his reason for the moment, as all of his rage came boiling to the surface, Bradly stood staring hard at the man in front of him—seeing through the man and consumed with hate.

The seaman realized his mistake in not taking this man seriously as he looked into his anger-contorted face. But too late he saw the danger in his opponent, for Bradly had already grabbed the man by the front of the shirt; a great bellow emerged from the depths of Bradly's chest and he shook him as though he were a giant rat. Then he let the man loose but before he could protect himself or get away from the madman before him, Bradly had smashed a hamlike fist into his opponent's face, smashing his nose with a crunching sound and sending him reeling across the room unconscious. Bradly had stood then, clenching and unclenching his fists, feeling some of the tension easing from his body at the sight of the seaman fallen on the floor.

For longer than a month he was driven so, never relenting in his search, combing the waterfronts and traveling to any port which he had heard might have pirates staying within it. But it was with a heavy heart and a weary body that Bradly finally put in at Louisiana. He had been told that a man called Jean Lafitte lived in New Orleans at times and that if anyone would know the whereabouts of Marco Radford, Jean Lafitte would.

He beat the streets of New Orleans, asking questions and offering money for information, but no one would give him the answers he needed. They thought him too dangerous-looking to try to fool and no one would really tell where Jean Lafitte stayed because should some harm befall him due to a man's eagerness for coins, that man would not live long in this town, which depended on the pirates for its livelihood.

It was late one evening and Bradly had about given up hope of finding out any information in New Orleans, when, finally, in a tavern after asking each man who came through the door, about Jean Lafitte, a young man said that he did indeed know the gentleman and in fact he himself worked for him.

Bradly could not believe this stroke of luck and asked the young man to join him at his table. After pouring each of them a drink, Bradly got down to his business, asking the man the whereabouts of his employer, if he had ever heard of a man called Marco Radford, and if perhaps he would know if Marco were still at sea or living in some town.

At the end of Bradly's tirade the young man smiled softly and held out his hand. "I am more than happy to meet you, Mr. Deveraux, my name is Mark Prescot and I shall be more than glad to help you to rescue your wife." Mark held no doubt that the man sitting opposite him was Katherine's husband. He looked exactly as he had pictured the man in his mind, and no man could be as interested in Marco as this man was without having a very good reason. Katherine was the best reason that Mark could think of.

Bradly's face paled from sheer relief, as he looked in disbelief at the young man before him. "But how do you know of my wife? Have you by chance seen her with this scoundrel Marco?" Bradly asked, daring to hope the man knew of Katherine.

"Indeed I have met the fair lady, Katherine, and I promise you that when last I saw her, she and her son were fine and no harm had befallen them," Mark replied, reading the joy and relief that passed for a slight minute across Bradly's face.

Then Mark commenced to relate to him how he had known Katherine in England, omitting the love he had held for the other man's wife and how seeing her in Marco's bed chamber, he had gone back the next day to call on her, after Marco was off the island. He told Bradly that he had sent a message to Moon Rise, telling him of his wife's whereabouts. He had also in this letter begged Bradly to meet him in New Orleans since he himself would not be going back to the island and would await him there.

Bradly could not believe his good fortune in having run into this young man. His head was reeling with the thought that he would be able to go to Katherine soon. "I cannot tell you in words what your loyalty to my wife means to me, Mr. Prescot." Bradly let out in a breath.

"There is no need, Mr. Deveraux, I wish to tell you now I will do anything in my power to help Katherine."

Bradly looked sideways at this youth in front of him. He could sense there was more to Mark's feelings than pure friendship toward his wife, but for this he could not discredit the man. He was hopelessly in love with Katherine himself and could well imagine another having the same feelings.

The two men talked way into the morning about how best to approach the pirate stronghold in order to rescue Katherine and Charles without having the whole island rise in an uproar and without being captured themselves.

Trying to catch any breeze which might find its way across the island, Katherine usually spent her afternoons reclining on the small garden patio, reading a book or just talking to Emily and relaxing.

It was on one such afternoon that Katherine sat reading from a book of poetry, when she heard loud shouts and laughter coming from the beach. She could imagine only one thing that would cause the island population to gather on the beach and that was the arrival of a ship. When, after a moment, she heard the cannon fire she was sure of it.

She set the book upon a small table and called for Emily to come quickly.

When Emily arrived she saw fear and agitation on the face of the woman she had grown to love and almost think of as a daughter. "What is it child? You look as pale as a ghost."

"Do you know if a ship has been sighted Emily?" she asked, clutching the folds of her gown.

"I don't know, honey." Emily shook her head from side to side.

"Hurry, Emily, and run down to the beach. Find out if those people are cheering for a ship and see if it is the one Marco is on." Katherine was beside herself, as she paced back and forth on the marble flooring.

"Right away, I will be gone but a short time." Emily hurried from the room, wishing she could break down and weep with pity for the lovely young girl. She knew how Katherine had dreaded the thought of Marco's return and she wished to God there was something she could do to help her.

Katherine walked the patio floor, her mind filling with terror each time she heard a noise about the house. Each minute she feared Marco would be coming through the door.

Emily had been gone only a moment before she came scampering through the front door. "It's him, Miss Katherine, it's him!" she shouted, running to the patio. "I waited until the first boat was dropped and then headed right back to tell you."

"Are you sure, Emily? Are you sure it's the same ship?" Katherine asked softly, feeling herself beginning to panic. "Did you see him, Emily?"

"No ma'am, I didn't see master Marco, but it's the ship he went on and everybody on the island is down there to greet them that's coming ashore."

Perhaps Marco had been killed. Katherine clutched at this thought. Perhaps he had been killed attacking the Spanish ship or he could have been drowned in a storm and be lying at the bottom of the sea at this very moment. She could only pray to God above to bring her this deliverance and to save her from her fate if Marco were to come back on the island.

Katherine excused Emily and then went upstairs to see Charles. She sat quietly beside the bed and watched her child peacefully sleeping. What could the future hold for her and her son? she wondered. What would become of Charles if he had to grow to his manhood here on this cursed island? Would he become as the others, turning evil and vile and roaming the seas as a scourge for his livelihood? And what of herself? Would she become a wretched-looking hag, as Rachel had? She had seen the girl twice since that day she had sent Emily to find her and to see if she would help her out of her imprisonment. At first Katherine had not recognized the woman, who was squatting on the ground outside and watching up to the house.

Katherine had looked closer in order to see what the woman was about and to her utter surprise, when the woman had looked up at the window where Katherine was, she had known at once that the dirty ragged creature below was Rachel Profane. At first, Katherine had thought to run and call to her from the door, to ask her to come in. But by the time she had reached the door and looked out Rachel was hurrying away, her dirty gray dress, which was twice too large, dragging in the dust.

It had been a terrible sight for Katherine to see and now she had to put herself in the other's place. Would she come to the same fate if Marco grew tired of her and cast her out? Would she then be thrown from the hands of one lecherous pirate after another, until she also looked like Rachel?

Or would she, like Emily, after having been violated by Marco, feel as though she no longer had the will to live? Would she feel degraded and not wish to leave this island again and face other people?

She could not picture herself, Katherine Rafferty Deveraux living the life of either Rachel or Emily. Somehow she would have to get off of this island; she would never be content to sit here and waste away, as others had.

She was abruptly pulled out of her thoughts by the slamming of a door downstairs and the pounding of bootsteps upon the stairs. She heard her own chamber door open and close and braced herself for the confrontation that was sure to come.

The door burst open and there standing on the threshold stood Marco Radford. "What the hell are you doing in here?" he stormed. "When I come home I expect you to be waiting downstairs as a mistress should when her man returns from a long journey. Have you not yet learned your proper place in my home?"

Katherine clutched the arms of the chair, her knuckles as white as her face. "I-I did not know," she stammered, fear ruling her words.

Marco looked her over from head to slippers. She was even lovelier than he had remembered on those long nights out at sea. He had a cruel nature but something of his softer side ruled him when he was around this woman; no other had ever affected him in this manner. "Perhaps, my flower, I have been a little rash. In time you will do my bidding with ease. You are new at this sort of thing, I realize, but now I have told you how to greet me; be sure you do so in the future." He stood quietly for a minute before he continued. "Now, my lovely Katherine, walk over here and greet your master as you should."

Katherine sat, not wishing to go to him as his pirate whore would, but she knew if she did not do this thing he wished he would use force to compel her obedience, and perhaps, being in her child's room, he would attempt to do some harm to him.

She rose slowly from her chair, swallowing convulsively and dreading what was to be. But before she took a step toward him, Marco crossed the room and grabbed hold of her, hurting her arms and bruising her lips.

Katherine's violet eyes poured out their hate as she pushed against him.

After taking his fill of her sweet lips, Marco released her. "I see you still have the same fire in you, Katherine, your eyes betray the anger you feel. But tonight my little tigress I shall have you purring like a kitten."

Katherine slumped back into her chair, her breasts heaving as she wiped the back of her hand across her mouth; her eyes were shooting daggers, which, if real, would have pierced his heart in half. "I will not play your mistress or your whore. I hate you more than I have ever hated anyone!" she hissed.

"Oh, we shall see what you play when I am through tonight, my beauty. You see, my dear, I enjoy a little force, it adds a little something to the game of love." He grinned. "I have to report to Jean about the cargo we brought back with us. I will not be gone much over an hour, so be dressed for dinner and we shall dine when I return," he said over his shoulder, as he walked from the room.

Only an hour, she thought. She watched her child for a long minute, then called Lucy, who had gone to the kitchen to help Emily prepare dinner, while she had come to sit with her son. Katherine left her son to Lucy's care, being sure to tell the black girl not to leave him even for a moment with Marco back in the house.

For modesty's sake, more than for the way it enhanced her beauty and set off her dark hair and deep violet eyes, Katherine chose to wear a rose taffeta dress, with a high lace collar and long full sleeves.

Having completed her dressing, she stood near the window, looking toward the sea and dreaming of Bradly. What could he be doing at this very moment? Was he still looking for her? Why had he not found her yet and why had she not heard again from Mark Prescot? Had they both just finally given up?

It seemed as if she had no choice but to go on with the evening ahead. But one thing was sure; no matter what, she would not easily be overtaken by that blackguard Marco. She would fight him until there was no more fight left in her, she swore this to herself.

Dinner was served in the dining room with only Katherine and Marco presiding at the table. The food was delicious but Katherine only forked her food about on her plate as she watched Marco, seated at the other end of the table, devour his. He seemed not to notice her at all while there was food in front of him. He attacked his meal as though he had been starving for weeks, stuffing food into his mouth and gulping down wine to wash the mess down his throat.

Katherine jumped when, having completed devouring what was before him, Marco gave a large belch and then proceeded to wipe his mouth with the back of his hand and brushing this on his trousers.

He pushed his chair back from the table and stared darkly at Katherine as he drank his wine.

Katherine felt unease grow in her as she sensed his eyes upon her so she kept her eyes on her plate, hoping to delay their confrontation because she hoped he would again drink himself senseless so that maybe she could defend herself against him.

But her hope was not to be realized this evening, she soon found out.

"You do not seem to be very hungry tonight. Could I take it that you are anxious about the evening ahead my beauty?" He walked over and placed himself in the chair next to Katherine's, pulling his over to sit beside her.

Katherine's hands began to tremble and she had to clutch them in her lap to keep from showing her fear.

"You shall enjoy it, Katherine." He brought one finger up to caress her jawline. "It shall not be as it was the last time, I promise you. You will not leave my bed like that morning before. You shall want to stay beside me."

Katherine shrank from his touch. "No,"

she whispered.

"But yes, Katherine, and since you do not seem to be interested in your food I suggest we go on upstairs now and begin your lessons on being the perfect mistress. I shall show you things you never dreamed of and you my little love will enjoy every minute of it, I promise you." He stood to his full height and grabbed hold of her, pulling her to him. "Yes, I think you shall enjoy what I have planned for you," he murmured in her hair as he pulled her into the main room and toward the stairs.

Katherine felt anger and outrage explode in her body; she pulled her arm out of his grasp and made a run for the front door.

But Marco was quicker and caught hold of the neck of her gown, tearing it down the back.

Katherine felt a fear she had never known before and tried escaping his hands. He was a monster, a mad monster, and she knew he would probably kill her if given the chance.

"You bitch!" He seethed. "I'll break that temper of yours and teach you to try and elude me." He grabbed hold of her waist from behind, lifted her off her feet, and started back to the stairs.

Katherine kicked out, flinging her arms wildly, screaming her hate and loathing at him.

"Those will be the last such words you shall screech at me, you slut," he roared. "After tonight you will not be able to curse anyone!"

Hardly able to breathe, with his arms about her, cutting off her air supply, Katherine's head was spinning dazedly by the time they reached the stairs. Her strength was ebbing from her very limbs and at that moment she realized that her fate was sealed and that no one was going to save her from this inhuman man.

As Marco reached the first step Katherine felt his grip upon her loosening. She gasped for air and with her dazed mind she thought she heard a deep voice talking on the other side of the room. She shook her head, trying to clear her brain, then with a sudden jolt she realized that it was not her mind playing tricks on her. A man was standing in the shadows of the room, speaking in a low deadly voice.

"Marco, you bastard, take your hands from my wife and come and meet me and take your death like a man." The low voice came from the main room. At first, Katherine could not make out the voice, so cold and deathlike were its tones. But the man standing hidden in the dark had said wife. Her mind shouted, wife! It was Bradly.

"Bradly!" she screamed, trying now with all the strength that was left in her to break Marco's grip and get to her husband.

Marco's look was black. His eyes searching out the room, trying to find his opponent. Then he gave a roar of cold, cruel laughter. "You think to take her from me do you, Brad? I will let you take something back to your

plantation with you if you wish and that is
your brat upstairs, but this lovely little
vixen"—he fondled her breasts slowly, as she
squirmed and pushed against him—"you shall
not have. She belongs to me now and I shall
have to kill you if you try to take her." He
reached to his side and drew up his cutlass.

Seeing his beloved, fighting on the stairs
against Marco, and seeing him touch her
breast, Bradly's blood turned to ice. There
would be no way out for the scum except
death, he swore to himself. No man could do
to his Katherine what this one had and live.
"Then come, you filthy swine, and I will have
an end to my long wish to cut your heart from
your repulsive body," Bradly bellowed, stepping out into the light.

Katherine gasped as she looked upon her
husband, never had she seen him or any other
man look so dangerous. He himself looked like
a pirate standing with cutlass in hand and feet
braced apart. His shirt was open to the waist
and his skin was a bronze color from the sun.
His hair was unruly and its dark mass now
hung over the collar of his shirt. Looking at
the dark beard he had grown over the past few
months, Katherine felt as though she barely
knew the menacing figure standing before her.

Marco wore a twisted grin on his face as he
set Katherine from him. "I see old friend you
are ready to feel my blade and go to your
maker, ha?"

Bradly did not speak as he waited for Marco

to reach him, but his cold gray eyes held a promise of death that would have discouraged and even frightened any other man, besides Marco. But Marco did not notice his eyes or the rage that encompassed his face; the only thing that he could think of was to kill this man he had hated for so long and then to take his wife up those stairs and to show her that he was her master.

Katherine stood numb, her hand clasped tightly over her mouth, so she could not scream and distract Bradly. Marco made the first move, swinging his cutlass in the air, missing Bradly and shattering a large vase that stood near the staircase.

The fight raged on, Bradly with the greater strength and weight and Marco with more experience in handling the sort of weapon with which they were battling.

Katherine's eyes never left Bradly's figure for a second. The two men were so engrossed in awaiting an opening to overtake the other that neither of them saw a small, dark figure steal through the door and huddle quietly in a corner.

Lucy had heard her master's voice and the fight going on downstairs and had silently, carrying Charles in the crook of her arm, made her way to her mistress.

The blows being struck were wearing on the two opponents but Bradly seemed to be holding up better than Marco. So far, he had only been struck on the arm, a small slice, between his elbow and his wrist. Blood stained his shirt as Katherine clutched the banister, knowing her husband did not even feel the pain as he pushed ever harder against his enemy.

Marco was breathing hard now as he tried to shield himself from the force of Bradly's blows. The raging force of Bradly's cutlass seemed to strike out harder than at the start of the fight and Marco could only back his way about the room, trying to keep Bradly's blade from making contact. Blood was streaming onto the carpet from a gash in his leg and a larger one on his shoulder, but still he thought he could win.

Bradly rained strokes down upon his opponent, not relenting in his attack, then with one huge burst of energy he drove with full force against Marco. Marco lost his footing and, as the blade came down at him, fell flat on his back so that he received a long deep gash across his chest.

Bradly stood panting over Marco's prone figure. Blood was seeping onto the floor from his chest as he lay there breathing his last breath of life.

Katherine ran to Bradly and threw her arms about him, tears streaming down her cheeks. "Bradly, Bradly," she wept. "I had thought I would never see you again, it has all been so horrible."

"I know, love, but you are safe now and no more harm shall ever befall you." He held her tightly against him, taking her lips and drinking of their sweet honey taste. At last, he released her and turned toward the stairs to Lucy and Charles.

Lucy ran to her master, her face aglow with happiness. "Master Brad, I done almost gave up on you ever coming and taking us from this hellhole of an island," she cried, as she placed the child in his arms.

Bradly looked down at his smiling son and then at his wife, his own eyes filling with tears. "Did you think for one moment I would not come to get what is mine?"

Katherine held tightly to his side, feeling safer than she had ever been in her life.

"We must hurry and leave before someone finds us here. I do not think I could stand off this whole damn island." He smiled.

They turned toward the door but Katherine, from the corner of her eye, glimpsed a small figure kneeling beside Marco. "Bradly!" she gasped, grabbing hold of his arm.

Bradly looked back to see a woman he did not recognize, talking insensibly to Marco.

"Why did you not take me and the love I offered you?" she wailed. "Why did you wish that bitch over me? I gave you everything, Marco. Why did you treat me as you did?"

Marco lay still, barely breathing, looking at the scarecrow of a woman leaning over him. "Get away from me, you hag," he whispered, barely getting the words out of his mouth.

"It is not too late. Let me take care of you. I

still love you, Marco," she screeched, trying to take hold of his hand.

Marco brought his head off the floor with an effort and spit a spurt of blood in her face. "Begone, bitch, get away from me."

Katherine looked in horror at Rachel's pathetic, bloodstained face. "Bradly it is Rachel. We cannot leave her here," she implored him.

Crossing the floor Bradly spoke softly to the girl, "Come, Rachel. You must come with us; there is nothing for you here." He reached down and took hold of her frail shoulders.

Rachel tried to beat his hands away, her distressed mind not wanting to believe what Marco had just said.

"Come Rachel," he pulled her, resisting, to her feet and all but dragged her to the door.

As the group started out, unknown to them, Marco pulled his pistol from his belt and tried with his last bit of strength to shoot and kill Bradly Deveraux, but Bradly on reaching the door had made the mistake of releasing Rachel over to Katherine's care and the girl in one last attempt to reach her love, broke loose from Katherine's hand, and ran toward Marco—at the same time he pulled the trigger of his pistol.

The room was filled with the sound of the gunshot; Katherine ran to Rachel as the girl slumped to the floor, a large hole from the bullet at the top of her stomach.

Bradly rushed to where Marco lay, thinking

to put his life to a sure ending, but only sightless eyes stared up at the ceiling; his breathing had stopped at last.

"I'm sorry, Katherine," Rachel coughed. "I loved him so and he promised me so much. I'm truly sorry for everything I have done to you."

Katherine tried to hush the girl but it was too late. Rachel closed her eyes and her life came to a stop.

"We must hurry, love," Bradly said softly, helping Katherine to her feet. "Mark Prescot is waiting outside and keeping watch. I'm sure someone will have heard that pistol shot."

Katherine was led to the boat that was waiting for them, hidden in a small cove along the beach. She felt a great sorrow at Rachel's death and wept softly for some time, wishing that she and the poor girl could have been friends and that things could have turned out differently.

The late spring days had a dreamlike quality at Moon Rise. The flowers about the house provided a multitude of colors and, like the roses twining about the veranda, their fragrant perfumes, sent heady scents in all directions. Birds chirped noisily as they went about their business of building nests, high in the tall majestic oaks. Deep velvety green lawns lay around the large house and extended to the plowed cotton fields, which were blooming white in the afternoon sun. Moon Rise was a quiet and comforting place of rest. Anyone who looked at it would think that perhaps God himself had touched down on this spot and taken his pleasure in the things about him.

"Is it not wonderful, my love? I can hardly believe that in only a matter of one day my father shall be joining us here at Moon Rise."

"Aye, my sweet. It shall be wonderful."

"You sound a bit gruff, Bradly. Is something amiss? Are you not pleased that my father shall be staying for a time?"

"I only worry for you, my darling." He patted her rounded stomach. "I fear you may try to do too much and do some harm to yourself."

Katherine's tender smile filled his very depths with warmth. "I had thought you would not worry so much now that we have already had one child. No harm came to me then and none shall with this one I am carrying."

"It is not the number of times, my precious. If the number be ten, I shall still have worries over you," Bradly said, reclining back on the bed.

Seated at her dressing table, Katherine had been brushing her hair. Now a small smile played about her lips as she viewed her reflection. Life for her had taken a full turn since she had left England. She had been a child then, but after almost three years of living as Bradly's wife, she was a woman.

Her father and old nurse, Biddy, had left

England soon after her stepmother's death and would be arriving at Moon Rise in only a matter of one day. She would be presenting him with another small grandchild soon; her joy was filled to bursting with this pleasant thought.

Oh she knew there would be more tears over the years, and some bitter disappointments and feelings of regret. But always there would be Bradly. No finer gift could she ever seek than he.

"What are you dreaming about my sweet? Come over here." He patted the bed. "I wish to partake of your dreams also."

As Katherine laid herself down next to him, his mind did soar. He at last had found his own Eden, here at Moon Rise, where his passions could fly up to the heavens although forever he could keep his love safely by his side and God willing many more Deverauxs would find the same contentment he had, here on this small patch of soil. Slowly he turned to the woman at his side. "You are my life, sealed in my heart, Katherine Deveraux, and forever more shall you stay so."

ENTRANCING ROMANCES BY SYLVIE F. SOMMERFIELD

TAMARA'S ECSTASY (998, $3.50)
Tamara knew it was foolish to give her heart to a sailor; he'd promise her the stars, but be gone with the tide. But she was a victim of her own desire. Lost in a sea of passion, she ached for his magic touch—and would do anything for it!

DEANNA'S DESIRE (906, $3.50)
Amidst the storm of the American Revolution, Matt and Deanna meet—and fall in love. In the name of freedom, they discover war's intrigues and horrors. Bound by passion, they risk everything to keep their love alive!

TAZIA'S TORMENT (882, $2.95)
When tempestuous Fantasio de Montega danced, men were hypnotized. And this was part of her secret revenge—until cruel fate tricked her into loving the man she'd vowed to kill!

RAPTURE'S ANGEL (750, $2.75)
When Angelique boarded the *Wayfarer,* she felt like a frightened child. Then Devon—with his gentle voice and captivating touch—reminded her that she was a woman, with a heart that longed to be won!

BESTSELLING ROMANCES BY JANELLE TAYLOR

SAVAGE ECSTASY (824, $3.50)
It was like lightning striking, the first time the Indian brave Gray Eagle looked into the eyes of the beautiful young settler Alisha. And from the moment he saw her, he knew that he must possess her — and make her his slave!

DEFIANT ECSTASY (931, $3.50)
When Gray Eagle returned to Fort Pierre's gates with his hundred warriors behind him, Alisha's heart skipped a beat: would Gray Eagle destroy her — or make his destiny her own?

FORBIDDEN ECSTASY (1014, $3.50)
Gray Eagle had promised Alisha his heart forever — nothing could keep him from her. But when Alisha woke to find her red-skinned lover gone, she felt abandoned and alone. Lost between two worlds, desperate and fearful of betrayal, Alisha hungered for the return of her FORBIDDEN ECSTASY.